PRAISE FOR
The Boy Toy

"An enchanting interracial rom-com. . . . Marsh eschews intense drama in favor of slow-burning anticipation, drawing readers in with vivid descriptions, witty dialogue, and a fleshed out depiction of Indian family culture. The result is a winning romance."
—*Publishers Weekly*

"Fun and sexy with just the right dash of family drama."
—PopSugar

"This tale of a one-night stand that becomes something more finds surprising depth and manages to spin an often-clumsy subject into gold."
—*Entertainment Weekly*

"If you're looking for a fun and sexy read that features an older woman and a younger man, the challenges of a multicultural relationship, and also a fair share of family drama, look no further than *The Boy Toy*. It's sure to please!"
—The Bookish Libra

"Not only was this book a hilarious read but it was very relatable."
—Harlequin Junkie

JOVE TITLES BY NICOLA MARSH

The Boy Toy
The Man Ban

NICOLA MARSH

THE MAN BAN

JOVE
New York

A JOVE BOOK
Published by Berkley
An imprint of Penguin Random House LLC
penguinrandomhouse.com

Library of Congress Cataloging-in-Publication Data

Names: Marsh, Nicola, author.
Title: The man ban / Nicola Marsh.
Description: First Edition. | New York: Jove, 2021.
Identifiers: LCCN 2021010500 (print) | LCCN 2021010501 (ebook) |
ISBN 9780593198643 (trade paperback) | ISBN 9780593198650 (ebook)
Subjects: GSAFD: Love stories.
Classification: LCC PS3613.A76986 M36 2021 (print) |
LCC PS3613.A76986 (ebook) | DDC 813/.6—dc23
LC record available at https://lccn.loc.gov/2021010500
LC ebook record available at https://lccn.loc.gov/2021010501

First Edition: July 2021

Printed in the United States of America
1st Printing

Book design by Katy Riegel

For the Anglo-Indian community around the world: our unique culinary dishes like devil fry, ball curry, pepper water, and beans foogath are the best.

1

HARPER DIDN'T BELIEVE in karma.

Unlike her best friend Nishi, the most beautiful bride she'd ever seen, who waxed lyrical about how meeting Arun at a Diwali celebration in southeast Melbourne had been fate, how they'd taken one look at each other and fallen madly in love, how a psychic had predicted this when doing her chart at the time of her birth.

Nishi had been her best friend since high school, so Harper didn't disillusion the loved-up bride. Her cynicism could easily explain Nishi's version of "fate": meeting Arun was random, it was lust at first sight considering they ended up shagging the night they met, and the tall, handsome, rich doctor the psychic predicted was a generic promise given to thousands of hopeful Indian parents after the birth of a daughter.

But Harper had to admit, being maid of honor and witnessing Nishi and Arun exchange vows earlier today, there'd been something almost magical about the couple so sure of their love they'd committed to each other in front of five hundred guests.

Five hundred guests who would hopefully take one look at the food she'd styled and gush on every social media app.

Harper needed work. Food styling may be her passion, but it didn't pay the bills half as much as her previous career in catering. She needed a big break, and Nishi had assured her that among the throng of five hundred were many online influencers. All it would take was one photo, one perfect pictorial image of her beautiful *bondas*, precise *pakoras*, or vivid *vadas*, and she'd be on her way.

As the guests mingled in the outer foyer of the Springvale Town Hall, she cast a final critical eye over the buffet tables. Two trestles lay end to end along an entire wall of the hall, laden with enough food to feed a thousand. The crimson tablecloths were barely visible beneath gold platters piled high with delicious Indian finger food, with squat ivory candles casting an alluring glow over everything.

She'd never styled a job this big and had balked when Nishi first asked. But her bestie had insisted, and it had been her gift to the happy couple. Everything looked perfect, and she blew out a breath, rolling her shoulders to release some of the tension. The edge of her sari slipped, but before she could pull it up, a hand tugged it back into place.

She turned and locked gazes with one of the groomsmen. She couldn't remember his name after being introduced earlier in the day, what felt like a lifetime ago, but she remembered his eyes, a mesmerizing, unique gray and currently lit with amusement.

"Can't have you unraveling and distracting the guests," he said. "Though personally, I wouldn't mind a little entertainment along with my entrée."

Harper bit back her first retort, that his flirting was wasted on her. She had a firm man ban in place, ensuring the last twelve months had been angst-free, leaving her to focus on her career and not a never-ending parade of dating disasters.

"Sorry to disappoint, but the only entertainment you'll be getting tonight is from the ten-piece band playing later."

If he heard the bite in her words, he didn't show it. Instead, he grinned, and something unfamiliar fluttered deep. That was the only downside to her ban; she missed the sex.

"Too bad."

His glance flicked over her, a practiced perusal from a guy who probably flirted with anything in a skirt. At six-two, with thick, wavy black hair, sharp cheekbones, broad shoulders that hinted at gym workouts, a killer smile, and those stunning eyes, this guy would be used to women preening under his attention.

When she frowned and didn't respond, an eyebrow quirked and he thrust out his hand. "We met earlier. Manish Gomes, but my friends call me Manny."

"Harper Ryland." She shook his hand and released it quickly. "Don't you have to go help the groom, *Manish*?"

He laughed at her sarcastic emphasis. "Arun's got everything under control. Besides, we're not exactly best buds. I think the only reason he asked me to be a groomsman was because we pulled two all-nighters in a row around the time he proposed to Nishi and I had biryani leftovers I shared."

Figured. Manish's confidence came from saving lives alongside Arun in the ER.

"Nishi's my best friend."

Her response sounded judgmental, like she couldn't figure out why Arun would ask some fellow doctor to be part of his wedding party when they obviously weren't close.

"You work together?"

She shook her head. "Best friends since high school."

"Right."

They lapsed into a silence that bordered on awkward. She may not be the most extroverted at the best of times, but she could hold her own in social settings. But something about this guy had her on edge, and she didn't like it. Not his fault he was gorgeous and charming; her latent insecurities made her want to rush to the bathroom and check her hair and makeup.

"Well, if you have any further sari emergencies, you know where to find me," he said, pointing at the head table, set below the stage. "I'm chivalrous that way, in case you were wondering."

"I'm not," she muttered, earning another grin. "Besides, you should be thankful I didn't slap you for fixing my sari when I didn't ask for your help."

His eyebrows arched in surprise at her snark as he held up his hands in apology. "You're right. My bad. I'll see you later."

Harper bit back a sigh as she watched him stride toward the foyer, all long legs and impressive shoulders shifting beneath a perfectly fitted kurta. She'd been envious when Nishi had told her what the guys were wearing; the slim-fitting pants and flowing top combo looked a lot more comfortable than the saris chosen for the women. She'd been in a perpetual state all day for fear of tripping over and causing the unraveling Manish had mentioned. But she had to admit the bridesmaids looked stunning in the cream silk shot through with gold thread, and she'd never felt so glamorous, even if she was one step away from a revealing disaster.

She'd been curt with Manish to the point of rudeness, and he hadn't deserved her brusque treatment. She blamed her nerves. This job meant everything to her, but deep down she knew better.

His perfection rattled her, and a man hadn't unnerved her in a long time.

Not that it mattered. Once this wedding was done, she'd probably only see him at the occasional function Nishi and Arun hosted: birth of their first child, baptism, that kind of thing. By then, she'd feign forgetfulness of their first meeting.

What Manny thought of her didn't matter. She had a job to do, and with the revelers soon lining up for the food, that's where her focus should be.

Bold men with unusual slate eyes should be forgotten.

2

"Manish, why are you sitting here talking to your old grandmother when you could be mingling and finding a wife?"

Manny slid an arm around Isadora Gomes and squeezed gently. "Because you're my plus-one and the most beautiful woman in the room."

"Get away with you." Izzy, as he'd called her since he could talk, slapped his chest but bestowed a warm smile on him. "I'm not getting any younger, you know, and it will be the happiest day of my life when you marry."

And the worst of his, considering he had no intention of ever entering the constricting bonds of matrimony.

"We've had this conversation many times, and it always ends the same," he said, pecking her cheek. "So let's enjoy Arun's wedding without the lecture, okay?"

Izzy puffed up in outrage, as expected. "I do not lecture. I merely point out you're forty and single when you could have your pick of women and make me a great-grandmother before I journey into the next world."

"Heard it all before." He rolled his eyes, a reaction that served to narrow hers.

"Manish, you need a wife."

"I need peace at the end of a long shift in the ER, so coming home to a nagging wife who resents my job because it takes me away from lavishing her with attention . . . no thanks." He shook his head, earning another narrow-eyed glare from a determined Izzy.

"You are too picky."

"And you are too fixated on marrying me off when I'm more than happy with my life."

It was the truth. He loved saving lives in a bustling ER in an inner-city Melbourne hospital, he loved his contemporary apartment in Prahran, and he loved being able to date freely.

His grandmother tsk-tsked. "Happiness comes with sharing your life with someone."

"Or from a bottle." He raised his glass, quarter filled with two-hundred-dollar whiskey. He hated to think how much Arun had spent on this wedding. The bride's parents might've paid for it, but Arun had contributed more than six figures if his boasting to a resident at the hospital had been right.

Manny would rather invest in real estate. Or a luxurious car. Just as many sleek curves without the hassle.

"You're incorrigible." Izzy whacked him on the chest again, but she snuggled closer under his arm. "But I love you."

"Right back at you."

Manny tightened his arm around his gran's shoulders, surprised to find her fitting more closely into him. Had she lost weight? But before he could quiz her, she straightened out of his embrace and pointed to a group of giggling twentysomethings poring over their cells.

"Go mingle."

The last thing he felt like doing was talking with a bunch of women over a decade younger than him, but he saw the determined glint in Izzy's judgmental stare. That's when he spotted Harper near the buffet table. She'd been prickly and standoffish and completely immune to his charms, which only served to intrigue him.

And she'd been right; it was totally inappropriate to snag the material of her sari and place it on her shoulder, but it had been an instinctive reaction, something he'd done for his mom countless times before she'd died.

He owed his grandmother so much, but if he had a choice between fake flirting with a bunch of immature women and verbally sparring with a recalcitrant maid of honor, he knew which he'd pick any day of the week.

"All right, have it your way." He pressed a kiss to her forehead. "I'm off to talk with a woman."

Izzy beamed as he stood, before waggling her finger at him. "Make sure she's suitable bride material."

He shook his head, shooting his grandmother a fond glance before heading in Harper's direction. Spending time with her would definitely get Izzy off his back, at least for tonight, though considering her nationality, maybe not. He knew when Izzy discussed his future bride she envisaged an Indian woman, not an Australian. Crazy, as he'd been born here and embraced it as much as his Anglo-Indian culture.

But he wasn't marrying anyone, least of all a woman who radiated serious hands-off vibes, so spending an hour or two seeing if he could charm her held a certain allure. With those big blue eyes, brown hair hanging halfway down her back in artfully styled waves, and curves highlighted by the sari, he knew exactly what Harper's allure was.

He'd been working manic hours in the ER lately and hadn't had a date in forever, so some harmless flirting with Harper beckoned.

He made a beeline for her, surprised she seemed to be hovering near the buffet table. The guests hadn't been directed to the food yet, so her positioning was odd. Either she was starving and wanted to be first in line, or she was avoiding the bridal table, where most of the wedding party now sat, apart from the two of them.

"Hey," he said, as he drew near. "Need some help guarding the food?"

He glimpsed a telltale flare in her eyes that implied she wasn't as immune to his flirting as she'd like him to think.

"I'm not guarding it."

Her response had a similar bite to earlier, like she didn't want him anywhere near her. But the eyes rarely lie, and right now she was gobbling him up and salivating for seconds.

"Sure looks that way to me." He smiled and gestured at the table. "Though who's going to want to touch all this fancy-schmancy stuff? It's way over the top."

Somehow he'd said the wrong thing again, as her eyes narrowed to glacial slits. "Is that right?"

"Absolutely. Indian food doesn't need dressing up. It's the flavor that matters, not the presentation."

"So you're an expert in food?"

"I hold my own in the kitchen."

He'd learned from the master. Izzy made the best *bebinka*, his favorite dessert, a rich, layered, coconut pudding that took hours to make and channeled her Portuguese-Goan heritage perfectly.

He could also make a mean pork vindaloo, *dahl*, and *aloo tikki*, the lentils and spiced potato patties something he'd lived on while in med school.

When he wasn't working manic hours at the hospital, he loved to cook for Izzy. His way of thanking her for the countless delicious meals she'd served him over the years, and a way to de-stress at the same time. No better way to vent frustration than dicing vegetables.

"You're very opinionated."

She sounded so disapproving he couldn't help but laugh.

"It's better to be honest, don't you think?"

"Yes, but someone took time to make this food look appealing for the guests. The least you can do is appreciate it."

He made a scoffing sound. "Styling food is overrated. As for prettying it up for this lot"—he pointed at the throng milling through the massive hall—"waste of time. They'll demolish whatever they can get their hands on in five seconds flat. Weddings make people hungry, and they don't want to stand around admiring the food; they want to eat it."

Her top teeth caught her bottom lip, and the damnedest thing happened. He wanted to do the same. Right here, right now. His gaze riveted to her mouth; the bow shape of it, glossed in crimson, the fullness. Man, he needed to get laid ASAP if watching a prickly woman gnaw unconsciously on her lip had him wanting to take her in the nearest private space.

She waged an inner battle. He saw it reflected in her expressive eyes, torn between berating him for his opinions and applauding. The war didn't last long—those luscious lips curved in a slow smile that had him sucking in air.

"I'm not hungry. Are you?"

Where had that sultry edge in her tone come from?

He shook his head. "No."

At least, not for food, but he wisely kept that gem to himself.

"Good, then let's get some fresh air."

She held out her hand, and rather than ponder her switch from bristly to flirty, he grasped it in his, ready for her to lead him wherever the hell she wanted.

3

THE MOMENT MANNY took hold of her hand, Harper had to resist the urge to yank him closer and knee him in the balls.

She thought she'd grown immune to insults since her vitiligo diagnosis thirteen months ago. Not that there'd been many, but she'd never forgotten her first phototherapy session to treat the white patches on her face and body. Being blasted with high ultraviolet rays for eighty seconds to re-pigment her skin hadn't been bad, but it meant she couldn't wear makeup entering the clinic. She'd felt naked striding into that place, and when a few teens skateboarding outside had fired off insults, it had hurt more than it should.

They were being smart-asses, trying to outdo their friends, so it shouldn't have registered. But every time she entered that clinic, three times a week, she made sure she wore her hair out so it half covered her face, along with a cap, and the minute her treatment was over she'd slather on foundation before heading out.

Like those bigmouth teens, Manny's insults regarding her food styling should've meant nothing too. But he'd hit her where she was most vulnerable—her floundering job—and she wanted to teach him a lesson.

She could've reacted by telling him where he could stick his opinions. But when she'd seen the way he looked at her mouth, like he wanted to devour her whole, she'd come up with another form of payback that would be much more fun.

If she could pull it off, that is.

Not dating for a year meant her flirting skills were subpar. She'd never been much good to begin with, so stringing him along for a little while would be challenging. But oh so fun, she thought as he fell into step beside her. She led him through a side door she'd used earlier when placing her tools of trade back in her car.

"Should I be worried?"

She hated to admit his deep voice did something to her insides, and it wasn't entirely unpleasant. "About?"

"You're dragging me away from hundreds of people into a dark alley. Maybe you're about to take advantage of me?"

"You wish," she muttered, and he laughed, the rich timbre of his chuckles as appealing as his damn voice.

"I like you, Harper, even if the feeling's not entirely mutual."

She arched a brow. "What makes you say that?"

"A hunch." He paused to close the door behind them, leaving them on a landing with six steps leading to a small car park beyond. "I'm just glad there were no carving forks on that buffet table, because I had the distinct impression you wanted to stab me in the eye with one."

Genuine laughter burst from her lips. Was there anything more attractive than a cute guy with a killer sense of humor?

"It's been a long day." She shrugged, dislodging the end of her sari again, and this time when he corrected it his fingertips brushed the bare skin of her upper arm, sending a skitter of heat through her.

"Phew." His hand swiped across his forehead in exaggerated relief. "At least it's not me."

"Oh, it's you too," she said, but this time they shared a conspiratorial smile devoid of ill feeling on her part.

"So what are we doing out here?" He surveyed the parking lot and the small row of shops beyond, mostly the Vietnamese cafés this area was famous for.

"Already told you, getting fresh air."

"You could've picked a better spot."

"Yeah, but this one's more private."

She bit back a triumphant grin as his gaze riveted to her mouth again. Maybe she wasn't so bad at this flirting caper after all.

"I can't get a read on you," he said, grasping her other hand in his, so she had to face him. "And I'm usually pretty good at it."

"Getting a read on people is code for prejudging them, right?"

The corners of his mouth twitched. "There you go again, twisting my words, making me out to be a bad guy."

"Are you?" She leaned a little closer and lowered her voice. "Bad?"

With a groan, he hauled her flush against him. She gasped—she hadn't expected her toying to escalate so quickly, and certainly not to this, where his mouth covered hers in a commanding kiss that left her reeling.

She shouldn't have let it get this far, but before she could stop it he sucked her bottom lip and nipped it, then soothed it with an assured sweep of his tongue that had her arms snaking around his neck to hang on for dear life.

Her lips parted on a needy whimper, and he took full advantage, his tongue challenging hers, taunting her, lashing her with the full force of an expertise she'd never known before.

Damn, the man could kiss.

She swayed beneath the onslaught of sensuality, grateful for his strong arms around her waist, until his hands slid down to her ass and pulled her flush against him, showing her exactly how far she'd let this game get out of hand.

She eased back and didn't know whether to be relieved or disappointed when he let her. Her ragged breathing matched his, and when she reluctantly dragged her gaze to meet his, the depth of his desire matched hers.

"That was some kiss," she murmured, hoping she could pull off coy, because that kiss had rattled her more than she liked.

She'd intended on toying with him, teasing him, then doing something excessively childish like rubbing his face in a dish of her perfectly presented *kulfi*.

But she hadn't expected the kiss, and now the thought of his face being covered in rose water–flavored ice cream made her think naughty thoughts of licking it off him.

"Yeah, it was."

He sounded as stunned as she felt, and when he reached out to tuck a strand of hair behind her ear, the tender gesture almost made her forget why she'd wanted to humiliate him in the first place.

Almost.

"Could you give me a hand?"

"Anytime."

She rolled her eyes at his naughty smirk. "I have some things in my car I need brought inside."

"Sure, lead the way."

Damn it, she even found his mock bow cute and resisted the urge to stomp to her car and kick a tire. He'd insulted her work. Worse, he'd belittled it, deeming it frivolous and unimportant. For that, he had to pay.

"Do you have a special gift for the happy couple?"

"Something like that," she said, popping the trunk and reaching into her bag of tricks.

When she attended styling jobs she used a giant briefcase, like the doctors' cases from the olden days that folded out. In it, she stocked every item she may need: knives, zester, peeler, mandolin, potato masher, pastry cutters, blow torch, wooden skewers, and hand mixer.

And a can of whipped cream.

With her back to him, she gave it a shake before swiveling to face him. He was peering into the trunk and didn't see it coming. With a deft press of her finger she directed the nozzle at him, releasing a stream of cream that covered his face.

He leaped back with a loud, "What the fuck?" and for a second Harper experienced genuine remorse. What a stupid, childish payback for some clueless guy insulting her food.

But then he wiped the cream from his eyes and fixed that glittering gray gaze on her, and she knew it would be okay.

Until she realized Manny wasn't angry.

He was intent on revenge.

4

THE FIRST RAUNCHY thought that entered Manny's mind when he saw the whipped cream can in Harper's hand was, *Lucky me, she's into some kinky shit.*

That was before she decorated him like a fucking meringue.

The woman was crazy, but before he got to the bottom of why she'd done this, he knew exactly how to deliver a little vengeance of his own.

"Oh no, you don't," she said, brandishing the can at him like a weapon.

"What are you going to do about it?"

Her eyes widened as she realized his intent a second before he kissed her again, this time smearing her face with the cream covering his.

She responded for a moment, those beautiful pliant lips pressing against his, before she pulled back and shoved him away.

"I can't believe you did that," she yelled, radiating anger like he was the bad guy in this scenario.

"Just like I can't believe your stealth cream attack on me."

Her chest heaved with indignation. Magnificent. Even now, when he knew she had to have a screw loose, he wanted his hands all over her . . .

"You've got to be kidding me," she muttered, flinging the can back in the trunk and reaching for a dishcloth from the same bag that held a mystifying array of kitchen implements. "Get your mind out of the gutter."

"From the way you kissed me before, I thought you liked it there."

"That kiss should never have happened." She slammed the trunk shut and dabbed at her face, doing little but spreading the cream around, before holding it out to him. "It wasn't part of the plan."

"What plan?"

She folded her arms and frowned. It did little to detract from her beauty, even beneath the layer of whipped cream.

"I'm a food stylist. You insulted me in there, so I wanted to make you pay."

Ah, so that was the reason behind her hissy fit. Now that he'd got over the shock of being decorated like an ice cream sundae, he could see the funny side of it, but by her glower, she didn't.

"Sorry."

"No you're not. You're an opinionated jerk who thinks his high and mighty job is more important than anything else, so I stupidly thought I'd take you down a peg or two by flirting, then humiliating you with that." She pointed at the cream covering his face, her shoulders slumping as she grimaced. "But it was lame and childish and I'm sorry."

"Apology accepted."

He bit back a grin because he didn't think she'd appreciate it. Yeah, what she'd done was something a kid would do, but it was funny as hell and perfectly warranted considering he'd insulted her job. "But for the record, I don't think being a doctor is better than anyone else's job, and I'm sorry if my jibes about yours made you feel that way."

He glimpsed grudging respect in her eyes before she blinked. "Wipe that stuff off your face. You look like a clown."

"So do you," he said, wiping his face before advancing on her to do the same.

But she sidestepped and held up her hands to ward him off. "I'll get cleaned up inside."

"You can't walk back in looking like that."

"I have a makeup bag in the room reserved for the bride, so I'll be fine."

With that, he watched the most infuriating, intriguing woman he'd met in a long time turn and run.

5

"I'm mortified." Harper covered her face with her hands as Samira and Pia tried to stifle their laughter and failed. "I acted like an idiot."

"Manny deserved it," Pia said, muttering, "Ouch," when Samira poked her in the arm.

"He wasn't being mean considering he didn't know Harper had styled the food."

Pia rolled her eyes. "You always defend him. If you weren't so hot and bothered for your sexy husband, I'd say there's something off with this friendship between you and the doc."

"Manny is so not my type." Samira's smitten gaze drifted past a group of revelers dancing a Bollywood version of the "Macarena" to focus on Rory, the host of Australia's latest hit reality TV show, *Renegades*. "Now him, on the other hand . . ."

Pia made mock gagging sounds. "How can you still be so in love after six months of marriage?"

"He makes it easy," Samira said softly, a satisfied smile curving her lips. "He's a great hands-on dad too, and Ronnie adores him."

Harper couldn't help a small stab of envy. She'd once harbored dreams of a family. Until her own had imploded and taken her faith in commitment with it.

"Rory and Ronnie, I don't know how you keep them straight," Pia said.

The women laughed. "Speaking of marriage, how are you and Dev going with counseling?" Samira asked.

When Harper had first met the cousins through Nishi, who loved calling impromptu wedding planning meetings as an excuse to drink margaritas and gossip, Samira had just married Rory and caused a minor scandal in the Indian community considering he was a decade younger, Australian, and had impregnated her out of wedlock. And Pia had been separated from her husband for several months. Pia had been surprisingly open about her struggles with infertility and how her husband's sterility had put a strain on her marriage, and with some not-so-gentle prompting from everyone in her family had made inroads to reconciling with Dev.

"The counseling is going well." A blush stained Pia's cheeks. "We're dating again."

"Good for you," Harper said, as Samira wolf whistled. "Are we talking 'dating,' cuz, or the horizontal bhangra?"

"Shut up." Pia elbowed Samira but laughed. "We're taking it slow."

"I'm so happy for you both." Samira gave Pia a quick hug. "Perhaps I should throw an informal dinner party or a barbecue, something to get us all together?" She slid a sideways glance at Harper. "Maybe I could invite Manny and make sure to secure the whipped cream under lock and key?"

"Don't remind me." Harper's cheeks burned again at the memory of what she'd done. She was never reckless or impulsive, so she had no clue what had prompted her to choose such a childish payback. "What I did was incredibly immature, definitely not my finest moment."

"He's a good sport," Samira said, eyeing her with open speculation. "But something tells me you wouldn't be this wound up unless there's more to this?"

Harper had no intention of telling the cousins about that toe-curling kiss and the all-too-brief follow up. The less time spent remembering the way her knees wobbled, her head spun, and everywhere in between zinged, the better.

"He rubbed me the wrong way, that's all," she said, glad her voice didn't give her away, because after that first kiss she knew exactly how the dashing doctor could rub her and where.

"He's too bloody charming for his own good," Pia muttered, but there was no malice in it. "The guy must have five nipples or an extra ass cheek, because how could someone like him be single at forty?"

Samira burst out laughing and Harper joined in, as Pia grinned. "Seriously. There has to be something wrong with him."

Apart from being opinionated and not afraid to express those opinions, Harper couldn't see any faults. Then again, she knew better than anybody that a perfect facade could hide a multitude of sins.

As if thoughts of her parents could conjure them up, her cell buzzed with an incoming call, and a glance at the screen had her heart sinking.

She loved her dad, she really did, but Alec Ryland, once the life of every party, never failed to bring her down these days. She contemplated letting the call go to voice mail so he could leave a message, but with DAD emblazoned on the screen and Samira and Pia casting her surprised glances as she hesitated, she felt obliged to take it.

"I'll be back," she mouthed, as she grabbed her cell and slipped out of the hall into a quiet corridor leading to the kitchen.

Taking a deep breath, she stabbed at the "answer" button and injected enthusiasm into her greeting. "Hey, Dad, everything okay?"

Rookie mistake and something she'd learned not to ask him since the shock separation from her mom fourteen months ago, because the question never failed to elicit a long-winded diatribe along the lines of, *How could she do this to me? Thirty-five years of marriage means something to me. Is there someone else?*

Harper had her own hurt to deal with after her parents' separation; she didn't have a lot left over to give.

"Not bad," he said, his morose tone belying the casual response. "Just thought I'd check in with my best girl."

Her dad never called after nine on a Saturday night, so Harper knew there was more to this.

"I'm actually at a wedding, Dad, so can't really talk—"

"Is your mother out on a date tonight?"

Harper's heart sank. She'd fielded various versions of this question for the last year, and thankfully, she could answer honestly because she had no idea about her mother's love life and didn't want to know.

"I've been busy, Dad, so haven't spoken to Mom since last week."

Another truth that hurt, because since her diagnosis Harper had withdrawn from her mother. Not because she didn't love her gorgeous, immaculately presented mom, but because spending time with her mom reinforced how flawed Harper felt.

Glamorous Lydia Ryland had always valued appearances and had taught her daughter the same. Ironic, that the professional makeup course they'd done together for fun ten years ago now came in mighty handy for Harper to hide the ugly white patches on her skin.

There was another reason, a more potent one, why Harper didn't hang out with her mom anymore. Deep down, where she didn't want to acknowledge the truth, she blamed her mom for causing her dad so much pain.

Big, bold, loud Alec had swanned through life like nothing bothered him. He'd openly adored Lydia but hadn't spent a lot of quality time with her; instead, he'd been at work or hanging out with his mates in their man caves. Yet when her parents were together they were happy. For as long as she could remember her parents entertained, their house constantly filled with people and laughter and food, heady stuff for an only child. She'd basked in her parents' love, proud of their solid marriage.

What a farce.

"You'd tell me if you knew anything, wouldn't you, love?"

If her mother was dating again, the last person she'd tell was her father. "How about I pop in tomorrow for a visit, Dad?"

"I'm playing golf all day. Maybe during the week?"

"Sure thing."

She liked how her dad tried to keep up his routine—beers in the man cave at a mate's house on a Friday night while watching the footy, takeout fried chicken night with his coworkers on a Monday, golf every Sunday—but she could tell he was doing it by rote rather than real enjoyment.

"Call me if you need me, Dad, okay? Anytime."

"Thanks, love. Bye."

He hung up, leaving her with the same heavy feeling in her gut she hadn't been able to shift since her folks had broken the news to her.

She may have had some dating disasters in her time, but nothing had shaken her belief in love and commitment as much as learning the parents who she'd thought idolized each other were separating.

Nobody had cheated or been abusive. They'd simply drifted apart; at least, that's what her mom had said. Harper thought there was more to it but hadn't delved; not when she believed the stress of being pulled in two directions, supporting both parents, had triggered the vitiligo, and she didn't need further angst. Selfish, maybe, but her world had tipped on its axis the day her parents separated, and a couple of months later when Colin had dumped her after she'd revealed her true self to him . . . she knew then she had to start taking better care of herself, and a self-imposed man ban was part of that.

So what was it about Manny Gomes that had snuck under her carefully erected guard?

What she'd done may have been immature, but she knew she wouldn't have gotten so riled up unless it had mattered what he thought of her. Disparaging her food styling had really hit home, and rather than walking away as she normally would've done, she'd gone down the path of game playing?

Definitely not her style, and she intended to avoid the dastardly doc for the remainder of the night.

She wandered back into the hall and looked around for Samira and Pia. They'd vanished from the small table where they'd been chatting earlier, and Harper caught sight of them on the dance floor with their husbands.

Rory and Dev had their arms wrapped around Samira's and Pia's waists, the women's wound around their husbands' necks, and both couples were staring at each other so intently the band could've stopped playing and they wouldn't have noticed.

And in that moment, standing on the outskirts of a wedding with five hundred people dancing and laughing and drinking, Harper had never felt so alone.

6

MANNY CAUGHT SIGHT of Harper standing at the back of the hall, her wistful gaze watching the people on the dance floor. She looked . . . lost, forlorn, and he experienced another twinge of guilt.

He hadn't meant to disparage her job. He'd sounded like a pompous idiot, and while getting a cream facial for his troubles had been extreme, he'd probably deserved it. Though he'd rather focus on what had preceded her impulsive action.

That kiss had blown his mind.

He hadn't been celibate since he'd graduated med school. Before that he hadn't had a lot of time for dating. But since, he'd more than made up for it. Long shifts and exhaustion didn't make for relationships, so he enjoyed the fleeting nature of his encounters instead. The women he dated knew the score and he had a few names in his cell, friends who were bonking buddies, fellow medicos who didn't have time for the complications of a relationship either.

Which meant he'd kissed a lot of women over the years, so what was it about Harper that had captured his attention so thoroughly?

"Why are you fixated on that girl?"

Trust Izzy to notice his interest in Harper. His grandmother had an inbuilt radar for an available woman within a five-hundred-foot radius.

"What girl?"

His feigned nonchalance earned a disgusted scoff. "That bridesmaid. You're staring."

He couldn't help it. Harper had something about her . . . a beautiful, cool exterior that screamed hands-off, hiding a feisty core if the way she responded to his kiss was any indication.

"We talked earlier. She's nice."

Izzy snorted. "Don't go getting any ideas."

"And what ideas may they be?"

"She's not for you." Izzy waggled her finger. "Mixed race marriages are complicated."

They'd had this discussion before, when Manny pointed out the entire Anglo-Indian race came about through mixed marriages. But Izzy had a hang-up about it and he rarely bothered correcting her these days; what was the point when he had no intention of getting married, ever?

"Then it's a good thing I'm not marrying her." He nudged her gently. "Surely you don't disapprove of me having a little fun?"

Izzy's nose crinkled. "Please don't elaborate."

"I won't, but I know you're not as shockable as you pretend."

She waved him away. "Go. Have your fun. But remember, you must find a wife before I die."

Considering Izzy was a sprightly eighty-six, he hoped that would be a long way off, ensuring he'd still be a happy bachelor at fifty and beyond.

"You're far from that," he said, "meaning the chances of me walking up the aisle anytime soon are zero."

Izzy's gaze slid away from his in a way he didn't like. Then again, most elderly didn't like thinking about their mortality. He hated contemplating a life without Izzy in it. His chest ached at the thought.

"I'm so proud of you." She spoke so softly he had to lean closer to hear her. "I've been blessed having you in my life."

His throat tightened at the glimpse of tears in her eyes. "Hey, weddings are happy occasions. What's brought this on?"

"The thought of me not being at yours," she said, clutching her chest, and winking.

Relieved she'd lightened the moment, he slid an arm around her waist. "You're one in a million, you know that, right?"

"I know," she said, leaning into him.

His gran was in a strange mood tonight, no doubt about it, and when he raised his head to glance toward the back of the hall again, Harper had vanished.

7

HARPER KNEW CATCHING up with her mom for a coffee the day after her dad's phone call wasn't a good idea. She might accidentally let slip how much he was still hurting after fourteen months of separation, because she couldn't get it out of her head how morose he'd sounded last night.

But that's exactly why she'd organized this late brunch. She'd been fielding too many similar calls from her dad lately, and she wanted to know what was going on in her mom's life so she could allay his fears, or confirm them, once and for all.

"How was Nishi's wedding?"

"Good."

Lydia arched a perfectly shaped brow. "Nishi's been your best friend for years, and there were five hundred people at the wedding. Surely, you can give me more than that?"

Harper wanted to say, *Surely you can give me more information about your private life*, but it wasn't the time. Their smashed avos had just arrived, and seeing as she hadn't eaten much at the wedding from nerves about her food presentation, she was starving.

"Nishi and Arun looked amazing; me, along with the other bridesmaids, rocked our saris; and the groomsmen were great."

One in particular, but she wouldn't dwell on that. She'd managed to avoid Manny for the rest of the wedding after their kiss'n'cream incident and had escaped as soon as the bouquet was tossed. But not before checking that every one of her thirty business cards had vanished from the buffet table. Seeing Nishi so happy had been the highlight, but watching people snap pictures of the food had come a close second.

"Why are you blushing?"

Trust her mom to notice. Before her separation, Lydia Ryland had been obsessed with Harper's love life. She'd offer fashion and hairstyling tips, would ask about every date and generally hang on every word of Harper's tales. Her mom had tolerated Colin, but Harper could tell there hadn't been any genuine liking there. Her mom valued appearances, and Colin slouched around in torn jeans and sweatshirts when he wasn't in his chef's whites.

Sure, her mom had made all the right *I'm sorry* noises after he'd dumped her, but Harper knew her mom was secretly glad and thought she could do better.

Since then, her mom had stopped showing interest in her dating life. She never questioned why Harper hadn't dated since Colin. Harper had initially been relieved and had assumed her mom had withdrawn to nurse her own hurt. Besides, the last thing she needed while struggling with the diagnosis of an autoimmune disease and the long-term effects to her skin and self-esteem was her mother's well-intentioned attention to detail with her appearance.

But as time passed and Lydia continued to become more insular, Harper had missed her mom's advice, no matter how nitpicky it had seemed at the time.

"I must be flushed because my latte is too hot." Harper blew on it. "But I need the caffeine hit."

Lydia obviously didn't buy her glib fib, but thankfully didn't call her out on it. Besides, thinking about Manny shouldn't make her blush. That kiss and its follow-up had been an anomaly, the practiced routine of a guy capable of getting any woman he wanted. But she didn't want. Her body's traitorous reaction to his kisses had been nothing more than visceral, courtesy of her man ban.

"So how are you, Mom? Haven't seen you in a while."

Harper didn't mean to sound judgmental, but Lydia's eyes narrowed slightly.

"I'm fine. Keeping busy. Can't complain."

"Which tells me exactly nothing. Are you still consulting at the beauty salon? Going out with friends?" She hesitated a moment before adding, "Seeing anyone?"

Lydia flashed a tight smile before focusing on making a vertical incision down the middle of her sourdough toast slathered in avocado and feta. "I pop into the salon once a week if they ask me. And yes, I've been to the National Gallery for a new overseas artists' exhibition, a concert at the Arts Center, and a high tea in the Dandenongs all in the last fortnight."

"Great," Harper said, making a mess while hacking at her toast, waiting for the all-important answer to her last question.

"As for dating, I'm not going to tell you because you'll tell your father and then he'll continue to bug me." Lydia forked a perfectly proportioned piece of square toast into her mouth and chewed, effectively buying herself silence. "More than he is already."

"We used to tell each other everything," Harper said, sadness making her stomach churn and effectively ruining her appetite. "Most of my friends were envious of us being besties. Even

Nishi, who's super close with her mom, used to mention how close we were."

"Are," Lydia corrected, dabbing at her lips with a napkin. Not that she needed to. Her mom's budge-proof coral lipstick remained intact, without a toast crumb in sight. "We are close, honey, but I've just been busy."

Probably with a man. Maybe her dad was right and her mom was dating someone? The sorrow in her gut congealed into a solid lump of misery because a small part of her, the part that still believed in the magic of rom-coms and meet-cutes and happily ever afters, hoped her parents might reunite.

"Too busy for your daughter?"

Lydia pinned her with a disapproving stare. "Don't go all judgmental on me. We both lead independent lives, and mine happens to be more hectic than usual at the moment."

Harper couldn't hold her tongue a second longer. "Who is he, Mom?"

"There's nobody," Lydia muttered, but this time her mom was the one blushing.

"You owe it to Dad to tell him if you're seeing someone, before he finds out from someone else."

And she'd rather that person not be her. Her folks still had a lot of mutual friends who hadn't taken sides after the separation. Then again, she could break the news gently.

"I don't owe that man anything." Lydia stabbed at her toast with particular viciousness. "We're separated, remember?"

Harper rolled her eyes. "How could I forget? What with you gallivanting all over town and too busy to catch up, and Dad calling me constantly to find out what you're up to, it's pretty hard not to notice you're estranged."

Apart from her hidden romantic, what had her holding out hope was the time factor. More than a year had passed since they'd separated, meaning her mom could file for divorce. But Lydia hadn't, and the one time Harper had asked her about it her mom had a mini meltdown.

"I'm sorry for not being around a lot lately." Lydia gave up the pretense of trying to eat and set her knife and fork together in the middle of the plate. "I'll try to do better."

"It's okay, Mom. I get it." Feeling rotten for sending her mom on a guilt trip, Harper reached across the table and squeezed her hand. "But for the record, I miss this." She swallowed the lump in her throat. "I miss us."

In reality, she missed everything. The occasional movie date with her folks, the family dinners where they'd end up having to order in because Lydia had tried some fancy recipe that always ended in disaster, the good-natured grilling about her poor choice in men. Being an only child, she'd always been close to her folks, and their insular family of three had made her feel loved in a way she'd never emulate again.

Pretty pathetic, being thirty and still lamenting the loss of her parents' marriage, but they'd never know how deeply their separation had cut her.

Because if Lydia and Alec Ryland, who were perfect for each other, couldn't make it after thirty-five years together, there was no hope for her.

8

It always amused Manny that his friend Samira, who'd spent over a decade living in glitzy LA, now resided in suburban, cosmopolitan Dandenong.

Melbourne had some high-end suburbs—Toorak, South Yarra, Malvern, Armadale—and considering the combined salaries of a physical therapist and TV reality show host, Samira and her husband, Rory, could've chosen to live pretty much anywhere. Instead, they resided in this modest, modern town house a few streets back from the cultural hub of Dandenong, where people of many nations mingled amidst the shops and marketplace. Considering their place was only one main road away from Kushi, Samira's mother, he figured regular free child-minding for their son, Ron, was part of the attraction.

He hadn't seen the happy couple for two months, discounting Nishi and Arun's wedding. Then again, he hadn't really been focused on his friends at that function, what with his hands—and face—full of a feisty food stylist and cream, respectively.

He hadn't crossed paths with Harper after he'd spied her looking so forlorn at the back of the hall, and he wanted to apologize again, this time saying it with flowers or chocolates. After a little reconnaissance via the Indian aunties, who knew everything about everyone, he garnered that while Harper was

Nishi's best friend, she also knew Pia and Samira well. He would've asked Arun, but the bozo was on his honeymoon with his new wife, hence his impromptu visit to another happy couple.

He knocked on the door and it opened a moment later, revealing a disheveled Rory holding a finger to his lips on the other side.

"Hey, mate, come in, but keep it quiet. Ronnie's only just gone down for a nap, finally." Rory rolled his eyes and dragged a hand through his messy hair. "Sleepless night with young Ronald and I'm knackered."

"You look it," Manny said, stepping inside and slapping Rory on the back. "Fatherhood suits you, mate. You look like you could do with a shave, a haircut, and a two-week nap."

"You look like shit too but please, come in anyway."

They chuckled softly, and after closing the door, Manny followed Rory toward the back of the house, where the family spent most of their time in a sun-filled rumpus room littered with baby paraphernalia, everything from early learning books to brightly colored blocks.

"Can I get you a beer?"

Manny shook his head. "I'm on call later, but you go ahead."

"Nah, beer will really send me to sleep." While Rory's eyes did indeed appear blurry from sleep deprivation, Manny knew the exact second Samira entered the room, because her husband's eyes lit up.

Manny turned to see Samira looking just as weary as Rory but sporting a glow best worn by a woman besotted with her man.

"Hey, Manny, good to see you." She crossed the room and gave him a quick hug, before making a beeline for Rory and kissing him full on the mouth.

"Man, you two make me sick with all this mushy, gushy stuff."

"You're just jealous I chose this magnificent specimen of manhood over Dr. Dickhead," Samira deadpanned, and the three of them burst out laughing.

When they'd first met, Samira's matchmaking Indian mother had been determined to see her only child marry an Indian man, though an Anglo-Indian doctor would suffice. And while Manny never had a genuine spark with the lovely physical therapist, Samira and Rory were a fiery conflagration ready to set alight. Samira had lied to Rory about marrying him according to her mother's wishes to drive the poor schmuck away deliberately, hence Rory's jealousy and nickname for him, which the happy couple had let slip one night when the three of them were hanging out at a local Indian vegetarian restaurant.

"I can't help it if you have exceedingly poor taste in men," Manny said, with an offhand shrug. "I'll have you know some women would much prefer brains over brawn."

Rory bore a startling resemblance to Chris Hemsworth and had turned women's heads around the country as the host of the newest reality show *Renegades*. The guy was smart too, considering he held an economics major, but they had fun ribbing each other.

"And some women prefer a guy with both," Rory drawled, cuddling Samira close, and the three of them laughed again.

"Take a seat." Samira waved at a chair. "What brings you by? We haven't seen you in ages."

"We saw him at the wedding yesterday," Rory said. "Two doc sightings in a week is two too many."

Manny flipped him the finger and Rory grinned.

"I'm actually heading to Auckland for a conference and thought I'd stop by because it's been too long since we hung out."

Samira studied him, her shrewd glance not missing a trick. "This is about Harper, isn't it?"

Dammit, sprung.

Feigning nonchalance, he said, "This is about friends who are too busy with their baby to make time for their other friend, so said other friend has to make a trip from the city all the way out to Dandenong."

"It's thirty minutes, you dufus, not a plane trip." Samira sank into the sofa next to Rory. "And cut the BS. I saw you checking out Harper at the wedding."

And by the cunning glint in her eyes, Samira knew a whole lot more.

"Did Harper tell you what happened?"

"About what?" Samira's eyes widened in faux innocence, and Manny knew he was busted.

"I acted like a jackass, and though I've apologized I want to send her something special."

"If you think I'm giving you her home address, you've got rocks in your head." She tapped her temple for emphasis. "Besides, Harper's not one of your bimbos you can screw around with."

"Harsh, but true," Rory added, with a grin.

"Do you two ever have a nice word to say about me?"

"No," Samira and Rory answered in unison, and laughed.

"Pathetic," Manny muttered, and Samira finally took pity on him.

"Look, the best I can do is give her your number. I'll explain what you want to do, and it's up to her whether she wants the contact or not."

"Fine." He huffed out a breath. It wasn't though, because he had acted like an ass from the moment he'd insulted her food presentation to kissing her like a caveman unable to control his impulses, and he seriously doubted he'd hear from the lovely Harper even after Samira gave her his number.

"Mate, take it from an expert in being hung up on a woman: there's nothing you can do unless she wants you to." Rory gazed at his wife in open adoration, and for a fleeting moment Manny wondered what it would be like to love a woman that much.

Before sending a silent prayer heavenward that he'd never find out.

As for being hung up on Harper, no way. It wasn't his style.

So why did the thought of not seeing her again make him wish for something he could barely contemplate?

9

HARPER HAD FULLY intended to call her dad when she got home from brunch with her mom, but she'd ended up being so drained from the encounter she fell asleep on the sofa.

When her cell rang she jerked awake, hoping it wasn't her dad because she needed her wits about her to field his usual twenty questions about Lydia. She didn't recognize the number on the screen and immediately felt guilty for being relieved it wasn't her dad. She hit the "answer" button.

"Harper Ryland speaking," she said in her best professional voice. She used her cell for business, and an unknown number, hot on the heels of all her cards vanishing at the wedding, could hopefully mean more work.

"Ms. Ryland, it's Wayne Storr."

She didn't know a Wayne Storr, but the name sounded vaguely familiar.

"Of Storr Hotels," he added, for clarification, and she sat up straighter.

Storr Hotels was well-known throughout Australia and New Zealand, famous for their quirky rooms, luxe facilities, and high-end dining.

Her pulse raced with the implication of what this call could mean, but she managed to keep her tone well modulated when she responded with, "What can I do for you, Mr. Storr?"

"I was at a wedding yesterday and was highly impressed with the food presentation, so I wanted to call you personally. That was you, yes?"

"Yes," she parroted, crossing the fingers on her free hand, the one not clenching the cell so tight she hoped it wouldn't shatter.

"Great. In that case, I would like to offer you a job. I'm opening a new hotel in Auckland, and another in Lake Taupo, and we're doing a full spread in major travel magazines that will be located in hotels all around New Zealand. We want to showcase the food in our restaurants, and your styling really impressed me, so what do you say?"

Harper wanted to yell, *Hell yeah*, but she settled for a sedate, "Thanks for the opportunity. If you could forward me the dates, pay scale, and exact locations, that would be great."

"I have your e-mail from your business card, so I'll send through all the relevant information, including your remuneration, now. Look it over, let me know if it's suitable, and we can move forward."

"Excellent," she said, glad her voice didn't come out an excited squeak.

A job like this would catapult her career into the stratosphere and ensure bigger jobs to come. She could move away from the occasional cookbook or newspaper magazine feature and focus on what she really wanted to do: prettying up food for glamorous publications seen the world over.

"I'll be in touch, Ms. Ryland."

Before she could say, *Call me Harper*, he'd hung up, a brusque, busy man who made billions, who'd called her personally rather than getting an assistant to do it because he liked her food so much.

A man who'd just offered her a dream job.

With an excited squeal, she leaped to her feet and did a happy dance halfway between a dab and a floss.

Styling food for Storr Hotels in New Zealand.

A massive coup that could take her business to a whole other level.

Finally, a change in luck.

And a much-needed break from the ongoing drama in her parents' lives.

10

It had been a day since Samira had texted Harper his number. Manny knew because he'd been there when she'd done it during his impromptu visit.

And nada.

Not that he'd expected an instant response, but his compulsive cell checking in case he'd missed a text was growing old fast. He never acted this way for any woman. And considering her over-the-top reaction to his offhand comments about her food, he should stay away.

Not that he wanted to date her per se; he merely wanted to apologize in a more demonstrative way. Then again, hadn't a kiss achieved that more than a bouquet or a chocolate box?

Damn, he couldn't get her out of his head, and rather than packing for his conference, he was sitting here mulling. He'd contemplated getting her information another way but had wanted to leave the proverbial ball in her court. But he'd always been a man of action, and sitting around waiting for anything bugged the crap out of him.

Doing what he should've done in the first place, he pulled up the search engine on his phone and typed in "Harper Ryland, food stylist." It took less than a second for the hits to pop up, and the first one gave him exactly what he wanted: a website. He hit the link and waited for it to load. When it opened, a dramatic photo of chili peppers, zucchini, and tomatoes arranged artistically on an ebony plate popped up. He'd never seen vegetables look so good.

The site had a portfolio button, media, a bio, and contact information. As much as he wanted to read her bio, he clicked on the "contact" button first. And he had it. An e-mail address and a cell number. Bingo.

A lighthearted text would do the trick, hopefully, and before he could second-guess the impulse to contact her, his thumbs tapped at the screen.

DEAR MS. RYLAND,

    YOUR WEBSITE IS MOST COMPREHENSIVE AND HANDY FOR PROCURING YOUR NUMBER.

    I'M HOSTING A HIGH TEA AND HAVE HAD SOME TROUBLE ICING 50 CUPCAKES.

    I HEAR YOU'RE A WHIZ WITH WHIPPED CREAM.

    I WOULD BE MOST GRATEFUL FOR YOUR ASSISTANCE IN THIS MATTER.

    NOT EVERYONE HAS YOUR LEVEL OF EXPERTISE.

    YOUR FRIEND,

MANNY

He grinned as he hit the "send" button. Surely, that would get a reaction out of her?

With the text sent, he hit the "bio" button and sucked in a breath. The professional headshot of Harper standing behind a kitchen bench covered in artistically arranged fruit and savory platters and smiling at the camera had him bringing his cell closer to his face.

She was beautiful, with those expressive blue eyes and wide smile, her makeup flawless and her hair glossy. Definitely more edible than her food.

He speed-read her bio, which didn't tell him a lot. Born and bred Melburnian, loved food from a young age when she'd baked brownies and made lemonade for a stall outside her house, had worked in catering for high-end social events before following her passion for food styling.

All very interesting, but he wanted to know what else sparked her passion . . .

With a groan, he flung his cell onto the bed and resumed packing. Maybe a week away in New Zealand for a medical conference on the latest and greatest ER advances would be just what the doctor ordered?

The fact he was resorting to lame puns even in his own head reinforced his need to get away and stop dwelling on a woman for the first time in forever.

11

HARPER HAD ALWAYS had a thing for hotels.

Ever since she was little, her parents would take her away with them wherever they went. They'd been on family holidays to Singapore, Bali, and Vanuatu, and while those trips had been great, she'd enjoyed the staycations in posh Melbourne hotels just as much. She'd loved everything about those long-weekend stays, from ordering indulgent room service to the tiny toiletries, from crisply tucked sheets to pay-per-view movies.

So as she stepped into the foyer of the new Storr Hotel in Auckland, she exhaled in relief, like she'd come home. Glancing around the opulent lobby, she didn't know where to look first. The funky curved stainless steel reception desk took pride of place along the far wall, which was covered in large asymmetrical wooden panels. A turquoise bar and aluminum-clad terrace to her right looked like the perfect place to chill with a drink while waiting for check-in. The striking red sofas and stylish white leather seats curved around low-slung Carrara marble coffee tables, while lush green plants invited the outside in.

She loved anything esthetically pleasing, and this hotel delivered. She inhaled, allowing the intoxicating smell of paint and new floor coverings to permeate her lungs, and knew this job could be the start of something big for her.

The hotel had opened last week, and she'd read rave reviews online. The restaurant, one of many high-end eateries around the world bearing the name of famous Scottish chef Jock McKell, had local diners flocking, and the thought of styling food for the major magazine campaign Wayne Storr wanted had her subduing an urge to dance a jig right in the middle of this plush foyer.

Jock McKell had been at the hotel opening, but she doubted she'd get to meet him. Probably just as well, as she'd had a major crush on the fifty-something chef ever since she'd started working in the food industry, and she'd rather not make a fool of herself when styling his food for photography was so important. She'd made enough of a fool of herself with that whipped cream incident at Nishi's wedding, and Manny's text on her cell had been burning a hole in her pocket since she'd received it four days ago.

She'd toyed with responding but couldn't come up with something that sounded as witty and lighthearted as his text. She'd never been any good at trading quips, and the fact that she'd embarrassed herself so totally with him made composing a response even harder.

She'd half expected him to send a follow-up text, but her phone had remained annoyingly silent. Then again, isn't that what she wanted? She needed to focus on doing a kick-ass job here and not dwell over a dashing doctor who'd annoyed the hell out of her but kissed like a dream.

After checking in and dumping her stuff in a room with a view of the impressive Sky Tower, she grabbed her laptop and headed for the function room where she'd be styling the food tomorrow. The hotel had several large banquet rooms they used for conferences, and judging by the number of men and women wearing immaculate suits with lanyards around their necks and heading toward the dining room, there must be a conference on now.

The head chef was waiting for her in the function room, and after introductions, he took her through the rundown for tomorrow: the order in which he'd be cooking dishes, the preparation times between each for photography, and any last-minute specifications from Jock McKell himself.

Perspiration trickled down the back of her neck as the implications of what she had to do set in, but the chef assured her the assistant they'd assigned her, a woman named Kylie, was experienced with food styling and the job would proceed smoothly.

However, she'd feel a lot more comfortable once she holed up in her room and studied up on Jock's green-lipped mussels with garlic and parsley, rack of lamb with red wine jus, whitebait fritters, and stewed feijoa ice cream parfait. She knew real inspiration wouldn't hit until she had the food in front of her tomorrow, but she always liked to prepare by studying various presentation methods online.

She'd touch base with the assistant too, because while she trusted the chef, she wanted to make sure there were no nasty surprises tomorrow.

After thanking the chef, she headed back to her room, where she typed Kylie's number into her cell and pressed "call." When the call switched to voice mail after ten rings, she left a message asking Kylie to call her back and hung up, trying to ignore the niggle in her gut. There could be any number of reasons why Kylie didn't answer: she was in the middle of a job, she had an appointment, she wasn't near her cell. But the chef had said Kylie was expecting her call and was free all afternoon, prepping for the job.

She was being silly. Kylie would call back and everything would proceed smoothly tomorrow.

She'd make sure of it.

12

As MEDICAL CONFERENCES went, this one had been more interesting than most. Manny liked keeping abreast of the latest
updates in emergency medicine, and the speakers at this conference had been some of the best from around the world. Advances in treatment for acute pneumonia, deep vein thrombosis,
upper gastrointestinal bleeding, prophylactic negative pressure
wound therapy, and croup had kept him riveted for the last
seventy-two hours, but he looked forward to having the next few
days off.

He rarely had vacation days at home, which meant whenever
he attended a conference away from Melbourne he scheduled
some time to relax afterward. He'd never been to Auckland, despite it only being a three-and-a-half-hour flight away, and he
looked forward to playing tourist.

After bidding farewell to fellow delegates, he headed for the
bar tucked into one side of the foyer. The glaring blues and stainless steel hurt his eyes, but they served a mean martini, a drink
he hadn't sampled since his early days as an intern, when one of
his supervisors had insisted his protégés attend Friday night
drinks at a pub near the hospital for those not on call.

He rarely drank these days, considering his life revolved
around the hospital, and being the chief ER physician meant he

had to keep his wits about him most of the time. But he had no such compunction here, and after ordering an extra dry martini, he pulled out his cell to check on Izzy.

His grandmother always answered on the third ring, like she hated keeping anyone waiting.

"Manish, my boy, how are you?"

"Good. Brain-dead from information overload, but good."

"You love it," Izzy said, her soft accent never failing to invoke memories of trailing after her as a boy, of rolling out parathas alongside her as a teen, of standing hip to hip at the stove while she showed him how to taste food by tapping the wooden spoon against his opposite palm. "But I hope you'll have some time to relax too. You work too hard."

"The conference wrapped up an hour ago, so I'll play tourist for a few days. How are you?"

He wasn't sure if he imagined the barest hesitation. "I'm fine. Old and decrepit, but fine. And I'd be finer if my only grandson would marry before I die."

"Not this again," he said, but there was no malice in his response. His gran had been saying the same thing for the last decade, since he hit thirty and showed no signs of finding a wife. "Trust me, you'll be the first to know if I ever lose my mind and slip a ring on any woman's finger."

Izzy tut-tutted. "You always make light of this, but I'm not getting any younger, Manish, and I don't want you to be alone after I'm gone."

Izzy had always been a bit of a hypochondriac, and he wondered if it was his gran's way of seeking attention since he'd graduated. He knew his long hours in the ER meant he didn't visit her as often as he'd like, but while she'd always have some medical complaint or another, she didn't mention death very often. Probably out of superstition, so hearing her say it twice in this conversation, after mentioning it at the wedding, seemed strange.

"Love you, Izzy. See you next week."

"Take care, my boy. There's an Indian dance next weekend, some extravaganza in Noble Park, that would be good for you to attend to meet—"

"I might be working," he said, the lie sliding from his lips before Izzy could drop names of prospective brides he had to meet at the dance.

He heard her disappointed sigh, so he tempered his response with, "We'll talk about it when I get home."

"Hmm, okay," Izzy muttered. "See you then."

She hung up, and he slid his cell back into his pocket before he'd be tempted to check it. Not that his fruitless search for messages during conference breaks had elicited a response from Harper as he'd hoped. She'd ignored his text, and while he'd never hound her, he'd been tempted to call on more than one occasion after a long day of listening to rambling lecturers.

Maybe their first memorable meeting had been their last and he needed to move on. He never did this. He usually went on one date with a woman, maybe two, and his longest relationship had lasted seven days. Harper wasn't interested. He needed to forget her.

As the bartender placed his martini on a coaster in front of him, a mini commotion near one of the function rooms captured his attention.

A woman who had her back to him was gesturing madly at a guy in chef's whites, brandishing her cell in one hand and oddly, a turkey baster in the other. The chef looked seriously freaked as the woman continued to gesture wildly, her arms windmilling. Crazy foodies.

Then the woman turned and his breath caught.

Harper.

13

HARPER COULDN'T BELIEVE this was happening.

She'd planned everything to the nth degree for the most important shoot of her career, and now this.

"What do you mean Kylie isn't coming?"

The junior chef took a step back, like he expected her to whack him over the head with the turkey baster in her hand. "She called in sick."

"Sick," Harper echoed, knowing it wasn't this guy's fault some flaky assistant had bailed on her, but wanting to clobber something anyway, and he happened to be closest. "Isn't there a replacement?"

"Uh . . . we've rung around, but nobody is available." The chef took another step back and glanced over his shoulder in the direction of the kitchen. "I really should be getting back to prepping the dishes for the shoot."

The shoot. The shoot she had to prepare for solo, an impossible task on her best day, but today, being tasked to make the great Jock McKell's dishes appear perfect so people all around the country would drool over them and flock to the Storr Hotels, she knew she was fighting a losing battle. That well-stocked minibar in her room was looking mighty tempting right about now.

"Go," she said, shooing him away, not surprised when he

bolted. She'd come on pretty strong, her disappointment and worry morphing into anger that the junior chef hadn't deserved.

She should've known something was up when Kylie hadn't returned her call yesterday. Illnesses happened, and in this industry, when you were sick it was best to keep away from food. But this job was huge for her and she felt like she'd screwed it up before she'd begun.

So much for her big break. If she couldn't pull this off, her name in the industry would be mud and she'd be back to catering parties for wealthy socialites. Ugh.

"You okay?"

She froze.

That deep voice laced with an underlying hint of amusement.

It couldn't be.

She turned and stared into startling gray eyes and the too-handsome face she'd last seen covered in whipped cream.

As if this day couldn't get any crappier.

"What are you doing here?"

Manny looked as shocked as she felt. "Medical conference. I'd ask you the same but it's obvious."

"It is?"

"You were at the conference too, but in the DIY artificial insemination lecture," he deadpanned, pointing at the baster in her hand.

An unexpected laugh spilled from her lips when it was the last thing she felt like doing. "I'm here for a big job. Wayne Storr, the owner of this hotel chain, was at Nishi's wedding and liked what he saw with the food presentation, so he hired me for a massive shoot. National coverage in travel magazines to be placed in all his hotels."

"Congratulations," he said, admiration in his potent stare. "I'm glad he saw the great job you did, unlike some other food Neanderthal who dismissed your hard work."

The corners of her lips curved upward. He had an inherent ability to make her smile when she felt like crawling into a corner, curling into a ball, and rocking. "You already apologized for that."

"Yet you didn't return my text?" He tapped his bottom lip, pretending to ponder. "Interesting."

"I didn't have time, what with organizing this job," she said, feeling her face flame at her fib. "A job I'm on the verge of screwing up, big-time."

"I thought you looked a little hot and bothered, and that guy you were talking to was petrified. What's going on?"

Just like that, the comic relief Manny had provided for the last few minutes faded away and the enormity of her situation crashed over her.

"For jobs this big, I require an assistant. We're shooting three dishes today, three tomorrow, and the amount of work required in preparation is massive. We need to shop for props, create props, arrange surfaces, unpack equipment, and that's before the real hard work starts."

She blew out a breath, annoyed by the burn of tears behind her eyes. "The assistant has called in sick, so basically, I'm screwed. I can't do this all on my own . . ." She trailed off, horrified to find her throat tightening. She cleared it and continued. "Anyway, I can't stand around chatting. I've got work to do."

"Let me help," he said, the concern in his eyes almost undoing her completely. "I can be your assistant."

His offer stunned her, and she gaped at him for a moment before reassembling her wits.

"Don't be silly. You've got more important things to do than take orders from me."

When his brow arched in amusement, like he'd enjoy taking orders from her in other rooms besides the kitchen, she added, "Besides, you don't know anything about food styling."

"I'm a fast learner." He shrugged, like his offer meant nothing, when she wanted to fling herself into his arms and hug him. "Seriously, if you want my help, I'm offering."

This was crazy. Why would a doctor she barely knew, and had thoroughly insulted by covering his face in cream then ignoring his text, want to help her?

She met his steady stare and her angst faded. Despite her previous assumptions, and her overreaction to his insulting her work at the wedding, Manny was a good guy. He didn't have to do this, but he'd offered to save her ass despite the way she'd treated him. She'd be a fool not to accept.

"I'm pretty bossy," she said, brandishing the turkey baster. "And I'll probably take an inordinate amount of pleasure in telling you what to do. Barking orders. Humiliating you. That kind of thing."

He grinned, and her heart did that weird little flip-flop thing it had done the first time he'd smiled at her at the wedding.

"I'm all yours, for however long you need me."

That's what she was afraid of.

14

Manny wasn't prone to doing crazy things to impress women. He liked a woman, he flirted, they reciprocated, they dated. Easy.

So what the hell was he doing, running around like a madman as Harper barked orders at him?

The last few hours had been manic, and she hadn't been kidding about needing an assistant. No way could she have done this shoot on her own. He'd helped lift heavy platters and fruit bowls, move tables, and arrange props. And that's when he wasn't handing her equipment so she could work at a frantic pace, making the dishes appear particularly delectable.

She made a rack of lamb look like a work of art; mussels look so fresh, like they'd just been pried off rocks; and whitebait fritters so pretty he wanted to gobble them in one go.

They hadn't stopped for a break over the last four hours, and the delicious aromas of the food, along with her immaculate presentation, made his stomach rumble. But Harper had made it clear: no tasting the food until they'd finished, and while cold lamb and mussels held little appeal, he'd happily eat the lot the minute she called quit.

A photographer buzzed around, changing lighting and angles, taking hundreds of shots. Manny couldn't believe this much work went into producing those food pictures in magazines. Once she'd arranged the dishes Harper didn't stop, ducking between the photographer to move a sprig of parsley or glazing the lamb to make it look extra juicy. She'd barely glanced his way, her focus so intent she could give some surgeons he'd worked with a run for their money.

When the photographer finally laid down his camera and said, "Good job," Manny was ready for a nap. Pulling an extra shift at the hospital had never drained him as much as this.

"Right, time to start packing up, Manny," Harper said, beckoning him over to the banquet table where the food had been set up. "You hungry?"

She leaned toward him. "This is the best part of the job," she murmured, pointing to the dishes. "Jock McKell's recipes are famous, and I can't wait to taste these."

"I'm starving," he said, offering her the plate of fritters before pouncing on them.

Harper took a bite and her eyes fluttered shut. "So good."

Manny's hand paused halfway to his mouth as he stared at the ecstatic expression on Harper's face. Damn, he'd give anything to see something similar but in the privacy of his hotel room.

As if sensing him staring, her eyes snapped open and when she saw him gawping at her, she blushed.

"As you can see, I love all aspects of food, especially the tasting," she said, raising her fritter in a toast. "Eat up."

He did as he was told, savoring the melt-in-the-mouth texture of the fritter but unable to process the flavor as he watched

Harper eat. There was something inherently beautiful about a woman who enjoyed her food, and he could've gawked at her all day. What was left of it, considering darkness had descended and they hadn't noticed.

After demolishing three fritters and two lamb cutlets, Harper wiped her hands on a serviette. "I can't thank you enough for today."

"My pleasure," he said, surprised to find he meant it.

When he'd first offered to help, he'd done it out of chivalry. She'd been genuinely upset, and the sheen of tears in her eyes had undone him completely. He could've spent the afternoon by the hotel pool reading for pleasure, something he rarely had time for. Instead, he'd run around after Harper like a lackey and hadn't minded. Watching her work had been eye-opening, and it solidified what he knew: he wanted to get to know her better.

"Once we pack up, can I buy you a drink?"

Her hesitation disappointed him. Surely, spending an hour or so chilling wasn't so arduous considering she'd been more than happy to have him around all afternoon?

"I'm exhausted and I need to plan for tomorrow's shoot, but sure, a drink would be nice after we pack up."

Buoyed by her answer, he mock frowned. "Pack up?"

"I'm not done ordering you around yet, mister," she said, with a smirk. "Now hop to it."

"Yes, ma'am." He saluted, adding a "bossy boots" under his breath.

She laughed, a pure, joyous sound that made Manny want to say screw the drink and invite her up to his room.

"Manny?"

"Yeah?"

"I owe you one."

She winked before turning away, leaving Manny staring at her gorgeous ass and thanking the karma gods he didn't believe in for this giant cosmic coincidence of placing Harper in his path.

15

As Harper sat across from Manny at the hotel bar nursing a mojito, she couldn't believe the events of today.

In what bizarre world did she lose an assistant for the most important job of her life, then have the man she'd berated yet who'd piqued her interest in Melbourne show up here and offer to help her out of a jam?

He'd been amazing, doing everything she asked of him, and only asking essential questions to ensure the shoot went smoothly. Not only had he saved her ass, he'd made the entire process easier than she'd anticipated and she owed him. Unfortunately, she couldn't get it out of her head that the way she'd like to repay him involved the two of them naked and sequestered in her room.

"Tell me more about your job," he said, sipping his martini.

"Haven't you seen enough of my work for one day? And besides, you're assisting me tomorrow too."

"How could I forget?" His nose crinkled. "I'd envisaged having a few much-needed days off after the conference to play tourist in Auckland but nooooo, I had to get up on my white horse and charge to your rescue." He smacked his head. "Schmuck."

She laughed. "I happen to like a knight in shining armor, especially one who knows the difference between a zester and a piping bag."

He smiled. "My grandmother likes to cook and I've learned a lot from her over the years."

He got this look in his eyes when he talked about his gran that made her melt. "I wouldn't think you'd have much time to cook, what with your hours at the hospital."

"Yeah, I'm busy, but cooking helps me relax."

"What's your go-to dish?"

"*Dahl.* I've been told it was my first solid food as a kid, and I've been addicted to the stuff ever since. Plus it's easy to whip up. Red lentils cook fast."

"I've never cooked it, but it's something I always order at Indian restaurants."

"Maybe I can cook it for you one day?" The glint in his eyes alerted her to the incoming zinger as he leaned in close. "It's an excellent breakfast dish too."

Harper laughed so loud nearby patrons turned to stare. "I can't believe you just said that."

"Why? The thought of the two of us spending a night together to indulge in some wild debauchery surprises you?" He wiggled his eyebrows, and she laughed again. "Because quite frankly, with the chemistry between us, it's inevitable."

"Keep telling yourself that," she said, patting his arm, realizing her mistake a second too late. In trying to be funny and condescending, she'd copped a feel of a very nice bicep.

"Haven't you heard? Assistants fall for their bosses all the time."

"And haven't you heard, that's a harassment case just waiting to happen."

"Lucky for you then, as of tomorrow evening I won't be your assistant anymore and you'll be free to take advantage of me as much as you want."

She'd always been a sucker for a sense of humor, one thing most of her previous boyfriends had been lacking, so it stood to reason she found his wit attractive—along with the rest of him. They grinned at each other and as their gazes locked, something indefinable, something altogether scary, arced between them.

"Thanks for the drink." She downed the rest of her mojito and placed the glass back on its coaster, annoyed by a momentary flicker of regret. She had a job to do, but for the last twenty minutes, having a drink with Manny, enjoying their sparring, she wondered what it would be like to date a guy like him for real. "But I really do need to prep for tomorrow. Meet you in the function room at ten?"

"I'll be there," he said, a hint of regret in his tone. "Harper?"

"Yeah?"

"There'll be plenty of time for you to take advantage of me tomorrow night when the job's a wrap."

The thought sent excitement skittering through her, and before she could react, he placed a far too chaste kiss on her cheek. "Sleep well."

Her cheek tingled where his lips had touched her skin, and she managed to say, "I will," before she bolted for the sanctity of her room, where she knew thoughts of Manny would ensure sleep would elude her.

16

"I can't believe we pulled that off," Harper said, collapsing into the nearest chair and blowing out a breath. "I really do owe you."

"I fully intend on calling in that favor sometime soon." Manny poured a glass of water and held it out to her. "But for now, I'm dehydrated, exhausted, and I'm sure being on my feet all day has given me cankles."

He rotated an ankle for emphasis, and she laughed. "There's nothing wrong with your ankles. Stop being a sook."

He pouted in mock hurt. "I'm sure they're swollen."

She rolled her eyes, their sparkle telling him she'd moved from tolerating his antics to enjoying their sparring.

It had been one hell of a day, with Harper snapping orders at him like she had yesterday but at a rapid rate considering they'd only had six hours to style three fancy dishes and the photographer had another job to go to. While he'd joked about his ankles, his feet did hurt, something that hadn't happened since his early stint as an intern, when he'd had to get used to being on his feet and rushing between wards for eight hours, sometimes longer.

His back ached too as he settled into a chair beside her, feeling every one of his forty years. He worked out when he could squeeze a visit to the gym between his hospital shifts and maintained his fitness, so feeling this blah surprised him.

"You okay?"

"Yeah, but what gave away my agony?"

She smiled and pulled a face. "The exaggerated wince as you sat down."

"I'm old. Don't mock me."

She snorted. "What are you, thirty-three?"

"It's rude to ask a gentleman's age." He waggled a finger at her, the simple gesture making his shoulder twinge. He really needed to make it to the gym more often if lifting a few heavy platters, albeit all day, made him this achy. "But thanks for the compliment. I'm forty."

Her hand flew to her mouth in mock surprise. "Forty? Wow, you're ancient."

"And feeling it." He shifted in the chair and grimaced as his back spasmed. "In fact, I've just thought of a way you can pay me back for my slave labor."

"How?"

"A full-body massage."

"Dream on."

"Already been doing plenty of that, sweetheart, and you're front and center in them all." He winked, enjoying their banter now that she'd loosened up.

She rolled her eyes, but the amusement playing about her mouth told him she was enjoying their wordplay as much as he was. "I'll pay for a massage at the hotel spa, and that's my final offer."

He crossed his arms and pretended to huff. "Not the same as having your hands all over my body."

"Take it or leave it."

"Maybe we can make it a couple's massage?" He wiggled his eyebrows and she laughed.

"Do you ever turn off the flirting?"

"No, it's my thing. Is it working?"

To his surprise, she nodded, a faint blush stealing into her cheeks. "A little."

"I like your honesty."

"And I like . . . the way you helped me out when you didn't have to. Thanks again."

She'd been about to say, *I like you*. He could see it in the sudden tension of her shoulders, in the glance away, and he wanted to tell her the feeling was entirely mutual. In fact, now that her job was done and he still had a few days of R&R left, he hoped they could indulge this mutual "liking" and see if it could turn into something more—like several nights of unbridled passion.

"You're welcome. So what are your plans now the job here is completed?"

"I've got another job lined up at Storr's newest hotel in Lake Taupo, about four hours from Auckland, then I'm sticking around for a few days, relaxing." She stared at him, the color in her cheeks intensifying. "But first, I wonder if you'd like to have dinner with me? My way of saying thanks for going above and beyond the last two days."

Thrilled by her offer, which definitely meant she felt this buzz between them and wanted to prolong their contact, he nodded. "I'd love to. Did you have somewhere in mind?"

"There's a great Indian restaurant not far from here, the best in Auckland apparently, and I have a hankering for some of that *dahl* you mentioned yesterday."

"Then Indian it is."

Though personally, he'd much rather be whipping it up for her, a cozy dinner for two, before feasting on her rather than food. Something to look forward to when they returned home, perhaps?

The moment the thought popped into his head, he wondered where it had come from. He'd never thought beyond one date, and dinner with Harper in Auckland could be classed as that. If they had sex after it, even better.

So what was it about this woman that had him contemplating cooking for her in the future?

"Great, you definitely deserve a treat after I've bossed you around for two days." Her eyes gleamed with amusement, like she'd loved every minute of it. "Shall I meet you back in the foyer in two hours and we can walk to the restaurant?"

"Sounds like a plan." If he could lever himself out of this chair, that is.

She stood in one fluid movement without a grimace in sight, which meant she was used to long hours on her feet and hefting sizable equipment around. Something in his expression must've given him away, because she held out her hand, a smirk quirking that mouth he'd love to devour again.

"Need some help, old man?"

"No," he growled, waving her hand away, before thinking better of it. Any excuse to touch her.

He pretended to struggle, hamming it up, until he heard her mutter, "For goodness' sake," before holding both hands out to him. He seized them and stood, ignoring the twang of his back as he tugged, pulling her flush against him.

"I'm feeling so much better," he murmured, plastering her hands to his chest and holding them secure. "It's a miracle."

"You're impossible," she said, but her admonishment came out breathy and barely above a whisper, and her gaze dropped to his mouth for a fraction of a second.

"Yet you like me anyway. Go figure?"

To his glee, she didn't object. Instead, she eyeballed him, so he could see every tiny speck of indigo in her stunning blue irises.

"I do like you, which is surprising, considering our cringeworthy first meeting. But I'm here to work, and this job is too important to me to lose focus. Got it?"

"I'm flattered I make you lose focus."

"You are definitely impossible," she muttered, with no malice in her tone. "Dinner, and that's it."

"Dinner, and we'll see what happens."

Before she could protest, he swooped in to press a soft kiss against her lips, using every ounce of willpower to rein in the impulse to kiss her senseless.

She sagged against him for a second before stepping back and tugging her hands free. He released her, but his chest burned where her palms had been, like she'd branded him.

"What was that?" A tiny frown grooved her brows, and she stared at him with uncertainty, like she couldn't figure him out.

"A prelude to dessert."

17

HARPER HAD INSTITUTED a man ban for a reason. Several reasons, actually, starting with too many bad dates before her first real relationship, and ending with Colin dumping her because she'd revealed herself to him.

She didn't like being single, which meant when a guy asked her out, she accepted. Friends of friends, guys she'd met at work while in the catering industry, even a few blind dates. Some of those dates had turned into relationships, but none had lasted beyond a few months, when she'd realize that while the guys may have potential they weren't "the one," and as her twenties ticked by, she became more discerning.

That's why Colin ending it had devastated her.

He was a chef at an inner-city restaurant determined to work his way up. They'd had a lot in common, from their love of thriller novels to a three Tim Tam limit while watching *Seinfeld* reruns. He'd been cute rather than handsome, with his reddish hair and easy smile, but he'd been sweet and sensitive, which is why she'd finally trusted him with the truth about her vitiligo.

Sadly, the first time he'd seen her without makeup in their relationship ended up being one of the last, because a day later he ended it. By piping "I'm sorry" in cream cheese frosting on a carrot cake he'd brought home from the restaurant. She hadn't been able to glance at carrot cake since.

Though she hadn't let him off that easily. Fuming, she'd shown up at the restaurant where he worked at the end of his shift, and waited until he'd almost reached his car before confronting him. The idiot had actually shied away from her, like he thought vitiligo was contagious or something. She'd demanded he tell her why he'd ended their relationship, and he'd mumbled something about not having genuine feelings for her and wanting to focus on his career.

She rarely swore, but yelling, "Fuck you," and seeing the dweeb flinch had been the closure she needed; that and flinging his stupid carrot cake at his windshield. That had been a particularly satisfying exclamation point on twelve wasted months with a jerk who didn't deserve her.

Being on her own for the last year had been cathartic. She'd proved to herself she didn't need a man in her life. Being single was fine and her job more than fulfilling.

Of course, her prolonged man ban could possibly explain her ridiculous infatuation with Manny, the gorgeous guy sitting across from her and eating with such gusto she wanted to sweep the table clear and lie in front of him so he could feast on her.

"Quit staring at me," he said, swiping a piece of naan through the rich *malai kofta*. "You'll ruin my appetite."

"Considering you've managed to stuff your face with two onion *pakoras*, two potato *bondas*, a lamb samosa, and three pieces of chicken tikka before these mains arrived, that's highly doubtful."

"I can't help it. Your bossiness made me ravenous." He smirked as he stared at her mouth. "For more than food, in case you were wondering."

She bit back a laugh, enjoying his flirting way too much. "I'm not. Now eat your dinner."

"Still issuing orders, I see," he said, grinning at her before popping the naan wrapped around a *kofta* into his mouth.

She did the same, savoring the explosion of flavor that made her taste buds dance. She loved the vegetarian *koftas*, a mix of potato, carrot, peas, and sweet corn, mashed together with paneer and formed into balls. The spicy gravy coating the *koftas* held hints of cumin, cilantro, turmeric, and garam masala, and the entire combination made her want to lick her plate.

She must've made an appreciative sound because when she glanced up from her plate Manny was staring at her like he wanted to drag her across the table and devour her.

Heat flushed her cheeks. Probably from the chili liberally used in the dish. Her excuse, she was sticking to it. "Now who's staring?"

"Do you know how incredibly sexy it is to see a woman with a healthy appetite?"

His low tone sent a ripple of desire through her. Damn it, she needed to deflect, to get this evening back on track to being a simple thank-you dinner, before she flung money on the table, grabbed his hand, and made a run for it back to the hotel.

"Perhaps if you dated real women rather than model types who exist on lettuce leaves, you'd find my appetite normal?"

"How do you know I date model types?"

She snorted. "Have a look at you. You look like you've stepped out of a magazine for hot doctors. Of course you'd date equally beautiful women."

His eyebrows shot up. "I'm not sure whether to thank you for the compliment or berate you for making me sound shallow."

"We all value appearances, and pretty people tend to stick with other pretty people."

"Once again, I'm glad you've noticed this magnificent facade"—he gestured at his face, his smile wide—"but I'm not sure where the prejudgment is coming from when you don't really know me."

She knew enough. She knew he was chivalrous and kind in coming to her rescue when he didn't have to. She knew he was a hard worker who took orders and executed them to the best of his abilities, even when he didn't have expertise in food styling. She knew he had a killer sense of humor and could laugh at himself; he hadn't brought up the whipped cream incident, but she couldn't get it out of her head. And she knew all these things combined to make her like him more than was good for her.

For the first time in over a year, she wanted to say screw her man ban and just screw him.

"Eat your *kofta*," she muttered, not surprised he didn't understand where her snark was coming from. She may have gotten over Colin a long time ago, but the reason he'd dumped her still rankled. Because every morning when she looked in the mirror, her face devoid of makeup, and she saw the white patches blotching her skin, it reinforced how everyone valued appearances. Would any man want her enough to see past it?

Sensing her distress, he kept silent. Another brownie point in his favor, knowing when to turn off the charm. Damn him for reeling her in with his many attributes.

When they'd demolished the *koftas* and the *dahl* she'd insisted they order, he sat back and patted his stomach, drawing her attention to it. His shirt wasn't fitted so she couldn't see the definition, but she bet it was as perfect as the rest of him.

"I'm so full," he said, with a little groan. "And I have to say, those *koftas* were almost as good as my gran's."

"I'm stuffed too. So no dessert?"

"I didn't say that." His eyes twinkled as he held up his hand, fingers spread. "Give me five minutes. Besides, haven't you heard we have two stomachs, one especially designed for dessert?"

"Remind me never to get treated at your ER," she deadpanned, and he laughed.

"Are you questioning my medical expertise?"

"Hey, if you believe that two-stomach thing, do you blame me?"

"It's nice to see you smile again."

Before she could move, he reached across the table and swiped his thumb across her bottom lip.

She let out a soft sigh, and he lingered for a moment before removing his hand.

"You had a naan crumb," he murmured, uncharacteristic embarrassment making his glance slide away.

"Or you couldn't resist touching my mouth," she said, her bluntness surprising him when his gaze locked on hers.

"That too."

Harper had no idea how long they stared at each other, oblivious to the clanking of dishes coming from the kitchen, the chatter of fellow patrons, and the soft sitar music piping through the restaurant.

But when he asked, "Shall we head back to the hotel?" it seemed the most natural thing in the world to nod and place her hand in his.

18

MANNY DIDN'T HAVE time for romance. Hell, he barely had time to date. So to find himself strolling Auckland's streets hand in hand with a beautiful woman who captivated him more with every passing moment had a distinct surrealism.

"Is this your first time in Auckland?"

"Yes. I've been booked in twice before for conferences here, but they ended up being transferred to Christchurch on the South Island. It wouldn't matter if I had been though, as the conferences are so full-on it means I see nothing of the city beyond the hotels I stay at unless I tack on a few vacation days at the end, which I like to do on occasion."

"Do you attend many conferences?"

"About three a year. The hospital values professional development as much as I do, so I squeeze them in when I can. What about you?"

He loved how Harper's nose crinkled when she pondered. "I spend countless hours poring over food magazines, checking out presentation and camera angles and lighting. Does that count?"

"Absolutely. Doesn't all that research make you hungry though?"

"Of course." She gestured at her body with her free hand. "Have you seen my curves?"

"Oh yeah, and I'm eternally grateful for them."

When she didn't respond, he stopped beneath a streetlight and grabbed her free hand, tugging her lightly to face him. "In case you hadn't noticed, I think you're beautiful."

She didn't believe him.

He felt it in the subtle stiffening of her hands in his, in the tiny frown that appeared between her brows, in the slightest downturn of her mouth. It confused the hell out of him, because she was gorgeous.

And it was more than her big blue eyes or her long brown hair. She had the glow of a woman happy to do things her way. A woman who took charge of her life and didn't allow others to dictate to her. He'd seen it before with some of the staff at the hospital, women who weren't as pretty as Harper but were strikingly attractive because of their inner confidence.

It made him wonder, who had dented Harper's confidence?

"You don't believe me?"

Her shoulders lifted in a shrug. "You're a charmer. Stands to reason you'd say something like that when we're out for a stroll on a balmy Auckland night."

Her dismissiveness annoyed him. "I'm not used to saying things I don't mean."

She snorted. "Yes you are. You're a practiced flirt, Manny, and a damn good one. It's okay. I like a bit of romance like the next girl, so keep paying me compliments, but please don't go all serious on me like you expect me to believe them."

He released her hands and took a step back, because being this close to her didn't help him think. He didn't like being labeled insincere. Nor did he like the tiny voice inside his head whispering, *why do you care?*

He'd always been this way. The class clown. The joker. The flirt. The only time his sense of humor had deserted him was after his mom died, and he never wanted to return to that dark time when he'd lost a shitload of weight and buried himself in work and nothing else.

It had been Izzy who'd snapped him out of his funk six long months later. She'd had a transient ischemic attack, and he'd realized that her worrying about him could rob him of his last remaining family member. His gran had recovered from the TIA quickly, but it had been the wake-up call he'd needed, and he'd started making her laugh again.

Over time, he'd reverted to being the guy everyone wanted at a party, the guy women liked being around because he made them feel good about themselves. Being that guy was the best because it allowed him to do the one thing he'd vowed after his mom died: to never let anyone get too close again.

Izzy often asked why he'd never married, why he insisted on being so stubborn in forgoing any lasting relationships, and he'd fobbed her off repeatedly. How could he articulate to his grandmother that the guilt over his mom's death still haunted him most nights when he lay in bed at the end of a long shift, ruminating on how he saved lives at the hospital but he couldn't save his own mother.

"I've insulted you." Harper laid a hand on his arm, and he allowed it to linger a moment, biting back the urge to tell her how badly he wanted her hands all over him, before shrugging her off. "Sorry."

He wanted to say, *No, you're not*, but being churlish wouldn't get this night back on track, and the last thing he needed with this woman staring at him with concern was to potentially blurt out why her offhand comment had stung so badly.

"Want to head down to the waterfront? I hear they've got some great cafés down there, and we could get a coffee?"

Thankfully, she bought his deflection. "Sounds good."

"Will you slug me if I take hold of your hand again?"

She tilted her chin up, a smile playing about her mouth. "Why don't you try it and find out?"

He slid his hand into hers, feigning a duck that made her laugh. "Come on, slugger, let's go get that coffee."

They strolled in companionable silence, along streets filled with restaurants and boutiques. He'd flipped through a brochure in his hotel room on the first day and seen the Viaduct was the place to be on the waterfront, and as they reached the harbor, he could see why. Restaurants, cafés, and bars lined the wooden boardwalks, overlooking the boats moored in a sheltered harbor.

The smell of sizzling onions, fresh sushi, and spicy Mexican mingled with a tempting aroma of coffee beans.

"This place is great," Harper said, picking up the pace and tugging on his hand like an excited child. "Shall we walk a little farther before having a coffee?"

He'd do anything she asked if it brought that excitement to her face, the kind that made her eyes glow and her cheeks flush.

"Sure." He pointed to a large wooden building at the end of a pier. "Pity the New Zealand Maritime Museum isn't open. I'm such a geek for places like that."

"Me too," she said, staring at him with wonder in her eyes.

"Careful there, Miss Ryland. It almost sounded like you admitted to having something in common with me."

She rolled her eyes, but she hadn't stopped grinning. "Pity I won't have time to check it out. I have to leave for Lake Taupo tomorrow."

Her grin faded and the light in her eyes dimmed. "I'm hoping the new hotel up there has lined up another assistant for me, considering Kylie has pulled out of this job completely."

Manny had never been prone to brain fades. He couldn't afford them in his line of work. Being in charge of a bustling ER meant having his wits about him at all times. So he had no idea what prompted him to say, "I could help you out there too?"

The moment the offer fell from his lips, he waited for regret to set in. He needed a few days' R&R desperately. What he didn't need was more time hefting platters and being told what to do and how to place hoki on a plate.

But the regret didn't come, and he knew why. The longer Harper stared at him with shock in her wide blue eyes, he knew he'd give anything to spend more time with her, even as her lackey.

"Why would you want to do that?" She gave a little shake of her head as if trying to clear it. "I mean, don't get me wrong, you really helped me out of a jam these last two days, but why would you want to traipse to Taupo and do more of the same when you could be chilling here?"

"Chilling's overrated." He shrugged, before tugging on her hand and bringing her closer. "Besides, having you order me around for another day or two won't be so bad if I get to spend time with you like this afterward."

That worried frown was back as she gnawed on her bottom lip. He could see indecision warring with hope in her expressive eyes, and damned if he didn't want to nibble on that lip too.

"I really don't see what you get out of this—"

"It's a genuine offer. Take it or leave it."

To his surprise, she flung herself at him, wrapped her arms around his neck, and buried her face against his chest, murmuring, "Thank you."

As his arms tightened around her waist, he should make light of her response. He should tease her about it, make her laugh.

But it was difficult to formulate any kind of answer with shock ricocheting through him that having her in his arms like this felt so right.

He liked helping people. He'd always been a rescuer. Valid qualities for someone in his profession.

But the feelings rioting through him had nothing to do with being a doctor and everything to do with falling for a woman for the first time.

19

HARPER HAD DATED extensively before her yearlong relationship with Colin. In that time, she'd been lucky enough to be taken on some pretty romantic dates. One guy had taken her to the ballet at the Victorian Arts Center, another had squired her to dinner at Vue de Monde on the fiftieth floor of the Rialto building. Even Colin had spent a small fortune on tickets for the *Harry Potter and the Cursed Child* stage play because he knew she'd read the entire series three times.

So how could sitting on a wrought iron bench overlooking Viaduct Harbor, holding a takeout coffee cup, trading quips with Manny, top all those in the romance stakes?

It wasn't like they were alone either. People strolled along the boardwalk regularly, stopping to admire the moon's reflection shimmering on the water. Muted jazz spilled from a nearby Japanese fusion restaurant. And the raucous laughter of a bunch of college kids sitting at outdoor tables at an upmarket bar frequently punctuated the peace.

None of it mattered, because sitting next to Manny on this bench, his shoulder touching hers, his knee occasionally grazing hers, the scent of his crisp cologne wafting toward her on the breeze, officially made this the most romantic night of her life.

She knew it was him more than anything. His generosity in offering to come to her aid again, his ability to make her laugh, his way of looking at her that made her feel like the most beautiful woman in the world.

Crazy and delusional, because she could never be that for him, but for tonight, in this gorgeous city, with the moon reflecting in the water's gently rippling surface, it was okay for her to have stars in her eyes.

"Tell me about your job," she said, needing a hard dose of reality before she clambered on his lap and kissed him.

"That's a date damper if ever I heard one."

"But we're not on a date."

"Could've fooled me." He opened his mouth in an exaggerated yawn, stretched his arm, then draped it across the back of the bench, resting lightly on her shoulders. "See? Date."

"That's the oldest, corniest move ever," she said, laughing at his mock outrage.

"I'll have you know it worked for Danny Zuko in *Grease*."

Her eyebrows rose. "You've seen *Grease*?"

"Hasn't everyone?"

"It's an oldie but a goodie."

"I've also seen *Pretty Woman*, *Notting Hill*, *Sleepless in Seattle*, and *Dirty Dancing* at least twice."

"You have not."

"Have too. I'm a metro kind of guy."

"You're just trying to impress me."

"Is it working?"

He had no idea how much. "Guys don't usually watch old romance flicks unless they've been duct-taped to the couch."

An odd expression akin to sadness flickered across his face

before vanishing so quickly she wondered if she'd imagined it. "When I first started med school, I'd often pull all-nighters to cram in the studying I had to do, and sometimes when I staggered out of my room I'd find Mom asleep in front of the TV because she wanted to stay up as long as I did. She loved anything romantic so on a rare night off I'd watch one of her favorite films with her."

Something inexplicable and altogether terrifying tightened in Harper's chest, making her want to haul this amazing guy into her arms and never let go.

"I bet she loved that," she said, not surprised emotion made her voice a tad huskier.

"She did. It's one of my best memories of her."

"How old were you when she died?"

"Twenty-five. I'd just qualified." He turned his head to stare at the water. "Turns out, no matter how good a doctor you are, you can't save everybody."

She'd been privy to charming Manny, flirtatious Manny, confident Manny, so hearing him sound so bitter, so broken, humanized him more than anything he could've said.

His jaw jutted, and a vein pulsed at his temple as he stared straight ahead, his gaze fixed, like he couldn't bear looking at her, so she made a segue.

"My parents separated about fourteen months ago, completely out of the blue, and while it's not as hard as losing one of them, it's tough."

Thankfully, his rigid expression eased as he turned to face her. "Sorry to hear that."

"Thanks. They'd been married thirty-five years and were one of the most committed couples I know, so it was a shock."

"I bet." He hesitated, as if unsure how to ask more. "Any particular reason?"

"Not that I know of. I used to have dinner with them every two weeks. Mom cooked a roast; Dad ate as fast as humanly possible before sitting in front of the TV to watch the footy. Then I rock up on this particular Sunday night fourteen months ago, they sit me down like I'm five, and tell me they're separating. Dad looked shattered, Mom resigned."

She'd never forget being ambushed by the two people she trusted most. For as long as she could remember, it had been the three Rylands against the world. Her friends had been envious of the bond she'd shared with her folks, and while she'd rebelled in her teens with the usual hanging out too late, attending parties she shouldn't, and leading Nishi astray, she'd liked knowing she had two people who had her back no matter what.

At the time they'd separated she'd thought it would be temporary. A spat they'd work through, and reunite. Some argument that had escalated to harsh words being exchanged. Both her parents were notoriously stubborn, so she'd thought once their hot heads cooled down they'd get back together. Fourteen months later, she was still waiting.

"Now Mom's acting like nothing's happened, and I think she may be dating again, and Dad's still heartbroken and putting me in the middle. I hate it . . ." She shook her head, embarrassed by the tears stinging her eyes.

Sensing her distress, his arm tightened around her shoulders. "Hey, you okay?"

She waited a moment until the tightness in her throat eased before responding. "Yeah. Anyway, enough of my family drama. Ready to head back to the hotel?"

"First, I'd like to make a toast." He raised his takeout cup. "To us and the start of a beautiful friendship."

"To us." She tapped her cup against his. "A couple of sad sacks who sure know how to ruin a first date."

"So this was a date?"

"No," she said, with a smile.

"Actually, you're right. When I take you on a first date, you'll know."

"How?"

He leaned in close, his warm breath tickling her ear. "I'm so into you that you'll definitely find out."

20

Manny sat on his balcony at the Storr Hotel in Lake Taupo, a beer and his laptop on the table in front of him. Beyond, a stunning vista stretched before him, the largest lake in New Zealand glistening in the late-afternoon sun. He should be relaxed. Instead, as he figured out the time difference between Taupo and Melbourne and waited for Izzy to wake from her afternoon nap before calling, a strange edginess gripped him.

What the hell was he doing here?

He should be back in Auckland, traipsing the streets, checking out art galleries, sampling some of the local cuisine, visiting the museum, even rappelling down Sky Tower. Instead, he'd signed on for another few days as Harper's assistant, and every time he tried to fathom his impulsive offer it gave him a headache.

He never went to these lengths for a woman, especially one who seemed to like him one minute and glare at him as if he had boy cooties the next. Though last night had been better and opening up about their families a tad had definitely brought them closer.

Not that he'd told her much. Because every time he thought of his mom, her death, and the role he'd played in it, he wanted to puke.

A ringtone sounded on his laptop, and he sat forward, glad

for the distraction. If anyone could take his mind off things, it was Izzy.

He pressed "answer" and her face shimmered into view. His gran had lost a lot of hair over the last few years after a perm gone wrong, and the lines bracketing her mouth had deepened, but her eyes were always the same: kind, serene, and filled with love.

"Hey, Izzy. How are you?"

"One foot in the grave, the other on a banana peel."

He chuckled at her standard greeting when she was feeling particularly ornery. "Your back playing up?"

She made a *pfft* sound. "Don't worry about me. Are you relaxing now the conference is over?"

"Absolutely. I'm actually spending a few days in Lake Taupo."

Her thinning eyebrows shot up. "Lake where?"

"It's about four hours south of Auckland. It's a beautiful town on the shores of a massive lake, the perfect place for relaxation."

"That was spur-of-the-moment."

"It was."

"Any particular reason?"

He recognized the cunning glint in Izzy's eyes. She thought his sudden jaunt involved a woman. Not that he'd confirm her suspicions. Izzy had already disparaged Harper at Nishi and Arun's wedding; he didn't need a lecture when he intended to enjoy this fleeting time with the beautiful brunette.

"Someone at the hotel in Auckland recommended it, so here I am."

Not a lie entirely, but if Izzy knew he'd not only been Harper's assistant in Auckland but was continuing his role for a few days here, she'd freak.

He didn't live his life according to what his grandmother wanted, but he didn't want to cause her unnecessary angst either. She hadn't had another TIA in fifteen years, but that had been a scary time, seeing her lying defenseless in a hospital bed, awaiting results of the CT scan and MRI. Getting her upset for nothing wasn't good for her health.

"As long as you enjoy yourself," Izzy said, with a demure smile, but the spark in her eyes meant she could see right through him. "And whoever she is, I hope you have fun."

"Gran—"

"Don't you 'Gran' me, young man. I've been able to read you like a book from the time you were in diapers, and whatever you're up to in Middle Earth, it definitely involves a woman."

He barked out a laugh. Only Izzy would make a *Lord of the Rings* reference. After all, she'd been the one to introduce him to the Tolkien series many years ago.

"You know me too well," he said.

"I certainly do." She made a shooing motion with her hands. "Go have your fun. Get it out of your system, because there'll come a time very soon when you'll have to settle down—"

"You're breaking up." He grabbed a stack of writing paper off the table and scrunched it, making crackling sounds. "Love you. Gotta go."

She grinned, tut-tutting as she waggled her finger at the screen, before it went dark.

He loved Izzy, he really did, but she had a one-track mind when it came to his love life, and if she had her way he would have an express ticket to Marriageville.

His cell rang, and when he glanced at the screen he found

himself smiling. How could Harper turn him into that guy, the guy who got a buzz just by seeing her name pop up on the screen?

He stabbed at the "answer" button with his thumb and raised the phone to his ear. "Hey."

"Hey, yourself. How's your room?"

"You could see for yourself if you popped in."

"Is that a line?"

"I don't know. Is it? Do you feel the compulsion to rush over to room 306 and see me right now? I promise I'll make it worth your while."

"Sorry, no compulsion."

"Too bad." He lowered his voice. "I'm still sore from hefting all those heavy platters in Auckland, and if you want me at the top of my beefcake game for your shoot tomorrow, you could give me that massage."

She laughed, a joyous sound that shot straight to his heart. Head. Gut. Wherever. "Nice try, but I'll pass."

"Your loss, sweetheart. Just think, you could be here right now, having me splayed on the bed at your mercy, all that bare skin to explore, running your hands over my pectorals, my biceps, my latissimus dorsi—"

"I hope that's not a fancy anatomical term for anything below the waist."

He guffawed, enjoying their sparring way too much. "You sure I haven't tempted you?"

She hesitated a moment, before replying. "Maybe a little, but I really have to prep for tomorrow. I'm meeting with the head chef in thirty minutes to run through the dishes, then I'll need a few hours to go through my planning."

"Anything I can do to help?"

"Just bring the beefcake at eight sharp in the morning."

"Yes, ma'am."

"And Manny?"

"Yeah?"

"If I ever lose my mind and decide to give you a massage, I'll be starting at your very impressive gluteus maximus."

21

HARPER COULDN'T STOP grinning as she made her way down the elaborate staircase leading to the hotel foyer. She'd never been good at comebacks, always thinking of a witty retort about ten minutes later than she should. But her parting comment to Manny before hanging up made her feel like punching the air. She just wished she could've seen his expression.

Of course, thinking about putting her hands anywhere near his glutes wasn't conducive to focusing on work, and she needed to get her head in the game to meet with the head chef shortly. She hadn't had much feedback after the job in Auckland. Not that she'd expected to hear from Wayne Storr himself, but it would've been nice to get some kind of response from his minions, who would've e-mailed him the layout and shots for final approval after the job was done.

On the upside, she hadn't received anything negative either, so she took that as a good sign. Thanks to Manny coming to her rescue, she'd done the job to the best of her abilities and had been happy with the result. The fact he'd offered to accompany her down here to help too . . . still blew her mind. Guys needed to get the Manny memo that chocolates and flowers weren't the way to a woman's heart; give her a gallant guy who wasn't afraid to take orders from a stressed-out woman any day.

As she traipsed down the final few steps into the foyer, she couldn't help but wish she landed these kinds of jobs all the time. There was something inherently luxe about the Storr Hotels, an understated elegance that welcomed and enraptured at the same time.

Whereas the new hotel in Auckland had a cosmopolitan vibe with a funky edge, this one channeled Hamptons chic. Cool and sophisticated met rustic beach casual. From the ash floorboards to the white-painted front desk, the pale blue sofas to the textured gray cushions, everything evoked a sense of serenity. She loved it.

Technically, the hotel wasn't open yet. It'd had a "soft" opening last week, meaning a few special guests had been invited to check it out. Not having many people around added to the exclusivity, and for a second she wished she wasn't here to work but had checked in with a hot guy for pure fun.

Ironically, she had the hot guy, and he was up for the fun, yet she was prevaricating. Silly, really, as this job should only take two days like the one in Auckland, but Wayne Storr had said she could have the room for longer. Extremely generous and a rare perk of the job. But Manny probably had to rush back to the hospital and wouldn't be up for a few days' R&R.

You won't know until you ask . . .

Telling her inner voice to shut the hell up, she headed for the bar, where the head chef had said they'd meet. Tucked into an octagonal alcove off the foyer, the bar boasted spectacular views of the lake through floor-to-ceiling glass windows. The ivory leather–covered bar was like nothing she'd ever seen before, with matching armchairs surrounding glass-topped coffee tables scattered throughout the space. The entire place channeled a posh

Hamptons' sunroom, the perfect cozy vibe for settling down with a few drinks.

Like the foyer, the place was empty, except for a guy in the far corner. As she made her way toward him, her heels clacked against the floorboards. He must've heard her, because he stood, turned, and her heart stopped.

Jock McKell. World-renowned chef. In the flesh.

From the times she'd seen him on TV, she'd drooled over him as much as his exquisite food. He wasn't tall, barely six feet, but his wiry body had strength, like he could wrestle gators. With a mop of unruly blond hair spiking in all directions, murky hazel eyes, and a road map of wrinkles, he shouldn't have been attractive, yet women the world over fancied him. She was one of them, and as she tried to focus on putting one foot in front of the other, she really hoped she wouldn't make an ass of herself.

"You must be the delightful Harper Ryland I've heard so much about," he said, the faint Scottish accent as appealing as the rest of him. "Jock McKell."

He thrust out his hand, and she was glad to see hers didn't shake as she extended it. "Yes, I'm Harper, nice to meet you."

They shook hands, and she couldn't be sure if his grip lingered longer than necessary.

"Please, have a seat and we can discuss the dishes you're going to style for me." He rested his elbows on his knees and leaned forward, like he was about to impart some great secret. "I can't wait to see what you can do."

He made it sound like she'd be undressing him, and with his eyes boring into her, a sliver of unease pierced her awe at meeting an icon of the foodie world. She admired this guy in the same way she "admired" Chris Hemsworth, Ryan Gosling, and

Bradley Cooper; from afar, her unrequited lust stemming from their unattainable movie-star quality as much as their looks. And while she may have a wee crush on Jock like most of the female population, she wasn't interested in becoming yet another woman in a long line of probable conquests.

Then there was Manny.

Would she consider responding to Jock if he wasn't around, if she didn't already have a thing for the dashing doctor?

She'd never know, because she liked Manny. Liked him enough to treat him with the respect he deserved, and that meant shutting down Jock if he had any ideas beyond her styling skills.

"I'm looking forward to working with you."

If he noticed her emphasis on "working," he didn't show it, his stare locked on hers increasingly disconcerting.

"I have the list of dishes to style. Are we sticking with that?"

"Yeah." He leaned back and draped his arms across the back of his chair, cocking one ankle and resting it on his opposite knee, in a classic *I'm the king of the world* pose. "But tell me about you."

Uh . . . no. Hell no. The thing was, when Manny looked at her like this, teasing with a hint of impropriety, she liked it. His flirting made her feel girly and appreciated, whereas Jock came across as arrogant and sleazy. He'd known her for less than a minute and he was coming on to her. While Harper knew she looked presentable, she wasn't a great beauty and didn't inspire grand passions in men, so Jock's behavior signified he did this with every woman in his sphere.

It made her dislike him, like finding out her idol preferred takeout over his sublime creations.

"I've got a lot of work to do, so let's just focus on the dishes," she said, her firm tone earning a raised eyebrow.

"No time for play?" His gaze dropped to her cleavage and lingered, before he dragged it back to meet hers, his mouth smirking.

Ugh. So he *had* been coming on to her. "No."

"Too bad. Aussie chicks are hot."

Chicks? Double ugh. But she couldn't screw up this job, so she mustered her best polite smile. "Are we starting with the mushroom risotto topped with roasted garlic shrimp?"

"You're no fun," he muttered, throwing up his hands in theatrical surrender. "Yeah, we'll start with that, followed by the beef ragù over creamy polenta, the John Dory with black truffles, the shellfish ravioli topped with pepper tuile, and finish with the chocolate arch and citrus cream."

Harper's mouth watered at the thought of tasting some of Jock's finest dishes after the shoot, and she hoped rebuffing him wouldn't deprive her of the chance.

"Sounds good. Shall we start at eight in the morning?"

"Make it seven," he snapped, eyeing her with ill-concealed impatience, like he couldn't fathom how she could turn him down.

So much for him being cool with her.

"Seven is fine."

He sat forward suddenly and reached across to grasp her knee before she knew what was happening. "Or we could stay up all night?"

Stunned by his audacity when she'd made it more than clear she wasn't interested, she stared at his hand before sliding back in her chair, effectively dislodging it. She could flip him the finger, tell him to eff off, call him names. But this job meant too much and she'd come too far to screw it up now.

"You're one of my idols, Jock. Your food is incredible, and I'm still pinching myself you're here in person and I get to work with you, but I have too much respect for your talent to mess with our professional relationship."

She'd aimed for the right mix of deference and ego stroking, leaving out the dash of kiss-my-ass she wanted to garnish with. Thankfully, he bought it, the disapproval in his eyes replaced by respect.

"See you at seven," he said, giving a brusque nod and standing.

Relieved, she said, "See you then," waiting until he strode out of the bar before slumping back into her chair.

A relief short-lived when a shadow fell across her and she looked up to find Manny glowering at her, his expression thunderous.

22

MANNY DIDN'T CONSIDER himself a jealous guy. He'd have to care a lot about a woman to allow the green-eyed monster to sink its claws into him, and he never let things get that far.

So the fact he wanted to pummel the jerk who'd had his hand on Harper's knee spoke volumes.

He cared about Harper.

More than he'd cared about any woman in a long time, if ever.

"Who was that?"

"One of the most famous chefs in the world." She pointed to the chair the prick had vacated. "Take a seat and stop towering over me. You're giving me a crick in my neck."

"You have to work with him?"

He sat, making it sound like she'd be giving the chef a private lap dance, and predictably, she bristled.

"I don't need you to go all caveman on me. I took care of him."

"He came on to you?"

"Yeah." She huffed out a sigh, her mouth downturned in disappointment. "He's one of my idols, and I can't believe I actually got to meet him. And in other circumstances I might've been flattered he made a pass at me, but this isn't a good time."

An interesting admission that made him want to punch the air. She could be referring to her work, but by the way she was looking at him, he knew it was more.

She'd rebuffed a famous chef, a guy she idolized, for him.

He'd definitely made the right decision in coming to Lake Taupo with her. But it wouldn't hurt to clarify.

"Because this job is too important to you?"

"That too."

She eyeballed him, daring him to make the connection, and it took less than a second.

He grinned. "You like me."

"Yeah, go figure?"

"And you chose me over some hotshot chef."

"Don't let it go to your head."

She poked out her tongue and he laughed. "You made the right choice, because he may be able to cook fancy-schmancy bite-size portions that'll probably leave you hungry, but can he make a good *dahl*?"

"I've yet to taste your fabled *dahl*."

"But you will, and I promise you, you'll be blown away."

A coy smile curved her lips, reminding him of how badly he wanted to kiss her again. "We're still talking about lentils, yeah?"

"Yeah," he said, though the thought of her lush mouth being anywhere near him made him hard in an instant.

"What are you doing down here anyway?"

"I knocked on your door, and when you weren't there I came looking for you."

A knowing glint lit her eyes. "Why did you knock on my door?"

Because he couldn't wait until tomorrow to see her.

Because he wanted to have her in his arms and see how far they could take this attraction sizzling between them.

Because he was a patient man usually, but she made him a little crazy.

But he couldn't say any of that, so he settled for, "I felt like a nightcap, thought you might like one too."

"Nightcap . . . right . . ." she drawled, making a mockery of his excuse, her smirk alerting him to the fact she knew exactly what he was thinking.

"I've got a whole range of those little booze bottles ready and waiting in my room."

She widened her eyes in faux innocence and pointed at the bar over his shoulder. "But we've got a smorgasbord of big booze bottles waiting for us. Why would we need to drink in your room?"

Damn, he loved her sparring.

"You want me to spell it out?"

Defiant, she eyeballed him. "Yeah."

They'd flirted long enough. Time to up the ante.

Manny stood, moved next to her chair, and crouched down so he could murmur in her ear.

"I want you. Naked. Panting. Hot. Writhing for wanting me as bad as I want you. Splayed on my bed so I can go down on you. Before we fuck all night."

She pulled back from him, her mouth a shocked O.

"Too much?"

She took a moment to respond, but the wicked smile curving her lips told him he'd like what she had to say.

"Not enough. All talk and no action." She stood and held out her hand. "Time to show me."

23

HARPER PULSED WITH heat from the tips of her toes to the top of her head, the throb between her legs surprising her as much as Manny's bluntness.

Until now he'd been flirtatious but not overtly blunt, and hearing him say what he'd like to do with her . . . big turn-on. Huge.

She clung to his hand as they took the stairs two at a time to the third floor. They hadn't wanted to wait for the lift. They didn't speak, didn't need to, the speed with which they ran down the corridor toward his room enough of an indication how much they wanted this.

His key card didn't work the first time, and he muttered a curse before trying it again. When the green light above the handle lit up, he all but wrenched it open. His ankle clunked against the door and he cursed again, but then they were inside and the door had barely closed before he had her up against it. His mouth ravaging hers. His hands everywhere.

Harper combusted. There was no other word to describe how she came alight, pushing against him, her hands plucking at his clothes, desperate to clamber all over him.

His tongue tangled with hers, masterful and challenging, and she groaned with the sheer pleasure of his kiss. He palmed her ass, half lifting her off the ground, and she snaked a leg around his hip. The position suited her just fine, the friction of his erection escalating her from turned-on to oh-my-god in a second.

A delicious vibration between their bodies almost sent her over the edge before she realized what it was. Her cell. She'd turned it to silent before her meeting with the head chef, and while she intended on ignoring it Manny wrenched his mouth from hers and eased back.

"Do you need to get that?"

"No," she said, but the sudden chill between their bodies allowed her common sense to override her blinding lust. The call could be about the shoot tomorrow. Hell, it could be Wayne Storr, and she couldn't let it go through to voicemail.

He stepped back, giving her more room, and she sighed. "Why do you have to be so damn sensible?" she muttered, as she slid the cell from her pocket and checked the screen.

Her dad.

She was tempted not to answer it, but even if she didn't, seeing his smiling face on the screen was enough of a damper on her sexcapades with Manny.

She screwed up her nose. "I have to get this. It's my dad."

"Go ahead." His rueful smile made her want to hug him for giving her this space. "I'll go take a cold shower."

She kissed her fingertips and pressed them to his lips before answering the phone.

"Hey, Dad, how are you?"

"Fine, love. You?"

"I'm in New Zealand for work. Did you get my text I sent before I left?"

"Uh . . . yes, I think so."

Her dad sounded more absentminded than usual, and for the first time since she'd landed in New Zealand she felt guilty for not checking in on him before she left. She didn't want to encourage his clinginess because it inevitably led to questions about her mom she couldn't or didn't want to answer. But her dad should be better by now, past this pining. It had been fourteen months since his marriage fell apart, and he had to move on.

"Have you heard from your mother?"

No, because her mom had a life and that meant she left Harper alone most of the time. But the moment the thought popped into her head she felt disloyal. Her dad was like a giant teddy bear, and he was floundering. He needed her.

"I haven't, Dad, but I've been busy—"

"She's probably seeing someone." He sighed. "Why is she doing this?"

Every phone call, every face-to-face chat with her dad had her fielding the same questions, and with Manny sitting on the bed, his back turned to give her some privacy, she'd had enough. The great Alec Ryland, the life of the party, big, bold, boisterous, had to grow a pair and make a clean break.

"Dad, it's time."

"For what?"

"To file for divorce."

Harper didn't know what was worse, her dad asking questions about her mom's dating life or this silence punctuated by what sounded suspiciously like sniffles.

"Dad, are you okay?"

"I'll talk to you when you get back," he said, and hung up, leaving her feeling more helpless than ever.

Wasn't she meant to be having life crises and her parents supposed to comfort her? This was all wrong, and she was tired of being caught in the middle. Her dad was right about one thing. When she got home they'd talk and she'd sort this out once and for all. Not that she had any say in their marriage or divorce, but she was tired of being pulled in both directions. She'd kept her opinion to herself, but it was time to voice it and make sure her parents moved on.

She crossed the room to lay a hand on Manny's shoulder. Only then did he turn, the concern in his eyes making her want to crawl into his lap for a hug.

"Sorry about that," she said, sitting next to him on the bed.

"You don't need to apologize. Family comes first." He reached up to brush a strand of hair away from her face. "You okay?"

"Yeah, but I'm tired of being caught in the middle. And of hearing my dad so down. When I get home I'm going to encourage him to file for divorce."

"He still loves your mom?"

She nodded, sadness for her folks making her throat tighten. "It's not my place to find out what went wrong with them, or try to fix it, but I wish I could. But that's obviously not going to happen, so I need to be up-front and tell them what I think. They need to move on."

He slid an arm around her waist and she rested her head on his shoulder, grateful for the silent comfort. She liked that he could be serious and supportive, and shelve his joker self when needed. Who was she kidding? She liked everything about this guy, way too much, way too soon.

"Do you want to head back to the bar for that nightcap?"

He was giving her an out, and she gratefully took it. Talking to her dad had definitely put a damper on their sexy time. And while she had full confidence Manny could rekindle their spark quickly, she wasn't in the mood anymore. Besides, she really should get some stuff ticked off her to-do list tonight, and if the prelude to sex with Manny had been any indication, she wouldn't get much done if they went the whole way.

"Thanks, but I should get back to my room and do some work." She cupped his cheek, brushing her thumb across it, savoring the rasp of stubble. "Sorry about all this."

"Nothing to be sorry for." He rested his cheek in her palm for a moment before straightening. "You've got some time off after this job, yeah?"

She nodded, and he leaned forward to brush a soft kiss across her lips, a fleeting touch that left her wanting more, so much more.

"Good, because once your work is finished, I have every intention of making that time count."

24

MANNY KEPT A close eye on that creep Jock McKell over the next two days. He'd wanted to punch the guy in the mouth for laying a hand on Harper. He'd hazard a guess she wasn't the first woman who worked for him who he'd tried it on. Bastard.

He abhorred jerks like McKell who used their power to intimidate women into wanting them. He'd worked with a neurosurgeon once, a chief of neurology, who'd made passes at every nurse, physical therapist, and doctor, regardless of their marital status. The guy had been a prized sleazebag, and Manny hadn't been surprised when the son of a bitch got a sudden transfer interstate, probably after the hospital had to field one too many sexual harassment cases.

But Jock had kept his distance from Harper while they'd worked the last forty-eight hours. Manny had no idea if Harper had factored him into a discussion with the chef, because the dickhead kept casting glowers his way the entire time.

Now, with the job wrapped up, Manny could focus on more important things, like wooing Harper.

He hadn't been proud of how he'd turned Neanderthal on her when he'd seen Jock coming on to her. He'd all but dragged her back to his room. Yeah, he wanted her that badly, but sex that night would've been about possessiveness as much as lust, and he didn't want to be that guy.

He wanted her to want him, and that meant wooing her properly.

Starting with a lakeside picnic at dusk.

"So that's a wrap?"

She flopped into the chair next to him and groaned. "Yeah, all done. I can't believe we pulled it off."

"You did most of the work. I was just the hired muscle."

"Who technically wasn't hired because I'm not paying you."

"Oh, I'll make you pay all right." He wiggled his eyebrows and she laughed.

"Right now, I'm too tired to slap you for that lame-ass comment."

"Are you too tired to be romanced?"

A spark of interest lit her eyes. "What did you have in mind?"

"A picnic by the lake."

"That sounds wonderful, but I really am exhausted. Rain check?"

"Tomorrow at dusk it is then." He tapped his temple, pretending to think. "So what shall we do tonight then, with the whole evening stretching before us, that doesn't involve being upright?"

He snapped his fingers. "I know. We could lie down. I've heard getting horizontal is excellent for tired muscles."

"You'll do anything to get me into bed, won't you?"

"You got that right."

They smiled at each other, reinforcing how in sync they were. After their less-than-auspicious first meeting, he hadn't held out much hope for them becoming civil, let alone this, and it made him want to punch the air in victory.

"Jock kept his distance." He made it sound like a conversational observation when he really wanted to make sure the creep had left her alone.

"Thanks to you."

"What do you mean?"

Her expression turned sheepish. "I might've implied you were my boyfriend and you had a black belt in tae kwon do."

He laughed. "While I like the boyfriend label, the closest I've come to martial arts is my first and last kickboxing session at the gym a few years ago."

"He doesn't know that though and it worked." She screwed up her nose. "I hate sleazy creeps. And I hate him for disillusioning me. I've admired his work for years, have watched reruns of his shows countless times, and he's spoiled that."

"Asshole."

"Ain't that the truth."

He had no right to delve into her past, but there was something in her eyes that prompted him to ask. "Has that happened to you before, being harassed?"

"Yeah, at my first catering job. I took care of it." She smirked and mimicked a sharp jab.

"Dare I ask how?"

"Let's just say a kitchen is full of sharp and heavy implements that can slip from my hands and end up almost castrating someone."

He winced. "Ouch."

"It worked though. The jackass didn't come near me again."

"Good for you."

"I can take care of myself." She squared her shoulders and flexed her biceps into a superhero pose. "So watch out, buster."

"You never have to worry about me overstepping." He held up his hands in surrender. "I've seen your arsenal of weapons, and it ain't pretty."

A faint blush stained her cheeks. "The first night we met, you saw my equipment bag in the trunk of my car."

"Yeah, the second before you creamed me."

She grimaced. "Not my finest moment."

"Yet here we are."

She studied him with an intensity that would've made a lesser man uncomfortable. For Manny, he was happy to have her look at him with an interesting mix of adoration and confusion.

"What?"

"You're some guy." She held up her hand and started ticking off points with the other. "As you so delicately put it, I creamed you at our first meeting. Then I don't return your text. Then you see me acting like a crazy person at the hotel in Auckland. And rather than enjoy a few days' relaxation at the end of your conference, you volunteer to save my ass."

She punctuated each point by flexing a finger. "And to top it off, you travel all the way here to keep saving my ass."

"Already told you, it's a mighty fine ass."

He expected her to laugh at his banter, but her expression turned solemn.

"Seriously, Manny, I can't thank you enough for what you've done for me. Nailing this job was vitally important, and you've helped me achieve that. Thank you."

Manny had received gratitude from patients before, or families of patients whose lives he'd saved. But nothing meant more to him at this moment than having Harper stare at him like he'd given her a precious gift.

"You're welcome."

She leaned over and pressed her lips to his in a sweet, too-chaste kiss that had him wanting more in a second. But he didn't want to ruin the moment with his relentless lust for her, so he settled for a smile when she eased away.

"So we've got a few days before we head back to Auckland?"

She nodded. "Yeah."

"Good, because I intend to make every second with you count."

25

WHEN HARPER OPENED her eyes the next morning and glanced at the alarm clock on the bedside table, she had to look twice. Eleven. Which meant she'd slept twelve hours straight. Impossible, so she blinked and refocused. The time didn't change, and she stretched before struggling into a sitting position.

Being a morning person, she never slept in. And since her diagnosis, it took more time to get ready in the morning before she could face anybody, so she always set her alarm extra early.

Shaking her head, she reached for her cell. Before she'd stumbled to her room in exhaustion last night, she'd made tentative plans to catch up with Manny for breakfast, but the time for that had well and truly passed.

She checked her messages. He'd texted once, just after eight, and called an hour later. She read the text first.

HEY SLEEPING BEAUTY, U STOOD ME UP 4 BREAKFAST.

He'd inserted a heart split in two emoji.

BUT I'LL SURVIVE. CALL ME WHEN U WAKE.

Smiling, she tapped the button to play his voice message.

"Hey, gorgeous, me again, your trusty assistant who gleefully resigned his position yesterday. If you're half as exhausted as I am you're probably still sleeping. Just to let you know I'm heading out to scout the local area for the perfect picnic spot. You know, for our D.A.T.E. later today. I'll probably skip lunch and go for a jog while I'm out, so why don't I meet you in the foyer around four? See you soon." He ended with a loud smooch that made her grin and press the cell to her chest.

Manny had a way about him that made her feel more light-hearted and carefree than she had in years. Technically, they were nothing more than two people attracted to each other making the most of a few days together. They'd end up in bed, she had no doubt, and she couldn't wait. But the way he made her feel surpassed what she'd had with Colin, and that surprised her.

Colin had been a nice guy. They'd had fun together. And despite him gutting her when she revealed her skin condition, she didn't think too badly of him. Their lives had melded for twelve months, and they'd emotionally invested, meaning she missed the intimacy more than him.

So how did Manny, a guy she barely knew, give her that same sense of closeness?

It didn't make sense, but for now she wouldn't question it. She'd worked her ass off the last few days; she deserved to have some fun during her remaining time in New Zealand.

She hit the "call" button next to Manny's name. He picked up on the second ring.

"Eager. I like that, Manny."

"Good morning to you too, Sleeping Beauty. Or should that be good afternoon?"

"It's still morning, though I feel like I've slept away the day."

"You must've needed it."

"Is that your medical opinion?"

"No. I'm off duty."

Just hearing his deep voice had Harper snuggling back under the covers, wishing he was next to her.

"Pity. Because I'm not feeling so good, and I was hoping you made house calls."

"What's wrong?"

"A distinct case of miss-you-itis."

"Damn it, if I wasn't halfway along this Craters of the Moon geothermal hike, I'd be there in a flash." He muttered a curse. "I know. I can give you a more accurate diagnosis over the phone if you do one thing."

Smiling, she said, "What?"

"Tell me what you're wearing."

Her thighs clenched as her smile extended into a grin. "My, my, Doctor, I didn't think this was one of those calls."

"You're in bed. You're missing me. What did you expect?"

"A little decorum."

"Yeah, sure."

"You're right. I want to torture you a little."

"A lot, considering I'm now envisaging you cute and sleep rumpled."

"What are you wearing?"

"Why?" he asked.

"Because I'm assuming there are families on that hike, and too much envisaging may lead to more than one tent pole in that national park."

He laughed so loudly she had to hold the cell away from her ear.

"You are really something else," he said. "And for the record? I miss you too."

"So I'll meet you in the foyer at four for our picnic?"

"Yeah. I found the perfect spot."

"Secluded?"

"Babe, you're killing me."

"Not yet, but maybe this will help." She lowered her voice. "I'm wearing nothing and I'm thinking of you."

She hung up on his garbled cry, grinning madly.

26

Manny had a shit night's sleep. He usually liked the tight corners of hotel beds, but he'd tossed so much he'd ended up yanking the top sheet free before kicking off the lot. When he'd eventually got a few snatched hours, he'd dreamed of Harper—lewd, erotic dreams that left him frustrated. Hence the excessive hiking today.

He'd almost been glad when she'd slept in and hadn't returned his text or call. It had given him time to burn off some energy. He'd already completed the Tokaanu thermal walk at the southern end of the lake, past hot mineral pools, spluttering mud pots, and beautiful native bush, and was halfway through the Craters of the Moon when she called.

With her voice husky from sleep, her banter, and her sexy parting comment, he knew completing the hike would be tough.

If she haunted his dreams, she consumed his every waking thought too. He may have wanted to woo her, but in reality they'd be having the fastest picnic on record later today before they busted every speed limit to get back to the hotel.

Yeah, he was that horny.

Forty-year-olds shouldn't be walking around with boners, and he had to hide behind a tree for a full five minutes after she hung up, ridding his mind of vivid images of Harper naked in bed.

When he got the situation behind his zipper under control, he speed-walked for the next twenty minutes to complete the exploration of the lunar-like landscape. But he barely noticed the bubbling craters, the steam vents, and the soils of many colors before he reached the end of the trail.

How the hell could he pass the time for the next four-plus hours?

At home, if he had a rare day off, he'd hit the gym, take Izzy out for a meal, then pore over medical journals, trying to keep abreast of the latest developments. He always lamented the lack of downtime in his job, but then he'd pull a twelve-hour shift and would be back on a high again. Saving people was his life. It had to be. Because all too often during those days off, when he was alone in his swanky apartment, he'd remember a time when he hadn't been able to save someone . . .

His mom had died because of him.

He'd killed Carla Gomes because he'd been young, cocky, and overconfident.

And he'd never forgive himself for it.

"Excuse me, have you visited the Otumuheke steam pools yet?" A teen in a ranger's uniform thrust a pamphlet at him and he took it, glad for the distraction from his self-flagellating thoughts.

"Thanks." He brandished the pamphlet. "I'll check it out."

Anything to keep memories of the past at bay.

However, soaking in a natural rock pool, overlooking the stunning crystal clear waters of Waikato River, New Zealand's longest, didn't have the desired effect. As relaxing as the hot thermal pools were, they allowed his mind to drift, right back to Harper.

He'd had it all planned out. A picnic on the shores of Lake Taupo at dusk tonight, followed by exploring Huka Falls tomorrow. Nice, friendly activities designed to get to know her better. Dating. A different experience for him, but she deserved it, considering they'd moved past his usual favored quickie the moment he'd offered to come to her rescue.

But all he could think about as he toweled off and got dressed was how fast they could eat the gourmet picnic he'd ordered before making it back to the hotel.

If they made it out of the foyer, that is.

27

HARPER'S PHONE CALL with Manny had left her hot and bothered, so after showering, dressing, and having a croissant and coffee brought to her room, she did the one thing guaranteed to take her mind off the hot doc until their date.

She Skyped her mom.

No surprise that when Lydia Ryland's face appeared on the screen, her mom was perfectly made-up, from her poppy-red lips to her mascaraed lashes, her sleek blond bob shiny beneath the lights in the dining room of her childhood home. Having a hairdresser for a mom had been fantastic growing up and her friends at school would often pop around so Lydia could fix their hair too. Those had been good times, their house filled with laughter and the smell of hair spray, and when her dad invariably came home with pizza for the lot of them, Harper had thought herself the luckiest girl in the world.

These days, not so much. Her parents were bugging the crap out of her, her diagnosis required ongoing treatment, and while she'd nailed this Storr job, she could be back to watching cents if no other work came of it.

"What's wrong?"

Trust her mom to take one look at her and figure she was in a funk.

"Nothing, Mom, just tired after finishing this big job."

Lydia leaned closer to the screen, as if trying to peer through it and figure out if Harper had lied or not. "How did it go?"

"Good. I met Jock McKell."

Lydia's eyes widened. "No way."

"I know, surreal, right?"

Lydia fanned her face. "Is he as hot in person as he is on TV?"

Harper could think of other words to describe Jock—creep, sleaze, jerk—but she settled for, "He's very dynamic, and his food is superb."

"You got to taste it?"

She nodded. "I always get to eat after a shoot is finished." She wanted to add, *You know that*, but her mom had lost interest in her job a while ago, around the time Lydia had dumped Alec and started focusing on herself.

"It all sounds very glamorous, flying to New Zealand, staying in the new Storr Hotels, meeting Jock McKell." Lydia let out a soft, wistful sigh. "My biggest claim to fame is doing a fancy updo for a third cousin twice removed of the lead singer from Human Nature."

Harper laughed. "You're making that up."

"What gave it away? The convoluted family tree?" Lydia smiled, alleviating some of the tension bracketing her mom's mouth.

"My job's not that glamorous, Mom. It's mostly a lot of hard work, long hours standing on my feet and stressing over whether a dish is perfect."

"I miss running the salon," Lydia blurted, crimson flushing her cheeks.

Surprised by her mom's admission, it was Harper's turn to

lean closer to the screen. She vaguely remembered her mom working when she was younger, but she didn't know she'd run a salon, let alone heard her lament the loss of it.

"Did you own a salon?"

Lydia nodded, biting down on her bottom lip. "Your father helped me purchase it before you were born. I ran it for about five years before you came along, then I sold it."

"Why?"

"Because your father's business was struggling, I was taking time off for maternity leave, and we could barely make mortgage payments." She sounded bitter, and her lips thinned. "I thought about going back to hairdressing when you were older, but it never seemed like the right time."

Stunned by her mom's admissions, Harper said, "You could go back to it now?"

Lydia snorted. "Who'd want to hire a sixty-year-old hairdresser who hasn't worked in three decades?"

"It's never too late to upskill, Mom, and if it's something you really want, why not give it a go?"

Lydia's eyes flashed fire. "What I want is for your father to—" She stopped abruptly, the color in her cheeks deepening. "Never mind. Was there any specific reason you called?"

Harper wanted to ask what that outburst about her dad meant. What did her mom want from her dad? But she'd learned early on during their separation that asking questions led to answers she'd rather not hear.

"I just wanted to check in and see how you are, Mom, that's all."

"I'm fine, don't worry about me and my ramblings." She waved away her concern. "When are you back?"

"In a few days." Days filled with Manny, naked, if she had her way. "I'll call you then."

"Okay." Lydia hesitated, and Harper willed her to open up, to tell her what the hell had happened between her parents to shatter their perfect marriage, to trust her.

Lydia had always been Harper's closest confidante and she'd cherished their mother-daughter relationship. But her mom had steadily withdrawn over the last year and nothing Harper said or did could change that.

But she tried one last time, because they were an ocean apart and she wanted to reassure her mom. "You know you can talk to me anytime, about anything?"

Lydia nodded, and Harper didn't know if it was the reflection of light on the screen or the angle of her mom's laptop, but she caught the shimmer of tears in Lydia's eyes.

"Talk soon." Lydia blew her a kiss and shut the call down, leaving Harper torn.

She'd got what she wished for, a distraction from her constant thoughts about Manny. But at what cost? There was something going on with her mom and when she got home she'd find out what it was. She was done being the diligent daughter, staying out of her parents' business because she didn't want to make things worse than they already were.

Her dad still wasn't coping well, and her mom may appear poised on the outside but her eyes hid a multitude of secrets.

She'd definitely deal with them back in Melbourne.

But for now, she had a date with a deliciously addictive doc to look forward to.

28

As HARPER STROLLED across the foyer toward him, Manny hoped he didn't look like one of those cartoon characters with his eyes bulging out and his tongue lolling to the floor.

There was nothing out of the ordinary with her paisley top, denim capris, and sparkly flip-flops, but the woman wearing the outfit made it exceptional.

She wore her hair down, flowing past her shoulders in tousled waves. Beyond sexy. She'd worn it up while working and he preferred this laid-back look. Her makeup was flawless as usual, and while he appreciated the effort, he couldn't wait to see her first thing in the morning, completely natural.

"Ready to be wined and dined?" He held out his hand as she got nearer and did a funny little bow.

"I've been looking forward to it all day."

She placed her hand in his and he raised it to his lips, pressing a lingering kiss on the back of it that made color rush to her cheeks.

"You look beautiful."

"This old thing?" She shrugged like his compliment meant little, but she beamed as her gaze swept him from head to foot. "You don't look too shabby yourself."

"High praise indeed."

He'd gone for a polo and denim. The jeans were a necessity if he couldn't keep his hands off her and he had a repeat of his inopportune boner on the walk earlier. "Shall we go?"

"We should, because if we don't leave this hotel right this very minute, I don't think we'll make it to the picnic at all."

His eyebrows rose at her bluntness. "So that phone call this morning affected you too, huh?"

"You have no idea." She winked. "How desperate to eat are you?"

Extremely desperate—to devour her. But he didn't want their time together to end up like all his previous encounters with women—brief, fleeting, and meaningless. He liked her too much for that, and she deserved a proper date at the least.

"I'm ravenous for you, but we'll need our strength, so food first, feasting on each other later?"

"Oh boy," she muttered, heat creeping into her cheeks. "Lucky you're a doctor, because I'll probably expire from combustion before then."

He ducked down to nip her ear. "Glad to know you're so hot for me."

"You have no idea." She turned her head quickly, sneaking a quick kiss that left him hankering for more.

With a glance over his shoulder to make sure they weren't being observed, he backed her into an alcove, hauled her into his arms, and plastered his lips to hers.

She moaned a little, opening her mouth, and damned if he didn't want to take her here and now. Her tongue tangled with his, hot and sinuous, and he throbbed with wanting her.

Her fingers tunneled through his hair, tugging, until his scalp tingled. He pressed against her, exactly where he wanted to be as she writhed and whimpered a little. So hot . . . *screw the picnic* . . .

He wrenched his mouth from hers, his ragged breathing matching hers. "Fuck, I can't get enough of you," he muttered, giving a shake of his head. Yeah, like that would clear it.

"We should go upstairs—"

"No. Picnic first," he muttered, knowing he'd regret this for the next few hours when he sat through the torturous process of putting food into her mouth while battling a distinct case of blue balls. "You deserve to be treated right."

Confusion clouded her eyes. "I want you, Manny. I don't need all the fancy trappings."

"This isn't a fancy date, it's low-key, and I want to spend some quality time with you."

The confusion cleared, replaced by amusement. "You sure you're not a woman trapped in a man's body?"

"Come on," he said, grabbing her hand. "Besides, the faster we eat, the faster you get to discover that my body is definitely all man."

She fell into step without having to be asked again.

"You DID GOOD, Manish Gomes." Harper raised a plastic champagne flute. "To the most romantic date I've ever had."

"To the most beautiful woman I've ever dated." He tapped his flute against hers before taking a sip. Champagne wasn't his drink of choice but he thought she'd like it, and he'd bought the most expensive bottle in the small liquor store.

"You don't have to lay it on too thick," she said, with a smile. "I bet you've cut a swath through Melbourne and beyond."

"I've dated a lot, if that's what you're asking."

"I know it's none of my business, but you're gorgeous, you're a doctor, you're half-Indian, and that means your gran is probably pushing you to get hitched. So why are you still single at forty?"

"Eat your quince paste and Camembert," he said, shoving a cracker into her hand.

"All the food in the world isn't going to distract me." She popped the cracker into her mouth, chewed, and swallowed. "If you don't answer me, I'll be forced to come up with a few answers of my own."

"Such as?"

"You're lousy in bed."

He almost choked on the grape he'd eaten. "That's not the reason."

"How would you know? Maybe those countless women you've dated haven't wanted to post online reviews?" She giggled, and the sound shot straight to his heart. "Or maybe they did and the news spread, hence your single status."

He mock growled. "Keep this up and you won't get to discover the Manny magic for yourself."

She burst out laughing. "I can't believe you just said that."

"Neither can I." Sheepish, he swiped a hand over his face. "Your fault. You completely discombobulate me."

"Discom what?"

"Bamboozle. Confuse. Drive me crazy—"

"I know what discombobulate means, but it's fun to watch you squirm."

"Bet I can make you squirm in a completely different way . . ." He touched her cheek, tracing the curve of it with a fingertip, along her jaw, and lower, to where her pulse beat crazily in her neck.

"You've made your point," she murmured, her breath hitching. "And if you're so keen for me to give you a review, we better hurry up and eat this feast."

He laughed and lowered his hand, not surprised to find it shaking a tad. She had that effect on him, and anytime he touched her he wanted more.

"So you like the food?"

"It's fantastic." She smacked her lips as she scooped up a dollop of beetroot dip on a gourmet cracker. "And the view isn't bad either."

She stared out over the lake, its still surface reflecting the stunning mauve, indigo, and pink sky as the sun set. He'd stumbled across this spot while driving earlier today, a small, secluded sandy beach with a vista to the town and beyond. A jetty jutted out into the lake and was probably used by locals in dinghies, but for now they had the place to themselves.

"This is surreal . . ." She gave a little shake of her head. "I haven't dated in a long time, and when I came to New Zealand to work, never in a million years did I dream I'd be sitting here with you."

"Would you have responded to my text back in Australia if we hadn't run into each other?"

She shrugged. "Honestly? I'm not sure."

"Ouch. Consider my ego wounded."

"I'm pretty sure your ego will survive." She turned away from the lake to glance at him. "You certainly made a lasting impression the first time we met."

"As did you." He made a grand show of moving the lemon meringue pie aside. "Just in case you get any ideas of topping that whipped cream effort with meringue."

She laughed, causing several birds getting ready to bed down for the night to take flight from a nearby tree. "After the way you've helped me the last few days, you're in no danger of bearing the brunt of my wrath again."

He swiped at his forehead. "Phew."

"But you are in danger."

"How so?"

In response, she cleared the artichoke and ricotta tart, the pumpkin and goat's curd mini quiches, and the mushroom frittata, and crawled toward him on the rug.

"Scared yet?"

"Should I be?"

"Yeah, because you're in danger of being leaped upon by a woman who hasn't had sex in over a year."

Stunned, he opened his mouth to respond, but she pressed a finger to his lips. "You don't need to say anything. But you do need to prove to me you've been worth the wait."

In a second he had her flipped and lying on her back, his body covering hers.

"You know we're in a public place, right?"

He gritted his teeth against the urge to ravish her all the same. "How fast can we pack up this picnic?"

"You've seen me dismantle my displays after styling the food. Either eat everything or throw it all into containers."

"Containers it is," he said, brushing his lips across hers once, twice, teasing her, driving himself nuts in the process, before straightening and offering a hand to help her sit up. "Besides, when you discover my prowess, you're going to be very hungry afterward."

"Promises, promises." Her eyes twinkled, and unable to stop himself he captured her chin and kissed her again. Slower this time. Nipping her bottom lip. Sucking on it. Sweeping his tongue along it to soothe and tantalize.

She moaned, and he knew he had to stop before he lost his mind.

Oddly shy, they didn't look at each other as they packed the picnic away in record time. Anticipation thrummed in his veins as he wondered when the last time was that everything a woman said or did seemed like extended foreplay.

He couldn't remember, which meant Harper had snuck under his guard when he least expected it. It could be the surroundings and the rare feeling of being on vacation. What happened in New Zealand stayed in New Zealand, that kind of thing. But he knew it was more, and he was kidding himself if he thought he could walk away from her when they got back to Melbourne.

Which meant he'd have to break the news to Izzy.

Hoisting the picnic basket into his arms, he asked, "Ready?"

"And raring to go."

She winked as she shook out the rug and folded it, joining him in a half sprint to the car.

Manny had never been so grateful for a small town, meaning they arrived back at the hotel in five minutes and were standing in the foyer with the picnic basket between them in six.

"Let's go to my room—"

"No!" Harper blushed and said, "Sorry, I'd prefer my room. I'm fussy about beds when I sleep."

He didn't point out they wouldn't be doing much sleeping.

But this wasn't the time to nitpick. He wanted this woman, any room, anytime.

"Let's go to your room then."

Her shoulders slumped in relief. "Sounds like a plan."

They rode the elevator in silence, and when the doors slid open he wondered what had really made her so tense. Was she having second thoughts? If so, he'd make it easy for her, no matter how much he'd been looking forward to this night.

As they stopped outside her room, he said, "If you're too tired, it's okay. We can do this another time and—"

"I want this," she murmured, eyeballing him, the depth of her desire ratcheting up his. "I want you."

"Okay." He exhaled a shaky breath as she slid her key card through the lock.

The green light blinked the first time, and as she pushed open the door he knew stepping over the threshold would take him into new territory.

With Harper, it was more than sex.

Damned if he was ready for it.

29

WITH MANNY IN the bathroom, Harper paced. From the door to the balcony and back again, over and over. It did little to calm her rampaging nerves.

She'd almost screwed up this night before it had begun.

Manny had looked at her like a crazy person when she'd freaked about going to his room instead of hers. She'd had it all planned out, how to ensure they hooked up here instead of his room. Lead into it gently, insist they go to her room, easy. Instead, she'd made up that lame-ass excuse about being fussy about beds. Major slap-upside-the-head moment.

He hadn't bought it either, but being the consummate gentleman, he'd offered her an out. He thought she didn't want this.

Like hell.

So she set about proving exactly how much she wanted him.

She'd pulled the covers back, dimmed the lights so only the balcony light remained on, and stripped down to her underwear. Plain old serviceable black cotton. She hadn't planned on hooking up with anyone in New Zealand, let alone Manny, and she hadn't had time to go out and shop for sexy lingerie. It had never been her thing anyway. With Colin, she didn't want him lingering over looking at her body once she'd been diagnosed. It had always been lights out. A smart move as it turned out.

That's why she'd insisted on her room tonight. She needed access to her makeup in the morning, to ensure Manny didn't see her face in all its patchy glory, and so she could control the lighting situation too. The latter wouldn't have been such a big deal in his room, though he might think her mad once she started running around turning off lights before they got down to sexy time.

Thankfully, he'd excused himself for the bathroom when they'd entered her room, giving her time to prepare. The sound of the bathroom door unlatching had her bolting toward the bed. She didn't know whether to sit or stand or lie down, nerves making her palms clammy.

This was ridiculous. She liked Manny. He was a good guy who'd helped her out of a jam when he didn't need to. He was funny and hot and beyond sexy.

She wanted him more than she'd ever wanted a guy, so why wouldn't her pounding pulse calm the hell down?

He stepped out of the bathroom, wearing nothing but a towel wrapped around his waist.

Broad chest dusted in hair. Strong arms. Delineated six-pack. Wow.

They gawked at each other for several seconds, his lopsided smile not what she'd hoped for when he first saw her semi-naked. His fingers toyed with the knot holding the towel up, and her breath caught as he undid it.

Her gaze riveted to that towel, and when he whipped it away with a flourish she didn't know whether to laugh or be disappointed.

"You seemed a bit freaked before, so I thought I might lighten the moment." He flung the towel away and did a bow. "Here I am, for your viewing pleasure."

This amazing man, standing in tight cotton boxers with his arms flung wide, had done this for her. He'd wanted to put her at ease. She wanted to hug him. But first, she had naughtier things in mind.

"You want me to objectify you?"

"Please." With a grin, he lowered his arms and snapped the elastic of his boxers. "But hey, I saved the best bit for you to unwrap."

She laughed, unable to remember the last time she felt this playful before sex. She'd been raised to present the perfect front, even before her diagnosis, so getting naked with someone always involved a lot of forethought for her. Had she waxed, exfoliated, moisturized? Was she wearing the right underwear? Was she thin enough, pretty enough?

Then Colin had seen the real her, and nothing mattered anymore. All the preparation in the world meant little when white patches on your skin made you look like one of those patchy cows.

These days, she did all the usual maintenance—waxing, et cetera—but it was for her. She didn't need a man for validation. But with Manny staring at her like he wanted to gobble her whole, she realized she'd missed this. Missed being appreciated. Missed being adored.

She hoped he intended on adoring her all night, repeatedly.

"Come here," she said, beckoning him. "Time for me to unwrap my present."

"I can barely see you," he said, pretending to flail his arms around blindly as he walked toward her.

"All the better to feel your way."

And that's exactly what she did when he got close enough: put her hands all over him. His chest. His shoulders. His waist.

"Don't move," she murmured. "Let me feel you."

He inhaled sharply as she slid her palms over every contour, exploring every dip with her fingertips. His skin was hot, his muscles hard, and he groaned when she slid her arms around his waist and grabbed his ass.

"I want to touch you," he whispered, his muscles quivering beneath her fingers as they traced the curve of his ass and skated along his waist to the front. "You're killing me."

"Patience." She stepped forward and pressed her lips to his shoulder, the tip of her tongue flicking out to lick him. He tasted salty, with a tangy undertone of citrus cologne. Her tongue traveled the length of his collarbone, lingered in the dip between, before doing the same on the other.

Only then did she slip her hand in the front of his boxers.

His breathing quickened and his lips parted as she delved deeper. He gasped as she wrapped her hand around him, all that hard perfection encased in soft velvet.

"Enough," he growled, stilling her hand. "My turn."

Harper liked taking charge in the bedroom because it gave her some sense of control when the rest of her life was spiraling out of it. But giving herself over to Manny's ministrations felt natural as he lowered her onto the bed and worshipped her with his mouth, his tongue, and his hands.

He unclasped her bra, sliding it over her arms with reverence as his mouth claimed one nipple, his thumb and forefinger twirling the other, sending sensation streaking through her body and pooling between her legs.

She writhed as he alternated between sucking and laving one nipple, and plucking at the other, until she didn't know where his mouth ended and her body began.

"So hot," he murmured when he eventually lifted his head, his eyes glazed and unfocused.

He slid down her body, taking her panties with him, leaving her exposed. She stiffened for a second, hoping he couldn't see all of her in the dark, before forcing herself to relax. There was barely a strip of light on the ceiling from the reflected glow of the balcony light. He couldn't see the patches unless he had X-ray vision.

With the first touch of his tongue against her clitoris, her worries evaporated. The second had her arching off the bed. The third had her hands blindly reaching for his head to anchor him in place. Then she lost all sense as he tongued her with the expertise of a man who knew how to please a woman. He slid one finger inside her, another, her pleasure building too quickly, not quick enough.

As his fingers mimicked what she yearned for him to do with the impressive appendage she'd had her fingers wrapped around not that long ago, he sucked on her clit and she came apart on a yell. Wave after wave rippled over her, setting her nerve endings alight.

She had no idea where he produced a condom from—magic Manny indeed—but the moment he slid into her, inch by exquisite inch, was pure heaven.

Harper hadn't known what to expect when she eventually had sex with Manny, but it sure wasn't this . . . this . . . tenderness. They'd been so hot for each other she'd anticipated hard and fast, but as he slid in and out, oh so slowly, giving a soft grunt every time, she gave herself over to the intimacy of it.

His lips fused to hers, his tongue sweeping into her mouth, testing, tasting. His hands slid under her ass, changing the angle, and soon she was climbing toward climax again. So close . . . just out of reach . . . he bit down on her lip and drove into her one last time and she flew, her orgasm crashing over her a moment before his breath shuddered out on a long, low moan.

When Harper could eventually get her brain to work in sync with her mouth, she said, "That was . . ."

"Magic?"

"Yeah, if that does it for you," she said, chuckling.

"You do it for me."

The amusement faded from his eyes, replaced by an emotion she dared not label for fear of reading too much into this.

So she deflected, something she'd become a master at.

"I'm glad you think so, because I intend on doing it for you all night long."

30

THE RICH AROMA of coffee woke Manny. He'd been having the most amazing dream . . . then he opened his eyes, blinked, and realized the reality far surpassed his fantasy.

Harper sat on the side of the bed and placed a steaming cup of coffee on the bedside table.

"Good morning." She leaned down to press a kiss to his lips but didn't linger. "I ordered coffee, but we've got a breakfast booking downstairs."

Disappointed when she stood and moved away, he sat up and reached for the coffee. "Thanks for this."

"My pleasure."

She crossed to the balcony and pulled the blackout drapes open, and only then did he see her fully. Dressed in jeans and a tank top, face perfectly made-up, hair slicked back in a low ponytail, like she was ready for a day of exploring.

Not quite the wake up he'd envisaged after the hedonistic night they'd spent together. How many times had they done it? Three? Four? Sex with Harper had been better than he'd imagined, and she'd matched him, wild and wanton in a way that had him hard just thinking about it.

Yet this composed woman standing before him was nothing like her wild counterpart, and he hoped he hadn't done something wrong. He never second-guessed himself. Confidence came with age; at least that's what he believed.

So why had she showered and dressed and made a booking downstairs when he thought they'd share room service this morning, preferably in bed?

"You're staring at me," she said, turning to face him, but with the sun at her back he couldn't get a read on her expression.

"That's because I'm besotted. I thought you would've figured that out after last night."

"All I figured out from last night is that you're a sex maniac." She took a few steps toward him. "And I like it."

"Good, because we can skip that tour of Huka Falls I mentioned and spend the day in bed."

He hoped she'd agree but her rigid posture screamed hands-off, as a hint of a frown appeared between her brows.

"You've worn me out, so how about we have breakfast, tour the falls, then come back here for an early dinner, and after that . . ." She gestured around the room. "I think I can handle you spending one more night here before we head back to Auckland tomorrow."

He couldn't get a read on her and it confused the hell out of him. She wouldn't have invited him back for tonight if she didn't want him, yet it seemed like she couldn't wait to get rid of him now.

"Is something wrong?"

She stiffened imperceptibly before broaching the remaining distance between them to sit on the bed. "No, I'm fine."

She captured his face between her hands, running the pads of her thumbs over his cheekbones, tracing a line toward his mouth, before pressing her lips to his. She tasted of minty toothpaste as she grazed her lips over his again and again, torturing him, taunting him.

When she eased away, he glimpsed regret mingling with need in her eyes.

"I can't figure you out." His voice came out rough, hoarse, as he reined in the impulse to haul her back under the covers and tear her clothes off.

"Nothing to figure out," she said, standing and moving out of arm's reach, eyeing the door like she couldn't wait to flee. "Apart from the fact I'm a starving woman who needs sustenance, so how about I meet you downstairs?"

Before he could protest, she was gone.

31

HARPER HAD MADE a complete mess of the morning after.

Manny must think she was a nutjob because of it.

Despite having little sleep, she'd set her alarm for five thirty, giving her plenty of time to shower and dress before he woke. Even then, she'd had the fastest shower on record and hoped he wouldn't knock on the bathroom door and ask why she'd locked it. Taking off her makeup, showering, and reapplying it meant she needed complete privacy, and she couldn't risk him walking in on her.

Ironic, that in the stark fluorescent lighting of the bathroom illuminating the white patches on her face and body, she felt nothing like the sexy, empowered woman from last night. Instead, in the harsh light, she wanted to shrink back into herself and don her camouflage before facing the guy who had rocked her world.

With a sexual attraction as intense as theirs, it stood to reason they'd be combustible in bed, but it had been so much better than she'd imagined. Manny was a skilled, considerate lover who gave pleasure before taking, who made her laugh before making her scream, who had an intimate knowledge of anatomy and used it to her advantage.

Heat flooded her body at the thought, and the fine hairs on the back of her neck snapped to attention at the memory of his hands and mouth all over her.

"Madam, can I get you a coffee while you wait?"

Harper startled and blinked at the waiter, who was barely out of his teens, before shaking her head. She'd already had one coffee and the last thing she needed before breakfast with Manny was to get more wired. "No thanks, I'm fine for now."

The waiter nodded and left her alone. Alone to think about how she could wrestle back some sense of normality when Manny joined her shortly.

She'd all but bolted from her room ten minutes ago. She'd aimed for casual by waking him with coffee but she should've known he'd be too astute, and he'd picked up on her jitters immediately. She'd tried to assuage him with that kiss, but all it had served to do was make her feel worse. What she wouldn't have given to strip and crawl back under the covers with him, but there was a reason she only had sex in the dark, and no matter how spectacular their night, he wasn't ready to see the real her yet.

He'd never get to see the real her.

This thing between them was a fling, an interlude born of close proximity in another country. It would be over as soon as it had begun when they headed back to Auckland tomorrow before boarding a plane to Melbourne the next day. Fleeting fun, just the way she wanted it.

So why did the thought of reinstating her man ban leave her feeling hollow, like all her insides had been scooped out and she was nothing but an empty shell?

She caught sight of Manny at the entrance to the restaurant and waved. He must've gone back to his room to shower and change, because his hair clung in wet whorls close to his scalp, and he wore khaki shorts and a white polo that set off his skin. But he hadn't shaved and the shadow along his jaw lent him a dangerous edge that made him sexier, if that was possible.

She watched him walk toward her, a saunter more than a stride, like he had all the time in the world—or maybe he didn't fancy sitting with the crazy lady at breakfast, the woman who'd welcomed him last night and retreated beneath her polished veneer this morning.

"Hey," she said, when he reached the table. "Hope you're hungry. They've got a wicked menu."

"Ravenous." He bent to kiss her before taking a seat, and that one small gesture went some way to calm her nerves.

She'd treated him pretty badly back in the room, but he obviously didn't hold a grudge as he picked up the menu and flicked through it. She owed him some kind of explanation, but anything she could come up with would sound lame. When he continued to study the menu, she fiddled with the cutlery, trying to compose something that wouldn't make her sound like a nutter.

Stilling her fingers, she folded them in her lap and said, "Sorry for being so awkward before. I'm not so good with morning-after etiquette."

He lowered the menu and eyeballed her, and she was relieved to see understanding rather than censure in his eyes.

"You don't need to feel awkward around me. I thought we got past all that around the time you used my face as a cupcake for your decorating skills."

She laughed, as he'd intended, and she wanted to vault the

table to hug him in gratitude for making this easy on her. "I'm a dork. What can I say?"

"You can say how spectacular I was last night. How you couldn't get enough. How badly you want a repeat."

"That too," she said, with a smile. "I had fun last night and despite running out on you this morning I'm looking forward to tonight."

"Phew, for a minute there I thought your sprint might've been a result of disappointment."

"I didn't pick you to have performance anxiety."

"I don't, but one more moment with you not wanting to be anywhere near me in your room and I might've developed a severe case."

Thankfully, the teen waiter approached again, and after ordering smashed avocado for her and hollandaise poached eggs for him, they fell into comfortable chatter. And it continued throughout their breakfast and on their drive to Huka Falls, New Zealand's number one tourist attraction.

But as Manny took hold of her hand before they started down the track to explore the noisy falls, she couldn't help but think she might've made a mistake.

She'd survived one awkward postcoital encounter this morning. What happened when there was a repeat tomorrow? Would Manny think she was completely bonkers?

It shouldn't matter as they'd be leaving, but it did, because what this incredible man thought of her meant something. The way she saw it, she had a choice. Go back to his room for a quickie before retreating to her room or invite him back to hers to spend the night, knowing he'd probably find it strange to find her fully dressed for a second morning in a row.

She could cite packing and an early checkout, but Manny was intelligent. He'd spot a bluff a mile off. Which meant she'd spend the rest of today dithering over her decision rather than enjoying her time with the sexiest man she'd encountered in a long while.

Freaking great.

32

MANNY THOUGHT BEING a doctor involved a certain amount of acting. Delivering bad news to a patient involved channeling his best poker face, standing up to a surgeon involved commanding every ounce of confidence, and breaking the news of a death to a family member required steeling his expression into one of concern while he may be crumpling inside.

Those acting skills had come in mighty handy today.

He hadn't given a flying fuck that Huka Falls was the largest falls along the Waikato River, that *huka* was the Maori term for foam, or that 220,000 liters of river gushed through a gorge and shot over eight meters to create a beautiful green-blue pool.

He'd faked it all right, showing interest as he held Harper's hand during the river walk, stopping at platforms to get the best view, expressing the right amount of awe at the beauty of Wairakei Park. But all the while he was trying to figure her out.

He'd done years of psychology as part of his undergrad degree and it meant squat, because Harper was holding out on him and he had no clue why.

Sure, she'd said all the right things at breakfast, citing her behavior as a result of morning-after awkwardness, but he wasn't buying it. There was something else at play and he hoped she'd open up to him when they made it back to his room soon.

"You sure you don't want something more substantial for dinner?"

"Takeout pizza is fine," she said, lifting the flat cardboard box to her nose and inhaling. "Plus it's vegetarian, so all that goodness counteracts the cheese."

He parked the car in front of the hotel entrance. "You're trying to bullshit a doctor?"

She flashed her best innocent smile. "Is it working?"

"Not a hope. Wait there."

Her eyebrows rose as he sprinted around the car to open the passenger door.

"Such a gentleman," she said, as he took the box out of her hands and waited until she got out before closing the door.

"That's not what you'll be saying when we get to my room shortly."

He winked but he didn't miss the slight falter in her step. This again? Would she make a fuss and demand he go to her room like last night?

"As long as I get to eat first, after that I'm all yours, and you can be as ungentlemanly as you like," she said, pinching his ass.

Relieved they'd got past the hiccup of which room to spend the night in, they speed-walked to the elevator and eyed the numbers as they lit up all the way to his floor. Once inside his room, he laid the pizza on the small dining table tucked into the corner and spun to face her.

"How hungry are you?"

The knowing glint in her eyes gave him hope. "For food?"

"No." He advanced on her, the tension of the day winding his muscles tight, and he knew the best way to unwind. "Pizza is just as tasty hot or cold, and I'm voting for the latter."

He heard the hitch of her breathing as he stopped in front of her, reaching out to toy with the strap of her tank top. His thumb grazed her skin, and her eyes widened.

"Cold is okay for me," she murmured, giving him all the go-ahead he needed.

After the way she'd blown his mind last night, being around her all day and not being able to slake his lust had been one long lesson in torturous foreplay, and he couldn't wait a moment longer.

Her frantic hands matched his as they plucked at clothes, tore them off, pushed them down. Her hands splayed across his chest as he slid a condom on, her eyes huge pools as she watched him do it. Hungry. Eager. Demanding.

Their mouths fused as he hoisted her into his arms, palming her ass, so she had no option but to wrap her legs around his waist. He sat on the bed and she straddled him, poised over him, before she slid down exquisitely slowly. Engulfing him in liquid heat. Shrouding him. Making him cry out with the perfection of it.

Her eyes never left his as she started to move, their bodies synced to the same rhythm, the friction driving him wild. Sweat slicked his skin as he let her set the pace, biting back the urge to grab her hips and pound into her.

Sensing his need, she whispered, "Don't hold back."

Lunging forward, he kissed her with every ounce of pent-up desire, holding her waist and thrusting upward. Over and over. Her hands groping, his anchoring, in a world turned topsy-turvy.

Her arms caged him, but he slid a hand between their bodies and touched her clit, stroking her, savoring the slickness. She picked up speed, wrenching her mouth from his, riding him with abandon.

He'd never seen anything so beautiful.

Her carnal gaze made him let go, driving them closer to the brink. The tremors started, and Manny pushed her over the edge as his orgasm slammed into him with a force that made him see stars.

When he could finally form a coherent word, he hugged Harper tight. "You are perfection."

She nipped his ear. "You know what else is pretty close to perfect besides me?"

"What?"

"Cold pizza, and I'm starving."

He laughed, and when she joined in he marveled that he'd finally found a woman he could be himself with, who laughed at his lame sense of humor, who got him.

The question was, what would he do with her when he got back to Melbourne?

33

THE MOMENT MANNY headed to the bathroom to take care of the condom, Harper sprang into action.

She couldn't let him see her naked, not when light from the setting sun filtered through the blinds. They'd been too caught up in the moment earlier for him to study her body. Their coupling had been hard and fast, just as she'd wanted. No time for him to see the patches on her body and ask probing questions. Not that he would. As a doctor he'd pick up on the vitiligo straightaway, and no way in hell did she want to go through the explanation of how/when/why she'd been diagnosed.

So by the time he came out of the bathroom, towel wrapped around his waist, she was fully dressed and brandishing a piece of pizza.

"Sorry, couldn't wait."

"You were right about being starving." He cast a quick glance over her clothes but didn't say anything as he pulled on his boxers and dropped the towel. "Save some for me."

"There's plenty," she said, taking a big bite to stop from blurting the truth: that she'd give anything to spend the night with him, that she wished he could see the real her, that she was grateful for the amazing time they'd spent together.

But this had to end, the sooner the better, before she became further invested.

Too late, her conscience cried, because the thought of walking away from this amazing man made her chest ache.

"Hey, slow down, you'll give yourself indigestion," he said, as she stuffed several bites into her mouth.

Chewing bought her a minute, demolishing the crust another, but she knew she'd have to say something eventually. She wiped her mouth with a napkin, balled it, and shot it into the trash, before raising her eyes to find him staring at her.

He knew. He had this look, like he expected her to run.

"What's going on?"

"We're leaving tomorrow and I need to answer work e-mails and check on another job for when I return and Skype my parents and—"

"You don't need to make excuses." Stone-faced, he pointed at the door. "You're free to leave anytime."

His blank features, his dull monotone, and his eyebrows gathered in a frown spoke volumes. Her needing to bolt wasn't new for him. He thought she was a flake, selfish, someone who took what she wanted and left.

Her throat thickened, the truth lodged there. She wished she could tell him she wasn't that person. That she'd fallen for him. That she wanted to trust him. But if anyone had learned the hard way about the pitfalls of trusting, she had.

She wouldn't make the same mistake twice.

"Would you believe me if I said I don't want to leave but I have to?"

"I don't know what to believe anymore." He scrubbed a hand over his face, but when he refocused on her, disapproval pinched his lips together. "Is it the sex? Because I think we're pretty fucking great together, but every time afterward you run."

Hell, she didn't want him thinking that, but he was perilously close to the truth. Would a smart guy like him put the puzzle pieces together and figure out he'd never actually seen her naked body and wonder why?

"Sex with you is phenomenal, the best I've ever had." Heat surged to her cheeks, and to some other choice places that would like nothing more than to strip and straddle him again. "But I guess I am freaking out a little. I like you a lot, but this has happened so fast, and I like my space."

His head tipped to the side as he studied her. "So you're telling me all you need is time?"

She couldn't give him false hope, not when she knew they'd be going their separate ways in Melbourne.

"I don't know what I need," she said, holding up her hand when he opened his mouth to respond. "And that's not your fault, you haven't done anything; it's just me."

"So you're saying what happened in Taupo stays in Taupo?"

"Isn't that what you want?"

She held her breath, willing him to make this easier on the both of them. When he shook his head, she should've known better than to think she'd get what she wanted.

"Usually I'd say yes, but I'm not going to pretend like the last few days have meant nothing."

"Of course it's not nothing. We like each other. But we'll be back in Melbourne soon, and we lead very different lives—"

"Do me a favor and don't preempt anything, okay?"

"What does that mean?"

"Let's keep our options open. You can leave now, no questions asked. But we'll be traveling back to Auckland tomorrow, with another night there before heading home, so let's ease up on the heavy talk and go with the flow."

Nice in theory, but she wasn't the grumpy one when she'd wanted to bolt a few minutes ago.

"You can do that?"

He nodded. "Absolutely."

"Okay then." She stood, unsure whether to kiss him or flee while she had the chance.

He took the decision out of her hands by standing too and placing a soft kiss against her lips. Her fingers ached with the urge to touch him, the fluttering in her chest indicative of either a heart condition or reluctance to leave him, and she knew it was the latter.

"I better go."

She willed her legs to walk rather than run, and when she reached the door, he called out, "Just so you know, me giving you space doesn't mean I'm giving up on us. Not by a long shot."

Hope flickered before she quashed it and left.

34

MANNY HAD DIAGNOSED some pretty rare conditions in his time as a doctor. Microdeletion syndrome, Feingold syndrome, and Wilson disease had all been picked up by him in patients desperately searching for answers, and he'd been lauded for it.

So why couldn't he get a clear read on what was bugging Harper?

Even now, thirty minutes after she'd all but run from his room, he couldn't figure out what had gone wrong. They'd had a fantastic time at the falls, they'd been so hot for each other they'd grabbed takeout dinner so they wouldn't waste time getting naked, the sex had been stupendous again, then he'd gone into the bathroom and come out to find her fully dressed, perched on the edge of a chair like she couldn't wait to leave.

Their discussion hadn't shed much light on the situation either. They'd gone around in circles until he'd realized nothing he said would make a difference. He didn't want to push her into wanting more from this relationship like he did; she'd have to figure it out on her own. Yet he couldn't shake the feeling that in letting her go so easily, he might've ended them before they'd begun.

He needed to clear his head, but he didn't fancy a jog after scoffing too much pizza. So he settled for talking to the most levelheaded person he knew.

Melbourne was two hours behind Taupo, and Izzy would be getting ready for her daily dose of American soap operas. Not an ideal time for a chat, but he needed to do something, and having his gran regale him with mundane details like the latest sale at the local Indian spice shop would ground him.

He hit the "call" button on his laptop and waited, relieved when Izzy's face shimmered into view.

"Manish, how lovely to see you," she said, peering at the screen. "But you look tired. I thought you were supposed to be relaxing after your conference." She tut-tutted. "You're one of those overachievers, always on the go, unable to unwind even when you get the chance. It's not healthy, you know."

He chuckled. This was exactly what he needed, a healthy dose of Izzy's life observations.

"Can I get a word in edgewise or do you want to lecture me some more?"

She waggled her finger at him. "You know I only do it out of the goodness of my heart. Who's going to care about you if your old gran doesn't?" Her shrewd eyes narrowed. "Especially when you don't have a wife, despite my insistence you rectify the situation stat?"

"Stop watching those hospital dramas," he said. "Nobody says 'stat' in real life."

The corners of her mouth tugged into a smile. "Don't distract me. Tell me what you've been doing since the conference ended."

He couldn't tell his gran the best part of his R&R, even though sex with Harper had definitely been the highlight.

"I'm doing all the touristy things in Lake Taupo. Hiking, soaking in thermal pools, checking out the falls."

Her nose crinkled. "Sounds boring." She tapped her lip. "Though as I recall, the last time we spoke a few days ago, I inferred there must be a woman involved in your jaunt to Lake Taupo and you didn't correct me."

"You know I never kiss and tell."

"Yet if you don't tell your dear old gran, how will I tell you if she's suitable or not?"

He refrained from pointing out he'd been choosing his own dates for a long time now. "I like her; that's all that matters."

Izzy's eyebrows shot up. "You've never told me you like any girl. What's so special about this one?"

Before he could respond, she jumped in with, "Is she Indian? Anglo-Indian?"

He should've known: the million-dollar question Izzy had asked repeatedly over the years when he'd admitted to taking a date to any number of hospital functions.

Usually, he'd fob off his grandmother. But Harper's funk had left him strangely vulnerable. He'd wanted to be distracted by Izzy, not have her catch him at a weak time.

"Actually, Harper was at Nishi and Arun's wedding."

Izzy's brow knit together in a formidable frown. "That Aussie girl you were panting after?"

She made it sound like Harper had been running around the wedding naked. Which would've definitely had him panting, now that he'd explored every inch of her delectable body.

"We ran into each other in Auckland. We've been out a few times. It's been fun."

Izzy leaned close to the screen, so close he could see every
wrinkle bracketing her mouth, the dark circles underscoring her
eyes. He expected another of her classic, *You need to marry a nice
Indian or Anglo-Indian girl, preferably in the medical profession like
you, a melding of the minds.*

"Fun. Yes. That's what you need after working so hard. And
that's what rest and relaxation is all about. Good, good." She
nodded in approval, but he knew what was coming. "Have your
fun, Manish, but at some point in your life you'll have to get
serious, and at forty, you're not getting any younger."

And there it was.

She pressed a hand to her chest. "And I'm not getting any
younger either. You know my greatest wish in life is to see you
married before I die, and that could be any tick of the clock now."

Yeah, more classic Izzy-isms.

Izzy adored him, and while she badgered him constantly
about getting married, she never overtly pushed. Her chastise-
ments were always done in jest, as if she believed mentioning his
marital status often enough would jar him into doing something
about it.

Now it was his turn to surprise her.

"What if I said I was serious about Harper?"

She pursed her lips in disapproval, with a disparaging *pfft*
sound. "You know my thoughts on this, Manish. You need a
woman to complement you. A woman befitting to be a doctor's
wife. What does this woman even do?"

"Harper is a food stylist."

He deliberately used her name because Izzy made "this woman"
sound like a hooker.

"A food stylist?" Izzy's nose crinkled. "What does that even mean? Food is for eating, not styling."

Manny sighed, wishing he'd waited until he was in the same room as his grandmother to have this conversation. But he liked Harper, and despite her bizarre behavior he had no intention of giving up on her, so the sooner his gran wrapped her head around the possibility of him dating her, the better.

"All those magazines you pore over, and those foodie sites online? The food is styled to look that good."

"Rubbish. The cooks present the food."

"No, the chefs prepare the food; the stylists make it look good."

He had no intention of telling her he knew this firsthand. Izzy would flip if she discovered he'd been Harper's assistant during his much-needed downtime.

"It sounds like a made-up job," she muttered, tut-tutting under her breath. "What do you mean you're serious about her?"

Damned if he knew.

He had limited time to invest in a relationship, which is why he hadn't done it before. Long hours at the hospital left him exhausted and with little time and energy to devote to anyone else. But Harper didn't strike him as the demanding type. In fact, if her runaway act after the few times they'd had sex was any indication, she wasn't likely to linger and loll around, wanting more than he could give.

Maybe they could make this work?

And maybe he'd be bungee jumping off the Sky Tower in Auckland tomorrow.

Not going to happen.

"Izzy, you know I date extensively but I don't do relationships, yet with Harper I'm willing to try."

She shook her head, disapproval surrounding her like an aura. "This is not what I want for you, Manish. She's all wrong for you. It will end badly."

"Shouldn't I be the judge of that?" He pressed a hand to his heart. "As you so consistently point out, I'm forty. Isn't it time I took a risk on love?"

"You love her?" Izzy screeched, her eyes bulging as her nose almost touched the screen. "You can't be serious."

"Settle, Izzy, I don't love her."

But the moment he verbalized the rebuttal, he hated the gut-deep twist that signaled he may be lying.

"We'll talk about this when you get home." Izzy waggled her finger at him. "I think you'll feel differently when you're back in Melbourne. Vacation romances never last."

Manny agreed, but in this case he had every intention of convincing Harper otherwise.

35

HARPER HAD WONDERED if Manny was too good to be true, and now she had proof.

He should've been pissed about how she'd bolted from his room last night. He should've taken it out on her in some form today during the four-hour drive back to Auckland.

Instead, he'd traded banter with her like nothing had happened. Not that he'd talked the whole way. Oh no, even his silences were companionable and not fraught with tension.

It made her like him all the more.

With Colin, any disagreements had meant he'd sulk for a day at least, sometimes two, and he never apologized. She'd eventually tire of his childish behavior and end up backing down or cooking his favorite meal. She'd hated it.

She should've known Manny would be more mature than that. Was it an age thing? She'd never dated a guy ten years older, and while his laid-back attitude and charming flirting made him seem years younger, she liked that with age came maturity. It gave her hope they could get through dinner tonight unscathed.

Wayne Storr had set it up as a thank-you for the great work she'd done; along with depositing her fee with a healthy bonus into her bank account.

For the first time since she'd started food styling, she had hope she could actually make a living from it. A recommendation from a mogul like him would go a long way to cementing her business, and updating her website was her first priority when she got home.

"We have a few hours to kill before dinner. Anything in particular you'd like to do?" He gestured at his body, his smirk making her laugh.

"You really meant it when you said let's go with the flow, huh?"

"Absolutely." He winked and pointed to the elevator that would take them up to their rooms. "As long as that involves the two of us naked again."

"Pervert." She swatted his chest, remembering exploring every inch of it with her tongue, knowing her telltale blush would alert him to her risqué thoughts.

"Takes one to know one."

"What are you, five?"

"You know exactly how mature I am," he said, capturing her hand and pressing a kiss to her palm before curling her fingers over it, the simple action sending a jolt of heat shooting straight to her core. "Perhaps you'd like to check out certain parts of me again to vouch for it?"

"Crude as well as a pervert," she said, grinning as she pressed the palm he'd just kissed to his chest. "Lucky for you, I don't mind a bit of rude banter."

"What about the rest?"

He covered her hand with his, and she could feel his heart thudding beneath her palm. "Someone recently said she'd had the best sex of her life, and I'm taking some of the credit for that."

"So that's all you took out of our discussion?" She rolled her eyes and wriggled her hand out from under his. "You're such a guy."

"I'm all man, babe, and don't you forget it."

They grinned at each other, and Harper could've leaped for joy that they'd reverted to their old sparring. He really was special. No holding grudges, no delving into her mini freak-out yesterday. Resuming their jaunty familiarity made her like him all the more.

"So getting back to your original question, how are we going to spend the next few hours before dinner?"

He clutched his chest like she'd wounded him. "As much as my ego is smarting that you don't want to spend the afternoon in bed with me, I was actually thinking of checking out Mount Eden if you're up for it?"

"Sounds like a plan."

"Meet you back here in fifteen?"

"See you then."

But before she could walk away, he grabbed her hand. "I meant it when I said let's go with the flow last night. I enjoy spending time with you. That's it."

His sincerity made her want to fling her arms around him. She settled for reaching up and cupping his cheek. "You're a special guy, Manish Gomes, and I like spending time with you too."

She didn't understand the intent in his eyes, and suddenly, the seriousness of the situation hit her like a frying pan to the back of the head.

Here was a guy who'd been witness to her flightiness, her fear, and he hadn't run. In fact, he'd gone to some lengths to set her at ease.

Harper hadn't been looking for a keeper, but maybe she'd found one regardless.

36

"You like hiking, don't you?" Harper flopped onto a bench at the top of Mount Eden and fanned her face. "Which is fine, because you're a doctor and you'd be into that 'exercise is good for your health' crap, but for the record, I'm a couch potato kind of girl."

"Noted." He sat next to her, pulled a bottle of water from his backpack, and handed it to her. "Now drink up. Fatigue makes you grouchy."

"Not grouchy. Thirsty," she said, uncapping the bottle and drinking deeply, drawing his attention to the elegant length of her neck and the pounding of her carotid pulse.

Before he could second-guess the urge, he leaned across and placed his lips over the pulse, giving a little nip that had her half gasping, half choking as she doused him with water.

"Are you trying to kill me? I almost choked," she said, elbowing him away, but there was no malice in her tone, and she pressed her fingertip to the pulse, a coy smile playing about her mouth.

"It's okay, I'd revive you with CPR." He puckered up and made smooching sounds. "A little mouth-to-mouth, combined with my hands all over your chest, you'd be just fine."

She aimed an elbow jab his way again and he laughed. "Sorry, I couldn't resist. You're gorgeous, even when you're sweaty."

"I am not sweaty. I'm perspiring." She dabbed at her top lip and grimaced. "Okay, I'm sweating like a pig, but whose fault is that?"

"If you ever quit complaining, you might thank me for the view," he said, surprised he could do this all day. Swap banter with her, tease her, make her laugh. It had become their thing.

Other women he'd dated hadn't sparked this level of interaction. They'd smile politely at his jokes or look at him with confusion, like they couldn't figure him out. But with Harper, there was none of that. She gave as good as she got, jibing like a champ. He loved it.

"I'm enjoying the view just fine." Her gaze started at his chest and swept downward, and damned if he didn't feel it like a physical caress.

"Stop looking at me like that. I'm wearing shorts."

She deliberately focused on his groin. "Oooh, that could be fun, seeing you sporting a boner—"

"Look at the view out there, now," he gritted out, already at half-mast.

"Spoilsport," she murmured, but did as he said, averting her eyes from him and looking out at the highest volcano in Auckland. "So what am I looking at?"

Playing tour guide would guarantee he'd take his mind off the situation in his pants, so he pointed at the harbor. "That's the Auckland Harbor Bridge, and Rangitoto Island. And in case you were wondering, the volcano last erupted fifteen thousand years ago and left a crater fifty meters deep."

"Fascinating," she said, but he heard the laughter in her voice.

"You're enjoying torturing me, aren't you?"

"A little." She held up her thumb and index finger an inch apart. "Is it working?"

"Spouting facts is guaranteed to get my mind off how badly I want to be buried inside you right now, so you can torture me all you like, but I read up on Mount Eden earlier this afternoon so I can recite tourist info all day."

When she didn't respond, he cast a sideways glance to find her tight-lipped, with flaming red cheeks.

He chuckled. "Now who's torturing who?"

"More facts. Now," she muttered, and he bit back a laugh as he saw her thighs clench together.

"Hmm . . . facts. Well, the volcanic peak we're on is known as Maungawhau, with views over the Hauraki Gulf. The suburb of Mount Eden is rather affluent and filled with trendy eateries. And the history is interesting—"

"You're the most fascinating man I've ever met," she blurted, turning to face him, hooking one leg under the other. "I just wanted you to know that."

"Thanks," he said, capturing her hand and squeezing. "I know we joke around a lot, which I like by the way, but it's nice to see you can be serious about your overwhelming feelings for me."

She laughed. "Yeah, that's me. Unable to control my feelings for you."

"You jest, but trust me, I grow on you."

"Like a fungus?"

"Hey, don't make light of that. I've seen some pretty bad fungi growths on parts of people that—"

"Gross."

"If geographical facts stop you from flinging yourself at me, I thought disgusting medical facts would do the trick even better."

"I'm not the one dealing with a rogue boner."

He laughed so loud she jumped, making him laugh even more. "Rogue boner? That's priceless."

"I'm glad I can amuse you." She tilted her chin in the air, feigning being offended.

"Hey, as long as you're not laughing at my rogue boner, we're good."

Their eyes met, and he wondered if Harper knew how truly special their connection was. Because he knew deep down if they stripped away the banter and the jokes and the sex, they'd still have something that was undeniable.

As if sensing the direction of his thoughts, she leaned forward and pressed her lips to his. Soft, tender, fleeting, yet the touch of her mouth on his twanged his heart, hard.

After his mom died, Manny didn't love. Yes, he loved Izzy, but she was family, and he wouldn't screw up with her the way he would if he let anyone else get too close.

But in this moment, with Harper showing him what her lips couldn't articulate, he knew he was in grave danger of letting her into a place he'd walled off years ago.

It scared the crap out of him.

37

HARPER KNEW WAYNE Storr must've told the kitchen staff to go all out with this dinner, because she couldn't believe the quality of every course. Seared scallops with charred scallions, slow-cooked lamb shoulder with fennel ricotta, grass-fed rib eye with polenta and salsa verde, finished with a tiramisu that made her eyes roll back in her head. At least, that's what it felt like, and if Manny's rapturous expression was any indication, he liked it too.

"That is categorically the best meal I've ever had." He patted his stomach and groaned. "And I'm not going to eat for the next week, I'm so stuffed."

"Me too."

But she knew a good way to burn off calories, and she couldn't wait a second longer. While the food may have been delicious, watching Manny eat had been torture. His lips wrapping around a scallop, his tongue flicking out to capture a dab of salsa verde on his lip, the small, satisfied groan as he spooned the final scoop of tiramisu into his mouth.

He'd driven her slowly but surely crazy.

It seemed like the entire meal had been one giant exercise in foreplay, and she'd been patient long enough.

Time for dessert.

In her case, greed was good.

"Shall we have coffee in my room?"

His eyes flared with awareness, turning the unique gray a deep pewter. "Yes."

He didn't speak as they stood and he took her hand. She liked that about him. For a guy who could be verbose and teasing, he knew when to shut up.

Electricity arced between them as they made it to her room, she closed the door, and he was upon her.

Pinning her against the wall. Hiking her dress up. Tearing her panties off. Unzipping and sheathing and sliding inside her on a low, guttural groan.

She clung to him, whispering all the things she wanted him to do to her, gasping when he drove harder and faster and deeper, just as she'd ordered.

He palmed her ass, lifting her off the floor, and she wrapped her legs around him, anchored in a world tipped on its axis.

He made her feel wanton. Wicked. Wild, as her fingers delved through his hair, angling his head away from hers so she could stare into his eyes, hoping to convey with a look what she could never say.

I'm falling for you.

Those beautiful slate eyes blazed with ferocity as he changed the alignment of their hips, his body rubbing her clit with every thrust.

He stretched her, filled her, and when her muscles spasmed, the pleasure so intense it almost blinded her, he was with her, thrusting into her one last time before her name fell from his lips in a long, drawn-out moan that made her shiver.

When he leaned forward and rested his forehead against hers, she battled the inexplicable urge to cry.

They were good together, almost perfect.

But Harper knew better than anyone there was no such thing as perfect.

AFTER SHOWERING, HARPER slipped into the old T-shirt she wore to bed and checked her face in the mirror one last time. She may have turned off the lights bar a single lamp before going into the bathroom, but who knew what Manny might've turned on while she'd been in here. But she couldn't slather on makeup because he'd become suspicious. Why would she shower last thing at night then reapply a face?

Thankfully, she'd learned the art of advanced makeup application about two months after her diagnosis. She'd paid a small fortune to attend a renowned celebrity makeup artist's class to learn the subtleties of application, and had spent many hours practicing, which meant she could achieve a barely there look with enough cover for her patches.

Satisfied that she looked like she wasn't wearing any makeup when she'd spent ten minutes achieving that exact look, she opened the bathroom door and exhaled in relief. Only the single lamp farthest from the bed was on, meaning she had a fair chance of pulling this off.

Asking Manny to stay had been a major turning point.

A big step for her. Huge.

She trusted him.

Not enough to reveal her true self yet, but after dinner and the way they'd connected during the frantic sex up against the wall she couldn't drive him away. Not again. He deserved better, and with this being their last night together she wanted to make it count.

"I was afraid you'd climbed out the bathroom window to get away from me."

She snickered. "I wouldn't fit."

"You would've tried if you were desperate enough, but I'm glad you chose to stay." He flicked back the bedcovers and patted the spot beside him. "Come here so I can impress you with how metrosexual I am and spoon you."

"You've impressed me enough," she said, with a coquettish smile, before slipping into bed and pulling up the covers.

"Come here." He wrapped his arm around her shoulders, and she snuggled in, terrified by how good this felt but loving it regardless.

"This is nice," he murmured, dropping a kiss on top of her head that made her eyes prickle with tears. "Much better than being abandoned, left to doubt my prowess and second-guess my obvious charm."

"Are you ever going to let me forget that? I asked you to stay this time, didn't I?" She gave him a gentle nudge with her elbow, and he clutched his ribs.

"You have my eternal gratitude. You'll also have my cardio-thoracic surgeon's bill when he checks me over for cracked ribs."

"Wuss."

"Bully."

She rolled her eyes and laughed. "You know, us swapping banter like this might be the best fun I've ever had in bed."

"Ouch, now you're really hurting me, considering we've already had sex in a bed."

She waved away his concern. "You know what I mean. This is nice. No pressure because it's our last night together. Just chilling."

When he didn't respond, she glanced up to find him staring at her with surprising solemnity. "Does it have to be our last night?"

"Considering we fly home tomorrow, yeah."

She'd deliberately misunderstood his question because she didn't have an answer for him. Not one that made sense. This had been fun because it was fleeting, with a guaranteed end date. But back in Melbourne, with the pressures of their careers, resuming treatment for her vitiligo, the worry about her parents and where her next job was coming from, she knew she wouldn't be this carefree.

"I know I said I'm not a relationship guy and I don't have time to date, but what would you say if I gave you a call when I'm between manic shifts?"

Good. He was on the same page as her. No time for a relationship. So why did the dismissive way he said it sting so damn much?

"I'd say call me, but if you think I'll be available for booty calls only, you might find yourself talking to my voice mail."

"I'm not that kind of guy," he said, feigning outrage. "What we're doing here? Conversing? Teasing? Proves it."

"What we're doing now is regrouping, because you're forty and old and you need time to recover between sexual escapades."

He laughed so hard she was pretty sure she glimpsed tears

leaking out of his eyes. "I am not old and I'm going to prove it to you. In another ten minutes or so."

She lifted the sheet, pretending to check out his package, and tut-tutted. "You may need twenty."

She joined in his laughter, thinking she'd be foolish to walk away from this when they returned to Melbourne. She didn't want a relationship; he wasn't offering one. So what would be so bad about the occasional hook-up between friends?

Deep down, she knew.

She wasn't that kind of girl.

She'd never had a one-night stand. All the guys she'd dated had been with the view to a relationship, the kind of steadfast, loyal relationship her folks had.

And look how that turned out.

"You can call me," she said, snuggling back into his chest. "I can't promise I'll answer, but you can call."

"Good, because I have a feeling I'm going to miss having you around every day when we get home." His arm tightened around her, and he rested his cheek on top of her head. "I don't like many people in this world because most of them annoy me with their foibles and hang-ups, but you, Harper Ryland, I like."

And damned if Harper's heart didn't swell with hope that maybe Manny could be the guy to get her to permanently shelve her man ban.

38

MANNY HATED EMOTIONAL airport scenes. He witnessed one every time he flew; a couple embracing like they'd never see each other again, squealing kids wrapped around a parent's leg, or a passionate interlude between two people who needed to get a room. He'd never understood the need to be excessively demonstrative, but as he watched Harper get into a taxi, he had the distinct urge to run after her and flag the damn thing down.

He'd offered to give her a lift, but she'd declined. It had annoyed him at first, but then he'd realized she might be struggling a tad over their parting and was trying to give them both an easy out.

As it was, their goodbye had been simple. As they'd exited the terminal, pulling their suitcases behind them, he'd stopped, opened his arms to her, and she'd stepped into his embrace without hesitation.

He'd hugged her tight, hoping to convey how much he'd enjoyed their time together. As if trying to do the same, she'd wrapped her arms around his waist and clung to him, her face buried against his chest, her body plastered to his.

He liked that they didn't speak, but as they'd eventually released each other he wished he could make sense of the feelings rioting through him. But he didn't like the confusion, and he sure as hell couldn't articulate it to her, so he'd dropped a kiss on her lips and smiled as she touched his cheek briefly before she headed for the taxi rank.

As the taxi pulled away from the curb, she slid her window down and waved. He tried to get a read on her expression, but at this distance he didn't know whether it was stoic or on the verge of crumpling.

He returned her wave and watched the taxi until it disappeared, feeling like one of those emotional airport schmucks he'd been judging earlier.

Being this out of sorts, he'd like nothing better than to head home, but he needed to check on Izzy. She may drive him crazy sometimes with her matchmaking but she depended on him, and he'd never shirk his duty.

He'd been lax once before, and his mom had died as a result.

Traffic was particularly bad on the freeway and it took an hour to reach the city, and another forty minutes to reach Dandenong, where Izzy had lived in the same house for the last thirty-five years. It had been his home too before he'd started med school and moved into dorms on campus. He always wondered why his mom hadn't found them a place of their own; he'd asked once, when he'd been about ten, and his mom said Izzy needed to be looked after and it was their duty considering his dad had died when he was two and he'd asked Carla Gomes to look after his mother.

A duty Manny had assumed after Carla died.

But he knew it was love more than duty that made Izzy such a big part of his life. He respected his grandmother, and she was the only family he had left. She'd been his rock after his mom died, and for that alone he owed her.

As he strode along the bricked path to the front door, he was surprised to see the garden appeared unattended, with the lawn an inch too long and weeds among the flower beds Izzy had once tended with such patience. These days, a gardener came once every two weeks, but it looked like he hadn't been in a month.

Manny had offered to buy Izzy a new house many times—something smaller if she liked, or even a fancy unit in a retirement village—but Izzy would have none of it. These days, whenever he brought it up she'd chastise him with *You need to bury me under the curry leaf tree out the back*, which ensured he'd inevitably change the subject.

When he reached the front door, he knocked three times before using his key to let himself in. The faintest aroma of fenugreek and garam masala clung to the walls, indicative of the many tasty Indian dishes Izzy had whipped up over the years.

"In here, Manish," Izzy called out from the lounge room. Not that she needed to; it was where she spent all her time, watching soap operas or playing games on her electronic tablet.

"Hi, Izzy . . ." His greeting faded as he caught sight of his grandmother, sitting in her favorite chintz armchair by the gas log fire.

She'd lost weight.

Enough that the red sweater hung from her shoulders and black leggings accentuated her twiglike legs. Her cheeks had a hint of gauntness too. How had he not noticed during their video calls?

Guilt niggled in his gut. Had he been too bamboozled by Harper, too caught up in his own pleasure, to notice?

"Stop gawking and come say hello to your grandmother," she muttered, holding open her arms for a hug.

When he wrapped his arms around her, it confirmed what he already knew. She'd definitely shed a few pounds. He'd last seen her at Arun's wedding, and that had been several weeks ago.

Unexplained weight loss at any age wasn't good from a medical standpoint, and in his grandmother it made him want to call the paramedics.

All the texts he'd pored over as an undergrad flashed before his eyes. Any number of conditions could result in weight loss: muscle wasting, overactive thyroid, diabetes, endocarditis, chronic obstructive pulmonary disease, inflammatory bowel disease, peptic ulcer, heart failure, and the big C. The thought of Izzy dealing with any of those made him feel sick.

He wanted to grill her, but he knew from experience Izzy didn't take kindly to being quizzed. She'd become defensive and shut down, and he couldn't have that happening, not when he needed answers.

Ironic, that he'd been worried coming here today because he'd expected an interrogation of epic proportions regarding Harper, and now he was worried for an entirely different reason.

"How are you?" He sat on the armchair next to hers, the old springs creaking. It had been his chair since he was a kid, and he'd read many a book curled up in it while Izzy and Carla watched Bollywood movies.

"The usual. Old and decrepit."

His gran's unusually morose answers had bothered him in New Zealand, but he'd dismissed it. Now he wondered if her responses were indicative of a deeper problem she didn't want him knowing about.

"Eating well?"

Predictably, she bristled, glaring at him like he'd asked her something ridiculously personal. "When you're my age, you don't feel like eating every single meal, so I might have skipped a few."

That could explain the weight loss, but Izzy had skipped breakfast or lunch for as long as he could remember.

"And you're feeling okay?"

"Fine," she snapped, but her gaze slid away, and he knew there was something going on.

He could hedge around it, but worry would gnaw at him until he confronted her, and if she needed more tests or special care, he'd rather know sooner than later.

"You've lost weight since I've been away."

"Nonsense," she said, waving away his concern. "Now tell me about this woman you were so distracted by. What was her name? Harper?" Her nose crinkled. "What kind of name is that?"

Of course Izzy would deflect. It was her way. He'd do better by answering her questions, then circling back to the subject of her health.

"I like Harper. We had a good time together."

"But now you're home." She dusted off her hands. "Time to put your vacation romance behind you and find someone more suitable—"

"Izzy, I've appreciated you not interfering in my life over the years. I always thought I was lucky being Anglo-Indian, so you weren't as relentless as the Indian aunties who make matchmaking a national pastime. So why the sudden obsession with finding me someone suitable?"

He made air quotes around the last two words and she frowned, making disapproving clucking noises under her breath.

"Because I want you to be happy."

"I am happy."

"I saw this Harper woman at the wedding. She's not for you."

"Why?"

It may be cruel getting her to spell it out, but he was lulling her into a false sense of security before getting back to the subject at hand: her health.

"She's Australian, yes?"

"Yes."

"And you said she styles food?"

"Uh-huh."

"Where is the common ground? Where are the shared interests?" She flung her arms in the air dramatically. "Where is the real connection? Culturally, you'll have little in common—"

"Izzy, I've been raised in Australia. I'm Australian."

"But your heritage is Anglo-Indian, and we're a dying race. It is better for you to procreate with someone of your own—"

"Whoa, who said anything about having kids?"

"You would make a wonderful father." Izzy's lips compressed into a thin line. "You are forty; it is time you started considering a younger wife, someone to have children."

Knowing it would antagonize Izzy but unable to resist, he said, "Harper's only thirty."

"Again with this Harper." She waggled her finger at him. "Women who indulge in flings don't make good wife material."

Manny didn't want to get into an argument regarding something that would never happen. He didn't want to marry, but that didn't mean he had to sit here and listen to Harper being disparaged when he happened to think she was pretty damn fantastic.

"Do you have any idea why you've lost weight? Because I think you were avoiding answering me earlier."

Izzy froze, her startled eyes flying to his, before she heaved a hefty sigh. "I have noticed. And I've been to my doctor, who ordered tests."

Izzy had gone to the doctor voluntarily? For as long as he remembered he'd had to badger her into getting an annual physical, let alone a doctor's visit if she was feeling unwell. She didn't believe in medication for colds, preferring the old-fashioned remedies of salt water gargles and drinking copious amounts of *rasam* or steeped ginger and turmeric.

Her visit to the local doctor, who she referred to as "that quack" on a good day, made him worry even more.

"What tests?"

"Comprehensive blood tests, and you'll be the first to know if they show anything other than I'm over-the-hill, but let's get back to this Harper woman."

"Izzy, I'm not going to discuss her with you, other than to say she's the first woman in a long time to spark my interest beyond a date."

Izzy's eyebrows rose so high her forehead wrinkled in a plethora of creases.

"I want to meet her."

"No."

"Why not? Are you ashamed of her?"

"Of course not, it's just that we've got busy schedules, so I'm not sure when I'm going to see her next."

Utter crap, because he had every intention of contacting the gorgeous Harper soon.

Izzy's head pitched to one side in a classic gesture he'd seen many times growing up. She'd never capitulate no matter how many times he gave her the brush-off.

"Rest assured, my boy, if she's as special as you say she is, I will meet her. And soon."

39

THE LAST THING Harper felt like doing after landing back in Melbourne was visiting her mom, but Lydia had left a message for her while she'd been in flight, and Harper didn't like the way she'd sounded.

Her poised mother rarely made demands, so the urgency in her tone imploring Harper to visit ASAP meant when the taxi dropped her home she dumped her suitcase inside, grabbed her car keys, and headed for the house she'd grown up in, in Glen Waverley. She only lived a few suburbs over, in leafy Ashwood, and the trip took less than fifteen minutes. She parked in front of her childhood home, a brick veneer California bungalow, and traipsed up the path, wishing she'd taken the time to check her appearance.

Nobody did the imperious head-to-toe sweep like Lydia Ryland.

While she loved her mom, growing up she'd hated the scrutiny. Lydia wouldn't overly criticize, but Harper would feel her silent disapproval if her skirt was too short or her top too revealing. Having fabulous hair courtesy of her mom made up for it somewhat, but ever since her diagnosis, Harper had become increasingly self-conscious.

Which made her invitation for Manny to stay over in her hotel room last night all the more significant.

Not that she hadn't been aware of the pitfalls. She'd turned out the lamp, and they'd made love twice before she woke early and slipped into the bathroom. It hadn't been a big deal because they had to check out at nine to head to the airport, and finding her showered and dressed hadn't fazed him.

They hadn't been able to get seats together on the flight, which gave her time to brace for their farewell. Crazy, because he'd said he'd call, and while she had no intention of making this into anything more than it was—a fun fling—she might or might not see him again.

But that hug at the airport had almost undone her. Being in his arms felt . . . right. And he had this way of holding her that conveyed so much more than words could. Silent strength. Dependability. Security. Things she craved in a man but had never been able to find.

Until now.

She'd cursed her independence as the taxi pulled away, and had almost told the driver to stop so she could take Manny up on his offer to drive her home. But that wouldn't have been conducive to getting her head back in the game of being home and making sensible choices, focused on building her business, so she'd managed a half-hearted wave while a tiny piece of her broke.

Harper had barely climbed the porch steps when she spotted a giant cellophane-wrapped basket in front of the door. It had a stuffed giraffe in the middle, a bottle of expensive champagne on one side, and a monster box of chocolates on the other. Her mom's new man had good taste.

She knocked before squatting to pick up the basket, and when the door opened, she presented it to her mom.

"From your secret admirer."

Lydia snorted. "It's from your father. It's his new thing."

Harper had no idea what that meant until she entered the dining room and saw their old mahogany table covered in baskets of various sizes, filled with gourmet nibbles to glossy magazines.

"So what was so urgent you had to see me now?"

"I need you to tell him to stop all this." Lydia swept her arm wide, her nose crinkling with distaste.

"It's sweet," Harper said, placing the basket on the table. Actually, she should've known it was her dad who sent it, considering he'd been the one to start her mom's giraffe collection years ago.

She'd been about eight, and they'd been at Moomba, one of those rare long weekends when her dad had been home for the three days. They'd watched the Moomba parade on the Labor Day Monday then strolled through the gardens, checking out the stalls. Her parents hadn't allowed her to go on any of the hair-raising rides, but her dad had played various arcade games to win her a prize. She'd loved her purple unicorn, but not as much as Lydia had loved the giant giraffe. Her mom had pretended to be embarrassed at first, having to cart a big stuffed toy back to the car, but she'd seen the way her parents kept looking at each other whenever the car stopped at signal lights, like they had stars in their eyes.

Ever since then, her dad would buy Lydia giraffes on every long weekend. Crystal, silver, even chocolate, and her mom kept them all.

It made Harper wonder if this one would end up in the trash.

"He loves you." Harper flung her arms wide. "When are you going to give him a break?"

Lydia must've had a recent shot of Botox, because Harper glimpsed a flicker of a raised eyebrow but not much moved above it.

"Why am I the bad guy in all this?"

"Because you kicked him out."

Anger pinched Lydia's lips. "You don't know anything about this—"

"Exactly, Mom, I don't know because you've told me nothing, and I'm sick of being caught in the middle. Either divorce Dad and put him out of his misery or sort this out if you want to. Either way, this limbo land you've both been existing in has got to stop."

Lydia gaped. "Tell me what you really think."

Harper blew out a shaky breath. "I haven't wanted to get involved because your marriage hasn't got anything to do with me. I love you both and I want you to be happy. And whatever the reason behind your shock separation, neither of you seem to be happy at all. Neither of you has moved on, which is pretty damn telling after so long, unless you've got feelings for each other still. In which case . . ." Harper shrugged. "Sort your shit out."

The fact Lydia didn't chastise her for cursing meant her mom had some serious stuff on her mind. After a long pause, Lydia's shoulders slumped, and her mom had never slumped a day in her life, her posture as perfect as the rest of her.

"I'll make us tea."

Harper didn't have the heart to say she didn't want tea, she wanted to know what the hell was going on, but she followed Lydia into the kitchen.

"How did things finish up in New Zealand?"

"Good. The jobs in Auckland and Lake Taupo went well. You already know I met Jock McKell, and the owner of the hotels, Wayne Storr, e-mailed me on a job well done, so I'm hoping to get more work out of it. And I got some downtime in Lake Taupo to look around; it was great."

Harper felt her cheeks heat at the memory of exactly how great things between her and Manny had been in Taupo, and her mom paused, halfway between setting out the china and spooning leaves into the pot.

Lydia's eyes widened. "Did you meet someone?"

Busted.

Harper knew she'd have to give her mom something or Lydia wouldn't let up.

"I ran into a friend over there actually. Total coincidence."

"A good friend, going by the color of your cheeks."

"I met him at Nishi's wedding, and he ended up helping me out with my styling jobs over there."

"Really? What does he do?"

Harper had hoped to leave Manny's job out of it because she knew what would happen once she announced it. Lydia would book the nearest chapel and reception hall.

"He's a doctor," she murmured, not surprised when the teacup in her mom's hand clattered against the saucer.

"Let me get this straight. He's a doctor and he volunteered to play your assistant styling food?" Lydia beamed. "He's got the hots for you, big-time."

"Yeah, well, the feeling is mutual, because he's incredibly hot."

Harper fanned her face. Like it would do much. Every time she thought about gorgeous Manny naked, she overheated.

Her mom wolf whistled. "This is a very pleasing development, sweetheart. After that blasted Colin, I thought you'd sworn off men."

"I could say the same about you, Mom."

"Touché."

The kettle whistled, and Lydia poured boiling water into the teapot and replaced the lid to let the tea steep.

"Are you going to see him again?"

"Maybe. Probably. He wants to."

"But?"

"I've got a lot going on, what with this Storr job just finished and me needing to use it to boost my profile. My savings aren't the best, and I'd like to change that fact."

Lydia waved away her concern. "Your father and I can always help you out financially. But how often do you find a hot doctor?"

"Is the tea ready?"

Lydia shook her head and poured. "You deserve to be happy."

"Once again, I could say the same about you."

As her mom placed a cup of tea in front of her, Harper glimpsed vulnerability in her dart-away gaze. "I will talk to your father."

"Good." Harper took a sip of tea and sighed. Nobody brewed like her mom, and she could thank Lydia for her tea addiction over coffee. "Have you thought any more about opening your own salon like we discussed?"

"That's one of the things I want to talk about with your father." Her mom's gaze drifted to the dining room and the many gift baskets on the table. "I know you won't understand this because you're too young, but when you live with someone for over three decades you become complacent. You get taken for granted. The resentment builds until one day you can't take it anymore."

"Is that what happened between you and Dad?"

"It's more complicated than that." Lydia gave a little shake of her head as if waking up from her musings. "Anyway, enough about me. Let's get back to this doctor of yours."

"He's not mine," Harper said, while a small part of her wished he was.

40

Being chief of ER had its perks, but picking up the slack when Manny's best doc called in sick wasn't one of them. He'd worked back-to-back shifts the last two days, snatching sleep in the break room when he could. He hadn't known whether to be relieved or annoyed he couldn't contact Harper in that time. As for Izzy, he'd taken her at her word when she said the blood test results wouldn't be in until today.

The moment he set foot in his apartment, he shrugged off his jacket, dumped his satchel, and reached for his cell. He'd checked it occasionally during his rare breaks, hoping for a call or a text from Harper, but she'd remained frustratingly silent. Then again, what did he expect? They hadn't made any promises to each other. They'd kept things casual. An "I'll see you when I see you" type of arrangement. It didn't stop him hoping she might've missed him enough to fire off a simple text.

He toed off his shoes and headed for the modular couch that took pride of place in his apartment. He'd fallen asleep on it more times than he could count. Long hours at the hospital didn't make for binge-watching the latest thriller series. He hit Izzy's number and waited. She usually picked up on the third ring; it took nine. The concern he'd kept at bay ratcheted up. Did she have bad news and didn't want to tell him?

"Hello, Manish. How's work?"

"Crazy busy, but that's not why I'm calling. Did you get your test results yet?"

"No, there's some delay at the lab, so it should be tomorrow or the next day."

"They couldn't give you a definitive time frame?"

In fairness, labs were overworked and all the demands in the world couldn't hurry up results—he'd tried many times.

"Manish, I'm of the philosophy that no news is good news, so why don't you take a chill pill?"

He barked out a laugh. "Where on earth did you hear that?"

"Felicia said it on my favorite soap opera last night."

"Watching those things will addle your brain."

"At eighty-six, soap operas addling my brain is the least of my worries, considering advanced-age dementia will do that regardless."

"Stop being so wise."

"And stop being a worrywart. What will be will be."

Manny knew his gran, and behind her flippancy was a hint of inevitability, like she knew something was wrong and was expecting the worst. It made his gut twist.

"You'll call me as soon as you hear anything?"

"Yes, yes." She made a disparaging snorting sound that had him grinning. "So you've been busy at work?"

"Manically so."

"No time to call that Harper then?"

Worse luck. "For someone who doesn't approve of her, you sure do like to harp on."

Izzy groaned. "Your puns are as woeful as they've always been."

"Love you too, Iz. I'm on duty again tomorrow, but call me anytime, okay?"

She grunted her agreement and hung up, leaving him helpless. He hated feeling like this. It had been the same after his mom's heart attack, when he couldn't do a damn thing to save her. That old feeling of inadequacy was back, making him want to drive over to Izzy's right now and demand she tell him what the hell was going on.

But he had to trust her. She said she didn't know anything, and he had to believe her. Besides, another day or two wasn't that long.

Resting his head on the back of the couch, he ran his fingers through his hair. Who was he kidding? Waiting to hear her test results would drive him insane.

Unless he had a suitable distraction . . .

He needed sleep, desperately, and the last thing he wanted was to treat Harper like a booty call. But losing himself in her beautiful body would take his mind off his worries . . .

Before he could second-guess his decision, he picked up his cell again and called Harper. She answered on the second ring.

"Hello, handsome."

His heart leaped irrationally at the sound of her voice. "I hope you've got caller ID on your phone and you know it's me."

"Isn't this Jock?"

He growled. "Don't you dare compare me to that asshole."

Harper laughed and it hit him in the chest. He loved how the sound of her laugh made him feel lighter instantly. He'd made the right decision in calling her.

"So how's my favorite doctor?"

"Exhausted after back-to-back shifts the last forty-eight hours."

"Is that your way of apologizing for not calling me?"

"You could've called me."

"I'm an old-fashioned gal and prefer the guy to do all the chasing."

"Babe, I don't need to chase anymore. I know you're a sure thing."

"I think you just insulted me."

"I complimented you." Damn, he loved her quick wit. "What are you up to?"

She hesitated, and he heard the faintest sound of traffic in the background. "I'm out, about to head home."

"Fancy some company?"

He held his breath like a lovesick teen asking the girl he secretly adored to the prom.

"Yeah, that'd be nice. But I live all the way out in Ashwood, and don't you need to rest after working so hard?"

"I can rest. Later."

"So this is a booty call, huh?"

"Only if you want it to be."

He heard her soft sigh. "I want to see you. What happens after that? Let's play it by ear."

Manny wanted to make light of it, to focus on the wordplay. But he wanted her to know how much it meant to him to see her, so he said, "I've been operating on autopilot the last two days, and I'm bone-deep tired, but I want to see you too. It's all I can think about."

"I'll text you my address," she said, her tone husky. "See you soon."

When she hung up, he grinned like an idiot before dragging his tired ass to the shower.

Soon couldn't come quick enough.

41

Harper hated the vitiligo treatment.

More to the point, the time suck it involved. The closest skin clinic that had one of the special phototherapy machines was thirty minutes away, so it was an hour return trip three times a week. And while the treatment itself didn't take long—she'd built up to eighty seconds being zapped like a roast chicken—she hated the vulnerability of it all.

Taking off her clothes. Wearing goggles to protect her eyes. Standing naked in the small cylindrical space while every inch of her body was blasted with high UV. She wasn't a big fan of the warnings either, that long-term treatment increased the risk of skin cancer. But she had no option. Either get treatment or risk the patches extending. The dermatologist said she was progressing slower than he'd like but she could see the improvement. He'd taken photos pre-treatment and at regular intervals since. The patches were shrinking, but she'd prefer them gone. He'd warned her that might never happen and she may need to continue treatment for however long was necessary.

She just wanted it to finish.

Stupid, really, because having an autoimmune disease meant she'd have this for the rest of her life. But the treatment would decrease with time and with it, some of her resentment, she hoped.

She loved her parents, she really did, but a small part of her would never get past how stress had probably triggered this and the timing coincided with their shock separation. Not that she'd ever tell them, but she knew her increasing annoyance with their situation stemmed a little from her resentment.

It didn't seem right to blame them; the dermatologist had assured her this kind of thing could be triggered at any time, and while stress was the most likely culprit, it could be caused by other stuff. But her life had been surprisingly angst-free fourteen months ago; she'd been in a stable relationship with Colin, she'd had a steady income from catering on the side while building her food-styling portfolio, and she'd been looking ahead to the future.

The only rough spot had been her parents' separation, so it stood to reason she blamed that as her stressor. She'd tell them eventually—not the part about blaming them, but about her disease. They'd been too self-absorbed since the separation to notice anything going on with her. Her dad wouldn't notice anyway, and her mom had simply made a comment once about her makeup application being flawless.

That's the thing about good foundation and concealer. They hid a multitude of flaws.

After having filled a script for the ointment she used on her face—it cost a small fortune, another not-so-fun part of the vitiligo—she'd headed for her car when her cell rang. When she'd seen Manny's name on the screen, she'd contemplated not answering for a moment. Having treatment didn't leave her in a great mood. But as it turned out, answering his call had been the best thing she could've done. There was something about Manny that never failed to bring a smile to her face, and the thought of spending some time with him would lift her spirits. She needed that lift.

After spending the last few days updating her website and adding the Storr jobs to her portfolio, she hadn't had a single call. Not that she'd expected instant success, but styling Jock McKell's food should lend kudos to her site. If there hadn't been a significant uptake in booked jobs by the end of the week, she'd have to go back to cold-calling, and she hated that. Nothing screamed "loser" like being told "thanks but no thanks" repeatedly.

She texted Manny her address when she got home, and he responded with a "c u in 45." It gave her time to have a speedy shower—she hated the smell of her skin after treatment, comparing it to slightly burned chicken—put her "mask" on, and do a quick tidy. Scooping clothes off the chair in her bedroom, flinging them into the closet, checking for stray bras, and finally lighting a ylang-ylang scented candle, serving a dual purpose of minimal lighting and making the room smell divine.

For she was in little doubt they'd end up in the bedroom.

Manny had sounded beat on the phone, so the fact he was willing to come over meant one thing.

He wasn't interested in talking.

Neither was she. She always spent an hour or two after treatment trying to distract herself, either with a favorite rom-com or a new book, anything to take her mind off the relentless mundane visits to the clinic.

Tonight, not talking and sex with Manny seemed like the perfect distraction solution.

When her doorbell rang, excitement sizzled through her and she bounded to the door like an eager puppy. Opening the door, she had to use every ounce of willpower not to fling herself at him.

He looked amazing.

Despite the shadows under his eyes from little sleep and the stubble peppering his jaw, he looked like he'd stepped off set from one of those medical dramas she never liked but her mom watched obsessively. Dark denim molded legs she remembered in exquisite detail, an olive-green T-shirt highlighted his chest, and those slate-gray eyes glinted with intent.

"I missed you," he said, soft, seductive, and she was a goner. His sincerity slayed her. No game playing. No bullshit. Just a genuine declaration of how he was feeling. Could this guy be any more perfect?

"Same here."

She opened the door wider and waited until he was inside before closing it and stepping into his arms. It was as simple as that. No words. Just a silent conveying of . . . something she daren't label for fear of getting it wrong and ruining everything.

The embrace reminded her of their parting at the airport. So much to say but neither wanted to take that final step to admit this thing between them may be more than a fling.

"You have no idea how much I needed that," he said, easing away to smile down at her. "It's been a rough few days."

"Come in, have a seat. Have you eaten?"

"You don't need to feed me," he said, a second before his stomach rumbled.

Sheepish, he shrugged, and she led him by the hand to the

couch. "Sit. Relax. I haven't eaten either, and it'll only take me two seconds to put a cheese platter together."

"Sounds good. Need a hand?"

"I've got it."

"Good, because I'm so exhausted I couldn't lift my ass off this couch if I tried."

She smiled and traced his cheek with a fingertip, incredibly pleased to be proven wrong. This wasn't just a booty call for him. He'd genuinely wanted to see her, and it made her want to hug him again.

"Be back in a sec."

She threw together some Brie, Camembert, cheddar, grapes, and quince paste on a platter and added a bowl of crackers, something to nibble on while they cozied up on the couch. A totally couple thing to do she hadn't anticipated, but now that he was here she wanted to make the most of it.

Besides, that candle in her bedroom was a big one and would burn for hours.

When she padded into the lounge room with the platter in her hands, Manny had his head resting on the back of the couch and his eyes closed, fatigue etched into the faint lines around his mouth. Tenderness expanded in her chest until she could barely breathe, and she contemplated taking the platter back into the kitchen and letting him sleep.

Sensing her scrutiny, he opened his eyes and sat up straighter. "Don't mind me. I'm an old man and need my regular naps."

"You're exhausted. You should be in bed."

He perked up, a spark in his gaze. "Is that an invitation?"

"I think you need to eat first to keep your strength up."

He pointed at his groin. "That doesn't need food to be up."

She chuckled. "Eat." She laid the platter down on the coffee table. "What would you like to drink?"

"Coffee please, strong black. Otherwise I'm in danger of falling asleep right here."

"What I said earlier, I meant you should be in bed at home. Why did you come over?"

"Because I had to see you." He captured her hand and pressed a kiss to it. "I wanted to make sure what happened between us in New Zealand wasn't just in my head."

"And?"

"It's real." He stood and reached for her, clasping her face in his hands, drawing her closer to slant his lips across hers. "Mind-blowingly real," he whispered against the corner of her mouth as his hands slid lower, over her shoulders, her torso, to cup her ass.

"I thought you needed coffee?"

"Later," he murmured, pulling her to him. "Much later."

42

MANNY HAD NO idea how long he'd slept, but when he woke he felt more refreshed than he had in a while. Long shifts after any time off kicked his ass, and it took him a week to acclimatize, which is why he didn't take a vacation often. He stretched and rolled over to find himself face-to-face with the reason for his supremely rested state.

"Good morning," Harper said, her coy smile alerting him to why he'd had such a deep sleep. A sensational orgasm was more powerful than any sleeping tablet. His medical opinion; he was sticking to it.

"It's a very good morning." He leaned forward to kiss her. "What time is it?"

"Almost five thirty."

"Crap. I've got a shift starting at midday, and I've got errands to run before that."

"No problem. You're free to leave at any time." She winked. "I'm not tying you to the bed."

"I wish you would."

"Maybe next time."

That was the best offer he'd had in a while. "So there's going to be a next time?"

"What do you think?"

She'd given him the perfect segue into what he'd wanted to discuss last night. Coming over to her place, deriving comfort in being here with her, reinforced what he'd known deep down when they'd parted at the airport.

He wanted more than a fling with Harper.

He wanted a relationship.

"I think we need to clarify what we're doing," he said, sliding his hand under the covers to capture hers. "Last night was special."

Either she misunderstood because he tended to deflect with humor or she deliberately chose to make light of what he'd said, but she lifted the top sheet a tad and peeked under. "I'll say."

"I know what you're doing." He squeezed her hand. "I'm the king of using banter to distract from the heavy stuff. But I'm not kidding around. And I'm not referring to the sex, because we both know how compatible we are between the sheets."

He pressed her palm to his chest, over his heart. "Last night was special because for the first time in my life, rather than avoiding company when I was feeling so crappy, I sought it out. And I wouldn't have done it for anybody other than you."

Her eyes widened and she nibbled on her lip. "What are you saying?"

"That I want to give this a go. You and me. Dating. Exclusively."

"Aww, you're asking me to go steady?"

He loved her sass. "Make light of this, but this will be my first relationship, so you'll need to go easy on me."

"You're forty. How can this be your first relationship?"

"Already told you, I didn't have the time or the inclination."

"You still won't have the time now. We're both busy and—"

"But the inclination between us is strong. Very strong." He shifted closer. "I know this is crazy because we've known each other for a short time. But I've never felt this way before, and I want to explore what we've got. So what do you say?"

She hesitated, and his heart sank. "I have to tell you something first."

"Uh-oh. You've got a long-lost lover returning to Melbourne? You've got a harem of guys in various restaurants around the city? You've decided to bone Jock McKell after all?"

She laughed and shook her head. "I've had a self-imposed man ban for the last year."

"A man ban?"

"Yeah, my last boyfriend, Colin, hurt me so badly I haven't gone near a guy since."

"So what was I? An aberration?"

"No, you were part of my Manny-banny."

He groaned. "That's woeful."

"Hey, the startling news that a man I think is the most gorgeous, intelligent guy I've ever met, and the best sex I've ever had, wants to date me calls for lame-ass puns."

"You're forgiven because you boosted my ego. But you still haven't answered my question. Are you up for dating a relationship-phobe and indoctrinating me into the ways of being part of a couple?"

This time, she didn't hesitate, her nod emphatic. "Let's do it."

He let out a whoop, wrapped his arms around her, and rolled

her on top of him. "I need to leave soon, but how about we have a rousing celebration first?"

Desire sparked in her eyes as she slowly, deliberately, writhed against him. "You know how much I love a good *celebration* with you."

43

HARPER STRODE INTO the small Indian café in Dandenong and immediately spotted Samira and Pia at a table by the window. The café only had ten tables but each one was taken, and the delicious aroma of spices made her salivate.

The women had their heads close together, looking at something on Pia's cell, and as she made her way toward them she heard Samira squeal, "I'm so happy for you."

"Hey, girls." Harper slung her arms around their shoulders and gave them a half hug. "What's going on?"

When she straightened, Samira nudged Pia, who had flushed crimson. "You tell her."

"Tell me what?"

"Sit first," Pia said, swiveling the phone toward her. "What do you see?"

Harper peered at the screen. "You and Dev draped all over each other in front of your place."

"Check the date stamp," Samira said, beaming.

Harper realized what all the fuss was about as she glimpsed the numbers. "You and Dev are back together?"

Pia nodded, her smile so bright it could light a room. "Yeah. It's taken us a long time to get here, but with the counseling and the dating, we're ready to move back in together."

"I'm thrilled for you both," Harper said, reaching out to give Pia's arm a squeeze.

"Thanks, we're thrilled too." Pia slid her cell back into her bag. "And we're planning a trip to India to check out adoption agencies."

"That's wonderful."

Samira clapped her hands. "If I was any more excited I wouldn't be able to eat, but that's never happened before, so I'm pretty sure I'll manage to squeeze in a *masala dosa*."

Pia laughed. "Have you had South Indian vegetarian food before, Harper?"

Harper nodded. "Nishi introduced me to the wonders of Indian food when we first met in school, and I've been hooked ever since."

"Shall I order three *masala dosas* then?" Pia asked.

"Yes please, and mango lassis," Harper added, as Pia headed to the counter to order.

"You're sounding like a pro." Samira smiled, surprisingly smug. "And something tells me you'll be eating a lot more Indian food in your future."

No way. How could Samira know about her and Manny when they'd only made it official this morning?

"How do you . . . I mean . . . when . . ."

Samira laughed. "Relax. You'll soon discover the Indian grapevine works faster than any smartphone."

Pia returned and sat. "What's the latest on the Indian grapevine?"

Smug, Samira gestured at Harper. "Our friend here has some news about a new boyfriend."

"Oooh, is he hot?"

Samira whacked Pia. "You've only just reunited with Dev."

Wincing, Pia rubbed her arm. "Yeah, but I'm a woman and I have a pulse so I can look." She focused on Harper. "Got a pic?"

As Samira continued to smirk, Harper heaved out a sigh. "Actually, you both know him."

Confusion creased Pia's brow. "We do?"

"It's Manny," Harper said, as Samira burst out laughing.

Pia's eyes widened in recognition. "Manny, as in Manish Gomes, the guy you humiliated at Nishi's wedding?"

Harper nodded as Samira continued to giggle like a schoolgirl. "His grandmother rang Mom, gave Kushi the full rundown about Manny chasing after some *Aussie* he met at Nishi's wedding all the way to New Zealand, and how he's mad for her and won't hear reason about settling down and marrying a nice Indian or Anglo-Indian girl."

"He chased you to New Zealand?" Pia's eyebrows rose, but Harper glimpsed the reservation in her eyes. "Just so you know, Manny's got a reputation as a pants man. He dates extensively, but he never chases after a woman, ever. So did he really follow you all the way to New Zealand?"

"That's practically a marriage proposal, you know," Samira said, snapping her fingers in front of Harper, who swatted Samira's hand away.

"Don't be ridiculous, nobody's getting married, and if you want to hear what really happened rather than listening to gossip, you two better shut up." Harper mimicked zipping over her lips, and the girls laughed.

Samira held up her hands in surrender. "Okay, okay, we'll behave." She leaned forward, her eyes sparkling. "Now tell us what happened, and don't leave out a single detail."

"Aren't you married to the hottest reality TV star in Australia?" Harper asked.

"Yeah, and your point?" Samira mock huffed. "Doesn't mean I don't love a bit of juicy gossip, and Manny falling for you definitely qualifies." She jerked a thumb at Pia. "Cuz is right, Manny doesn't do commitment, and we're not trying to scare you off by saying it, just telling you how it is."

"He told me that himself when we both stipulated having a fling while we were overseas, but things changed . . ." Harper felt heat creeping into her cheeks, and she resisted the urge to press her hands to them. "We had a good chat this morning, and turns out we're trying the relationship thing."

"Good for you," Pia said, a second before Samira added, "So tell us more about this fling."

Harper grinned, happy to have something to impart rather than being a bystander as usual. While she'd known Nishi forever, she'd only met Samira and Pia through her friend, and they'd caught up regularly in the lead-up to the wedding. She liked the cousins and they had bonded over a shared love of *Gilmore Girls* reruns, Ryan Gosling flicks, and masala chai. It was a bonus that Samira happened to be a friend of Manny's. And Harper was sure that had nothing to do with Samira organizing this catch-up today. Yeah, right.

"Well, you know about the wedding debacle."

Samira nodded. "Not the most auspicious beginning, but you must've had a lot of fun resolving your differences." She made a lewd sign with her forefinger moving in and out of a circle formed with her opposite thumb and index.

"You are so immature." Pia elbowed Samira and rolled her eyes. "Now quit it so we can get the lowdown."

Appearing suitably chastised, Samira clasped her hands together and rested them on the table. "Okay, I'll be good."

"At the Storr Hotel in Auckland, I ran into Manny. He'd just finished up a medical conference, I was freaking out over losing my assistant, and he volunteered to help me out."

Samira's and Pia's jaws dropped in unison, like those clowns at a sideshow where you popped Ping-Pong balls in their mouth.

"He what?" Pia asked.

"He helped me out of a jam. Was really sweet about it, actually. Took orders like a pro, and if it wasn't for him I would've made a mess of the job."

Biting back a grin at their matching shocked expressions, she continued. "He was taking a few days off after the conference, and I had another job to do at the new Storr Hotel in Lake Taupo, so he offered to accompany me down there too."

Samira's eyes narrowed in suspicion. "Let me get this straight. He helps you out of a tight spot, takes orders from you, you fall for his gallantry, and suddenly you're dating?" She shook her head. "I don't buy it. What aren't you telling us?"

Aiming for bashful, Harper shrugged. "Well, there may have been a few romantic dates here and there, and some sexy time."

Pia whistled. "Look at your cheeks. They're fire-engine red."

Samira wiggled her eyebrows. "That good, huh?"

"Better," Harper murmured, remembering all the ways Manny had pleasured her, not surprised she'd become addicted so quickly. "He's a special guy."

"He's one of the good ones," Samira said, but Harper detected a hint of recalcitrance.

"What aren't you telling me?"

Samira cast Pia a quick sideways glance before refocusing on her. "I like Manny. He's fun. But he does have a reputation among the Indian community as being the unobtainable bachelor."

"Some of the aunties call him the Unicorn behind his back," Pia added.

As proof of where Harper's mind was at when it came to her new boyfriend, mentioning unicorn had her thinking about his impressive horn and she struggled not to snicker.

"So you think he's just fooling around with me?"

Samira hesitated, before saying, "We don't want to see you get hurt."

"Thanks, that's sweet, but don't worry, I'm going into this with my eyes open."

Thankfully, the arrival of their *dosas* and lassis put paid to further conversation about her relationship. But as Harper tore into her paper-thin crispy rice pancake and scooped up the spicy potato filling, she couldn't help but wonder if she'd been too quick to accept Manny's spiel about her being an exception to his no-relationship rule.

And what that might spell if he'd spun her a whole lot of BS she'd fallen for.

44

AT THE END of an eight-hour shift, the last thing Manny felt like doing was having drinks with other couples. He'd much rather have Harper all to himself, in his bed preferably, but while he may not have had a real relationship before, he knew it meant making sacrifices.

At least he knew Samira and Rory, and Pia, though he hadn't met her husband, Dev, yet. Harper had been pretty chuffed about them reuniting, and from what Samira had told him, Pia and Dev had been through the wringer trying to conceive, and infertility had precipitated their separation.

So he could do this. Play nice for an hour, make small talk, then whisk his girlfriend back to his place for some raunchy one-on-one time.

"You're awfully quiet," Harper said, as they strolled along the Yarra River to an upmarket Southbank bar.

"It's because I'm still processing. The aunties really call me the Unicorn?"

"Yeah, because you can't be captured. A figment of the imagination of a thousand pining brides-to-be, apparently."

"They're always trying to matchmake, regardless if you welcome it or not, and I do not," he said, wondering why Izzy hadn't mentioned the nickname over the years.

Though it wasn't exactly flattering, and he'd hazard a guess the aunties had never used it in front of his gran. She'd always been fiercely protective of him, and in a battle of Izzy versus the aunties he'd have his money on Izzy every time.

"You're Anglo-Indian though, so arranged marriages aren't part of your culture. Why do they feel the need to interfere?"

"Because it's a skill born of a lifetime's practice," he said drily, remembering countless functions where he'd been introduced to an endless parade of "suitable" women.

Doctors were considered the Holy Grail for matchmaking mothers, and he'd been successfully dodging them ever since he graduated.

"I can't wait to show you off to the community," he said. "Having a girlfriend will finally get those old crows off my back."

"So that's all I am, huh? A prop in your dastardly plan to foil the aunties?"

"You're also incredibly talented in bed," he deadpanned, cracking up when she bumped him with her hip, hard, and he staggered a step. "Hey, don't be so brutal. I'm coming off a difficult shift and I'm only doing this because you asked so nicely."

The memory of how she'd asked, by giving him a blow job as a prelude, had him wanting to finish these obligatory drinks in thirty minutes rather than sixty.

"It's our first outing as a couple," she said, her smile surprisingly shy. "It's kind of nice."

"You know what would be nicer?"

He lowered his head to whisper in her ear every filthy thing he'd do to her later, and by the end of it she was leaning into him, her breathing accelerated.

"You don't play fair," she muttered, tilting her face up to his. "The least you can do is kiss me."

"I'm not into PDAs in the middle of Melbourne," he said, struggling to not laugh in the face of her outrage.

"You better give me some kind of public display of affection right here, right now, mister, or I'm going to torture you."

"How?"

"By telling you I'm going commando under this dress and your naughty wordplay means I won't be sitting down the entire time we're in the bar."

With that, she strutted up the steps in front of him, leaving him with a raging hard-on and lamenting his urge to tease, because Harper had matched him quip for quip while upping the ante.

She was magnificent.

He bounded up the steps after her in time to hold the door open, and she smiled sweetly before entering.

"There they are." She pointed to a corner of the bar where the other couples had nabbed a tall table surrounded by stools. "Behave."

"After that stunt you just pulled?"

"Who, me?" She batted her eyelashes and he laughed. "As I recall, you started it with your dirty talk."

"Stop it. I can't walk up to these people with a boner."

She tapped her lip, pretending to ponder. "And here I was thinking I took care of that situation about an hour ago."

"You. Are. Killing. Me," he said, through gritted teeth.

"Hey, they've seen us." She waved and slipped her hand into his. "Just stand behind me till you get that thing under control."

"That thing is going to make you very happy later."

They grinned at each other, electricity arcing between them with the promise of what was to come. He loved her mischievous side, and he could imagine them having a lot of fun together for however long this lasted.

Not that he was envisaging an end date just yet, but he was a realist. Never being in a relationship meant he would screw up eventually. And if she didn't have the patience to guide him through, they'd be over. But he didn't want to think about that yet. He intended on enjoying every scintillating second with his gorgeous girlfriend.

She always looked good, but tonight she'd outdone herself. Smoky eyes, crimson lips, hair in a sleek curtain halfway down her back. The simple black dress covered more than it revealed—high neck, long sleeves, mid-calf—but it caressed her curves like a glove, making his palms itch to do the same.

Not helping the situation behind his zipper.

As they reached the couples and greetings were exchanged, with an introduction for him and Dev, he liked that Harper didn't release his hand. It bound her to him in a way that appealed to his inner caveman. *All mine.*

"What would you like to drink?" He squeezed her hand. "Or would you like me to choose you a decadent cocktail to make you tipsy?"

"A mojito is fine," she said, tugging him closer to whisper in his ear. "For the record, you don't need me tipsy to take advantage of me. I'm all yours."

Unable to stop himself, he kissed her on the lips, not caring about the cheers and whistles from their friends.

When he released her, he couldn't help the goofball grin spreading across his face. "Everyone else right for drinks?"

"We're fine, mate, but you better get extra ice in yours to cool the fuck down," Rory said, and everyone laughed.

"Back in a minute." He touched the small of Harper's back, his fingertips drifting lower to stroke the curve of her ass, before he stepped away and through a gap between people at the bar.

When he glanced over his shoulder, she was staring at him with the kind of smile that took his breath away. Half promise, half infatuation, all in.

His heart kicked hard and damned if he cared.

So what if he'd fallen for her?

About bloody time.

As he made his way back to her, mojito in one hand, light beer in the other, he wondered when the last time was he'd been this happy.

If ever.

45

"So tell me, Harper, what do you see in this bozo?" Rory raised his beer in Manny's direction, and everyone grinned. "You know he hit on my wife too many times to count before she chose the better man."

"Hey, watch it, man. Those fake biceps don't fool anyone." Manny jabbed him in the arm and winced, making everyone laugh.

"Well, I happen to think this guy's pretty fantastic," Harper said, slipping her hand through the crook of Manny's elbow and looking up at him. "So quit it."

"Oooh," Samira said. "Someone's very protective of her man."

"And I love her for it."

Everyone stared at Manny in shock, including Harper.

Surely, he didn't mean that? It had to be a figure of speech, a throwaway comment.

Manny's guffaw sounded forced before he said, "So, who's getting the next round?"

"I will," Harper said, needing to get away from the curious eyes swinging between her and Manny.

"Want some help?" he asked, ducking down to whisper in her ear. "Don't look so frightened. When I say I love you it won't be in front of these busybodies."

When.

Not *if.*

More discombobulated by the minute, she said, "You stay here. I'll go order drinks and get the barman to bring them over."

"Okay." He kissed her, not caring who saw. Another thing she liked about him: the confidence in his own skin. She wished she could be half that confident. "And by the way, how you stood up for me? Big turn-on. And I'll show you exactly how much of a turn-on when we ditch them soon."

A shiver of longing shot through her. "Counting on it," she said, before heading off to order drinks.

A crowd had built up in the bar over the last half hour, and patrons lining up were three-deep, so she sidled her way to the farthest corner near the restrooms and waited for the people in front of her to move.

A light touch landed on her shoulder. "Harper?"

She froze.

No way.

Colin hated the bar scene. He'd never wanted to go out when they'd been dating, saying he preferred to chill at home after long hours at the restaurant, and he certainly wouldn't pay the exorbitant bar prices for the Shiraz he liked.

She turned and fixed a polite smile on her face. "Colin."

He looked the same, though his hair skimmed his collar these days rather than the short back and sides he'd favored when they'd dated. His blue eyes were warm, his smile endearing. Colin channeled the boy-next-door perfectly, but she knew firsthand the sweetness hid a shallow soul.

"Small world, huh?" He had the audacity to touch her arm, and she gritted her teeth before stepping back a fraction.

"Yeah, too small."

His eyes widened at her sarcasm and she continued. "Funny running into you in a bar. It's the last place you'd usually frequent."

He shrugged, sheepish. "I like to mix it up these days."

Translated, he was only a boring old fart when he was with her.

Screw you, Colin.

A frown dented his brow, and for a moment she wondered if she'd spoken out loud.

"You look incredible," he said, searching her face with an intensity that made her want to squirm. "Absolutely stunning. The patches all gone?"

Harper could play this game. She could be polite and make small talk and pretend like what Colin thought of her mattered. But she'd been done with him the minute he turned his back on her because she didn't fit his image of perfection, so she was finished with playing nice.

"None of your fucking business."

He reared back like she'd poked him in the eye. "Hey, where did that come from?"

Harper tapped her lip, pretending to think. "Let's see. Probably from the same place that thinks you're a weak prick for dumping me when I showed you those patches."

"That wasn't the reason." The lie slid easily from his lips, but he couldn't meet her eyes as he said it.

"Yeah, it was, and even now you don't have the balls to admit it."

He threw his hands up. "I just wanted to say hi, but if I'd known you were still hung up on me, I wouldn't have bothered."

"Hung up on you?" Harper laughed so loud several people nearby turned to stare. "News flash, Col. See that gorgeous guy at the other end of the bar, the one who's about five inches taller than you? He's my boyfriend, and he's one hundred times the man you'll ever be. And for the record?"

She held her hands about a foot apart. "Those five inches in height isn't the only measurement where he's got you beat."

Colin flushed an angry puce, before stomping away. Applause rang out from a few women nearby, and Harper flashed a sheepish smile before slinking back in the direction of her group. She'd find another spot to wait to order.

However, she'd barely made it ten feet before she ran into Manny.

"You okay?"

When he touched her arm, she melted and craved his touch all over.

"Yeah."

"Who was that guy?"

"My ex."

"What did you say to him?"

"Why?"

"Because I'm pretty sure I glimpsed tears as he stormed out of here."

She chuckled. "I may have insulted his manhood by saying you had five inches on him in all aspects of anatomy."

Amusement lit Manny's eyes. "Five inches, huh? I'm not sure whether to be flattered or to make sure you're not prone to exaggeration."

"Hey, I tell it how it is."

Not wanting to waste another thought on Colin, she slipped

her hand in his. "My ex is a shallow prick and not worth talking about. So how about you and I make our excuses to the gang and leave so I can get out my ruler and validate those inches?"

He laughed and pulled her in close. "You are one of a kind."

"Is that a yes?"

"Let's go."

46

IT WOULD'VE MADE sense for Harper to stay over at Manny's place, considering his apartment was closer to Southbank than her house, but she'd insisted she needed to be home in the morning for a delivery. Manny hadn't cared. He'd go wherever she wanted if it meant spending the night in her arms.

She'd been surprisingly quiet on the thirty-minute drive to her place, and he wondered if it had anything to do with her ex. While Manny hadn't been dating her long, and talking about an ex wasn't high on his list of priorities, seeing the guy's reaction and hearing her label him a shallow prick meant there was a story there beyond two people growing apart.

They were a few streets away from her house, and he couldn't contain his curiosity any longer.

"I know it's not kosher to discuss previous relationships, but considering this is my first and you can't quiz me, I think it's only fair I get to interrogate you."

Her hands, resting in her lap, tightened, making her knuckles stand out. "Talking about Colin is the last thing I want to do."

"At least the *shallow prick* has a name."

He'd expected her to laugh. She didn't.

"How long did you two date?"

"About a year."

"You mentioned he dumped you?"

"Yeah."

"The guy's obviously a dickhead." He wanted to ask the all-important "why" but had to lead into it. "Did you live together?"

"He wanted to, but my house is my haven. He rented near the restaurant where he worked, so it made sense for us to hang out there anyway." She snorted. "I think he only suggested moving in together to cut back on rent."

"So he wasn't the love of your life?"

"Hell no."

He cast a quick glance at her, and she was tight-lipped, her silhouette rigid.

"Why did you break up?"

There, he'd asked the million-dollar question, but as he turned into her street, she remained silent.

"Harper?"

"Talking about old boyfriends is a real mood killer," she muttered, folding her arms and slouching. "Drop it, okay?"

More intrigued than ever by her recalcitrance to talk about it, he turned into her driveway as his pager went off.

"Are you on call?"

He shook his head and picked up the pager, groaning when he saw the number. "This is from my office, which can only mean one thing."

"What?"

"Problems."

He slid his cell out of his pocket and called the number, not surprised when his second in charge said two of their doctors had come down with gastro and there'd been a major pileup on the Western Ring Road, meaning patients would be flown in to their ER as first point of call.

"I'll be there in thirty," he said, and hung up, before turning to Harper. "Sorry, but I have to go. Staff shortage at the hospital, and a stack of incoming trauma patients."

"Go," she said, her stiff posture finally relaxing as she reached out to cup his cheek. "I think it's beyond cool you save the world."

"I can't save everyone."

The bitter retort popped out before he could stop it, but before she could delve deeper, he said, "I really have to go. I'll call you."

"Okay."

They met halfway across the console and exchanged a quick kiss that felt obligatory rather than passionate. He hated it. He didn't want their evening to end like this, with her feeling defensive about his probing for information about her ex, and him remembering how he couldn't save the one person he'd wanted to.

He waited until she'd unlocked her front door and slipped inside before reversing out of her drive. She hadn't looked back, and it made him wonder if he'd screwed up this relationship before it had barely begun.

47

MANNY DIDN'T CALL.

Then again, Harper heard about the multicar pileup on the news late last night and first thing this morning, and she guessed he would still be working.

She couldn't fathom having such a high-pressure job, where a split-second decision could literally mean the difference between life and death. She loved his sense of humor, but it made her wonder if he used it as a defense mechanism to deal with the trauma he saw on a daily basis.

He'd been defensive last night when she'd made the offhand comment about saving the world. It had been stupid, in hindsight. He probably thought she was making light of a serious subject.

Their whole conversation in the car last night had been a drag. Not that they'd said much. She'd been stewing over her run-in with Colin, and he'd taken his cue from her, remaining silent until they'd almost reached her place.

She'd been angry at herself more than anything, for giving Colin the satisfaction of caring about being dumped by him. She could've handled it better, like pretending he didn't exist. But she'd lost it when he'd stared at her, admiration with a hint of something more in his eyes, like she was back to being beautiful after revealing the ugliness. It had triggered her in a way she hadn't anticipated, though her comeback about inches had been snidely clever.

Harper didn't give a crap about height or size; if she had, she wouldn't have dated Colin. But it had been a low blow criticizing his lack of . . . ahem . . . inches, just because he'd resurrected her old feelings of inadequacy by focusing on her looks.

As she toyed with her cell, contemplating sending a text to Manny for when he finished his shift, it rang and Samira's name popped up.

Glad for the distraction, she answered. "Hey."

"Hey yourself. I've got Pia on the line too, conference call."

Ah . . . so this would be a dissection of last night's drinks at the bar. She should've expected it, but she'd been too busy wasting time mulling over Colin to think about it.

"Hi, Harper," Pia said. "You and Manny disappeared pretty fast last night."

"You two are seriously loved up," Samira added, making smoochy sounds. "So how are things in Lovesville?"

"He got called into the hospital last night, so just peachy."

"Someone sounds a little shitty because they didn't get any loving last night," Samira said with a snicker.

"Don't listen to her," Pia said. "I heard about that multicar pileup on the news. Must be tough dealing with that."

"I was thinking the same thing." Harper liked these women, but Pia was definitely the more intuitive. "You're both in the health industry. Does it ever get you down, dealing with people's problems all day?"

"I do get sick of it sometimes," Samira said, sounding surprisingly somber. "Every patient who walks into my office is in pain and wants to be fixed. When I mention the E word so they can help themselves, they equate exercise with lying on the couch and doing nothing proactive."

"Speech therapists don't get as much of the heavy stuff," Pia said. "Especially working in private practice like I do. But speechies in hospitals deal with a lot of poststroke rehab, so teaching people how to swallow again, that kind of thing. It can be draining."

"Why are you asking this? Did Manny say something?"

Harper shook her head before realizing the girls couldn't see her. "No, but seeing him rush off last night while I chilled in bed with a book made the vast differences between us more noticeable."

"Between your jobs, you mean," Samira clarified.

"Yeah, I guess . . ." Though that hadn't been all, and Harper knew it. Seeing him so focused after that call last night, watching him dash off, clarified that to someone like him, his job would always come first.

Not that he'd ever make her feel second-best; he wasn't that kind of guy. And she'd never put him in the position of having to choose between her and his job, but being head of an ER in a major hospital came with responsibilities, and she had a feeling last night would be the first of many times Manny would be called away from her.

Crazy, to be having these thoughts after they'd only been officially dating a few days, but Colin had often made her feel second-best and she knew some of her residual angst stemmed from that.

"For what it's worth, by what we saw last night, if Manny had a choice between going into work and spending time with you, there's no contest; he'd choose you every time," Samira said.

"He only has eyes for you, that's for sure," Pia added. "After you left, Sam and I chastised Rory and Dev for not looking at us the way Manny looks at you."

Harper chuckled. "Girls, we haven't been dating long. They don't call it the honeymoon period for nothing."

Besides, she'd give anything to have what Samira and Pia had: keepers. A guy around for the long haul. A guy to accept her, every flawed inch. A guy who would always choose her.

"It was nice hanging out last night. When Nishi gets back, we should get her and Arun into our cozy clique too," Samira said. "It's great to have a group where everyone gets along, the guys and the girls."

"Sounds good," Pia said, "but don't expect to see us every week. Dev and I are technically back in that honeymoon period."

Samira made a gagging sound. "Okay, all you loved-up couples can stick to your honeymoons while I wrangle a baby and a husband who's auditioning for another role that will take him away from home for a few months."

"Auntie Pia is always available for babysitting . . . after the honeymoon," Pia said, and they laughed.

An e-mail popped up on the laptop screen in front of Harper, with JOB OFFER in the subject line.

"Thanks for the call, girls, but I have to go. Work beckons."

"Bye," Samira and Pia said in unison, before hanging up, leaving Harper to check her e-mail.

She'd been asked to style a hospital fundraiser, a silent auction charity night at a swanky Docklands venue. Full buffet of fancy finger food. The kind of job she didn't like because it was finicky and all it took was one canapé to look off center and the whole platter suffered. But she couldn't afford to turn her back on any jobs at this stage, and she fired off an acceptance with her fee. Confirmation arrived surprisingly quickly, and after making note of the date in her diary, she pondered the booking.

She'd never done any work for hospitals before, and while the hosting hospital wasn't Manny's, what were the odds of landing a job like this after she'd started dating a doctor? Had he put in a good word for her?

She didn't know whether to be grateful or annoyed. He'd already helped her out enough with the New Zealand jobs. She wasn't some charity case. But she immediately felt bad for being prickly. Who cared how the referral came her way? She needed the work, she needed the money; she should be thankful rather than self-sabotaging.

Was she trying to find faults with Manny because he was too perfect?

And did his perfection accentuate her imperfections, playing into every one of her insecurities?

She had to be careful, because if she got too caught up in analyzing their differences, she could ruin the best thing to happen to her. She wanted to believe in him, to be grateful for this new, sparkly relationship.

But could they ever have a real relationship if she withheld the truth?

It was too early to reveal her true self to him, but there'd come a time soon when she would have to, and that day terrified her.

48

MANNY HAD WORKED twelve hours straight and wanted to head home, have a shower, and fall into bed. But the moment he glimpsed Izzy's text message on his cell, "please come see me," he shelved his fatigue and hightailed it to her place.

She must have her test results.

She wanted to deliver them in person.

Which could only mean one thing.

Bad news.

How many times had he been on the opposite side of this scenario, the one imparting the bad news? Too many to count, and it never got easier. No matter how calm his voice, how stoic his expression, how much he steeled his nerve, watching the faces of patients' loved ones crumple when he imparted a serious diagnosis never failed to gut him.

Now he could be on the receiving end, and he couldn't contemplate a world without Izzy in it. She'd been his rock, his everything, for so long. She'd got him through the dark time after his mom's death, when the guilt threatened to overwhelm him. She badgered him and nagged him but she loved him irrevocably, and the thought of her having a terminal illness made him want to retch.

Considering the badly injured, mutilated patients from the

car pileup he'd attended to for the last twelve hours, he shouldn't speed, but he made it to Izzy's in record time. He parked out the front and turned off the engine, then sat in the car for a full minute, gripping the steering wheel and resting his forehead against it. Exhaustion made his head spin, but it was more than that. Being light-headed stemmed from what he'd face when he walked inside his grandmother's house.

After dragging in several calming breaths, he straightened, shook out his arms, and got out of the car. Mustering every ounce of calm, he strode to the front door and let himself in. He couldn't avoid this any longer. He needed to know what they were dealing with. Now.

The aroma of beef masala chops emanated from the kitchen, and he followed the tantalizing smell. They'd been his favorite from childhood and reserved for special occasions. He hated that he'd forever associate something he loved with the news he knew wouldn't be good.

"I made your favorite," Izzy said, tapping a wooden spoon against the edge of the pot before re-covering it. "Thought you might be hungry after a long shift."

He crossed the kitchen to drop a kiss on her cheek. "How did you know I was on a long shift?"

"Because you would've been here thirty minutes after my text otherwise."

"True," he said, glad she'd brought it up rather than hedging around the news she had to impart. "You got your results?"

"I did."

"And?"

"Sit. Have some masala chai."

Manny didn't want tea. He didn't want anything other than

good news, but he'd given up wishing for things that could never happen around the time he'd pushed his mom to exercise and she'd dropped dead of a heart attack.

"Okay," he said, knowing this was part of a ritual, a long-established way of Izzy getting her nerves under control. He'd seen it countless times before. The day he'd got a scholarship to attend a lauded private school. The day his final high school grades came out. The day he was offered a place at college to study medicine.

He'd drunk a lot of cups of masala chai with his gran over the years so he waited, clamping down his impatience as she went through the ritual of boiling tea leaves with cloves, cinnamon, cardamom, a pinch of pepper, and ginger, adding milk and way too much sugar before pouring the steaming concoction into chipped glasses.

When she placed the glass in front of him and pulled up a seat, the scent of the spices made his throat clog with emotion. The smell of comfort. Of home.

He reached for the tea and took a sip to ease the tightness in his throat, the milky sweetness evoking so many treasured memories.

Izzy waited until he'd drunk half his tea before speaking.

"The doctor suspected endocarditis when I first saw him, and the blood tests and the transthoracic echocardiogram I had yesterday confirmed it."

Manny returned his glass to the table, his hand trembling, as every snippet of information about inflammation of the heart's inner lining flooded his brain.

Usually caused by bacteria. Uncommon in people with healthy hearts, which meant Izzy's wasn't. Symptoms could develop slowly over time, so could go undiagnosed too long.

"Stop imagining the worst," Izzy said, poking him in the chest. "It's not the end of the world."

"Endocarditis can be fatal," he blurted, immediately ashamed those were the first words he uttered after his gran revealed her diagnosis.

He should be comforting her, offering her pragmatic advice, not scaring her. Then again, Izzy was too stoic for her own good, and he needed to ensure she knew how serious her condition was.

"I'm well aware of that," she said. "I may call my doctor a quack, but he's far from it."

"What symptoms have you had?"

Her gaze slid away, furtive, guilty. "You were right: I have lost weight. And I've had night sweats, joint pain, with occasional nausea. I thought I'd lost weight because I haven't felt like eating much the last few weeks." She shrugged, fatalistic. "Then my heart started doing some weird jumpy thing, so I thought I better get it checked out."

"It's bacterial, so it will be treated with antibiotics for a start—"

"The echocardiogram showed I have heart valve damage and a lot of scarring around it, which allowed a buildup of bacteria."

Manny was pretty sure his heart skipped a beat. Valve damage in itself could be fatal too.

"How bad are the valves?"

Izzy's nose wrinkled. "Bad. Apparently, I have prolonged infective endocarditis, so there's a lot of damage. Dead tissue around the valves, fluid buildup, debris from the infected tissue. I need the valves replaced."

Manny felt the blood drain from his face. "All of them?"

"They've booked me in for surgery in two days."

Fuck. This was serious, and he knew enough that if Izzy had a case of prolonged infective endocarditis, replacing the heart valves wouldn't mean she'd be fine.

Complications from sustained damage were common: blood clots, atrial fibrillation, kidney inflammation, and the more severe stroke and heart failure.

"Please get that look off your face." Izzy sighed and reached out to clasp his hand between hers. "I'm old. I've lived a good life. What will be will be."

Tears burned the back of his eyes as he searched for something to say other than curse the injustice of this. He had nobody, apart from Izzy.

Though that wasn't entirely true. He had Harper now. And the thought of having someone to confide in, to vent to, went some way to alleviating the pressure in his chest.

"But you know what this means, don't you?" Izzy squeezed his hand before releasing it, the old twinkle in her eyes.

"What?"

"You'll have to get married before I die. It will be my deathbed wish, and I'll haunt you forever if you don't."

"Stop this talk about dying," he muttered, harsher than intended as her eyebrow rose.

"You of all people know what I'm dealing with, Manish, so please don't patronize me or sugarcoat the truth. My doctor clearly outlined the seriousness of my condition, so I'm under no illusions."

She clutched at her chest, and Manny could've sworn his heart stopped. "Are you okay?"

"I'm fine, but seeing you married would be the best medicine."

He managed a laugh. "You're incorrigible."

"Made you smile though."

He shook his head and pulled her in for a hug. She clung to him, and as he pressed his cheek to the top of her head, he wished he could impart his strength to her.

His beloved grandmother would need it for what she had to face.

49

HARPER HAD RECEIVED a text from Manny yesterday afternoon, saying he'd worked twelve hours and had to crash for the rest of the day, and he'd call her today. She tried not to read anything into the brevity of the text. What did she expect, some overly effusive missive when the guy had spent half a day patching up people? She'd almost asked him about the hospital job that had come her way but knew the last thing he needed at the end of a long shift was to trade texts, so she'd bided her time until today.

He must be having one hell of a sleep, because he hadn't called by midday, and she knew this would be another downside of dating a doctor besides being ditched for emergencies: not being able to call him for fear of waking him. A selfish, irrational thought, considering the work he did and how he devoted his time to her when they were together. Manny made her feel special in a way she never had, like she was the only girl in the world. She needed to remember that the next time she felt a little sulky.

Her mom had invited her over for lunch, and Harper hoped Lydia had taken her advice and sorted things with her dad. Seeing those gift baskets the other day had made Harper sad in a way she hadn't expected. Her dad truly loved her mom, his devotion absolute. So what the hell had happened to keep them apart for so long? If there was the slightest chance they could reconcile their differences, Harper would be all for it.

The first thing she noticed when she parked in front of her childhood home was a new car in the driveway. A black compact hybrid. Her mom's small SUV was parked in front of it, so it wasn't an impulsive buy by Lydia, and she hoped her dad hadn't gone overboard and upped the ante from his gift baskets. Or worse, it signaled her mom was about to introduce her to a new man.

The door opened as she reached the porch, and Harper struggled not to gape. Her immaculately presented mother who never had a hair out of place, always wore makeup, and wouldn't be seen dead in a leisure suit, wore her hair loose and tousled around her shoulders, not a bit of makeup on her face, and black yoga pants topped with a gray hoodie.

But Lydia's eyes sparkled in a way Harper hadn't seen in a long time, and her smile . . . she'd never seen her mother this happy.

"Who are you and what have you done with my mom?"

"Come in," Lydia said, waiting until Harper had stepped inside and closed the door before flinging her arms around her.

"Mom, you're scaring me. What's going on?"

The moment she asked the question, she knew.

The strange car in the driveway.

Her mom's disheveled appearance.

Lydia definitely had a new man, and they'd barely made it out of the bedroom.

Harper shuddered and Lydia released her.

"I've got a surprise for you," her mom said, leading her by the hand toward the kitchen.

The first thing Harper glimpsed as they passed the dining room was no gift baskets. Yep, it was looking more likely by the minute that her mom had a new man.

The second thing she saw as she entered the kitchen was her dad, wearing a tailored suit of all things, with a tie and expensive Italian loafers.

When her father smiled, his proud gaze swinging between her and Lydia, Harper knew what the surprise was, and she let out a whoop. Her feet flew across the kitchen, and she flung herself into her dad's open arms, bursting into tears as he hugged her tight.

"I guess this means she's happy about our decision," Lydia said, completing their family hug by pressing against Harper's back like she used to when Harper was little and it was the three of them against the world.

There were sniffles all round before they disengaged and Harper stood between her parents, her head swiveling.

"You two owe me an explanation."

"We love you, darling, but we don't owe you anything," Lydia said, standing beside Alec, her hand in his. "But we want to tell you what's happened, because we know you've been worried about us."

"That's an understatement," Harper said, pulling up a chair at the table.

She couldn't be happier that her parents had reunited, but a small part of her wished she could reboot her vitiligo as easily. They could return to normal, but she never could.

"You're looking awfully slick, Dad."

Alec shrugged, bashful. "I was trying to impress your mother, be the man I thought she wanted me to be, but it turns out my clothes had nothing to do with it."

"Let's have a drink." Her mom sloshed bourbon into three glasses and added ice before joining them at the table.

Another anomaly in a day tipped topsy-turvy. She'd never, ever seen Lydia touch a spirit; her mom was a chardonnay drinker any day of the week.

When they all had a drink, Lydia raised her glass. "To the Rylands."

"To you and dad," Harper said, clinking her glass against her parents'. "Now, would someone like to give me the lowdown?"

Her dad couldn't take his eyes off her mom, so Harper knew Lydia would be the one to talk.

"Your father and I had a good marriage for the most part, but when you live with someone long enough, resentment can set in. While I gave up my career by choice to save your father's business, I envisaged going back to it one day. But your father got used to having me around as an adjunct to his business, entertaining his cronies, throwing parties, and I knew having a salon again would never happen."

"But I thought you loved entertaining," Harper said. "Some of my fondest childhood memories are the big parties you guys hosted here. We were always having people around. The food, the music, the laughter, I cherished all that."

"What I didn't realize was your mother had to do all the work to make those parties a success," her dad said, suitably shame-faced. "I was the life of the party, but your mother did it all. The preparation, the food, the cleaning up." He shook his head. "I was hopeless."

"I gave up asking him to help after a while but that wasn't good, because as my resentment built I seriously started to dislike your father."

"So what happened last year to push you over the edge?"

"You know I consult at the local beauty salon every now and then?"

Harper nodded.

"An opportunity came up for me to help with a bridal party. Hair, makeup, the works, but it meant traveling to Albury for the weekend. Turns out I'd done one of the bridesmaid's hair and she was opening her own beauty salon and wanted me on board for hair. But when I told your father, he said that was the weekend his partner was hosting the hardware store owners, and we had to be there otherwise his business would suffer."

Lydia huffed out a breath. "Once again, his business came first. I'd felt neglected for years because of his bloody business, and that was the last straw."

Alec rested his hand on Lydia's knee. "I'm so sorry."

Lydia flashed a grateful smile. "We've been over this, Alec. Let me tell Harper the rest.

"You know what triggered me the most? Your father never really *saw* me. He didn't see how excited I was about the opportunity. He didn't see my devastation when he told me about his event. It was like I'd become invisible over the years, and that hurt the most, after I'd devoted my life to making his easier." Lydia shrugged. "I'd finally had enough. When I initially kicked him out, I wanted to give him a wake-up call, to show him how he'd been taking me for granted."

"It worked," Alec muttered, shaking his head. "I was such an idiot."

"But a funny thing happened when I had the house to my-self," Lydia said. "I liked it. I began to do the things I wanted to do, things I never had a chance to when your father was around, like playing loud rock music and eating in front of the TV and staying up till two a.m. I felt . . . free."

"While I was bloody miserable." Alec bumped Lydia with his shoulder. "I used to sit out the front sometimes, hearing you blast that music, and imagine you were partying with some bas-tard two decades my junior."

Harper bit back a smile. "Stalker much, Dad?"

"Your father never stopped caring."

The speed with which Lydia defended Alec showed Harper more than words could say. They were definitely a team again.

"So what changed? What led to this?" Harper gestured at the two of them, sitting close, shoulders touching.

"Those blasted gift baskets," Lydia said, shooting Alec a fond glance. "Your father wrote me a letter and tucked it into the last one. It was the first time he didn't beg for forgiveness or ask to come home. But he listed every reason he thought why our mar-riage had floundered and asked for another chance to make it better." She rested her head against his shoulder, utterly besot-ted. "He showed insight I wasn't sure he was capable of and made me realize what we had was worth fighting for after thirty-five years. So we both want to do better."

Lydia straightened and pointed to her face. "I'm going to stop putting on a front all the time, trying to live up to an idea of perfection that's in my own head."

"And I'm going to semi-retire," Alec said. "Cut back to twenty hours a week so I can devote the rest of the time to working on our marriage and putting your mother first so she never feels second-best again."

"Wow." Harper pressed her hands to her chest, where love for these two amazing people swelled. "I'm incredibly happy for you both."

"Thanks, love, we're happy too." Alec slipped an arm around Lydia's shoulders. "And if you don't mind, we have a lot of catching up to do."

"Are you kicking me out? What about lunch?"

"We'll take you out for a Happy Meal sometime next week," Alec deadpanned, and they all laughed, remembering it was their go-to bribe when she was little.

"I'll leave you two lovebirds alone." Harper stood and moved around the table to kiss her mom and dad. "I love you both so much."

"Right back at you, kid," her dad said, while her mom squeezed her hand.

As she left the house and headed for her car, Harper realized she hadn't told them about Manny. She'd planned on filling in her mom on her new relationship status and telling her dad at a later date.

But it didn't matter; she'd tell them another time. Seeing her parents reunited reinforced her belief in love again.

And maybe, just maybe, she could have a happily ever after of her own.

50

MANNY HAD SLEPT poorly last night. He'd been physically and mentally exhausted when he'd gotten home from Izzy's and had barely mustered the energy to text Harper before falling into bed. But it took a long time for slumber to come, considering Izzy's diagnosis and her fatalistic approach reverberated around his head.

He'd tried to take the emotion out of it and analyze it from a purely medical perspective. It didn't help, because if Izzy were any other patient and not his grandmother, the prognosis would still be the same.

Not good.

Her age, combined with the length of time the endocarditis had gone undiagnosed, meant the risk of complications was high. Even if she survived the surgery, she could be in danger.

His grandmother could die, and there wasn't one damn thing he could do about it.

He'd only felt this helpless once before, when his mom had died in his arms. Back then, he'd been consumed by guilt and uselessness.

This time would be different.

He could give his grandmother the one thing she wanted so badly.

He had it all planned out.

He just hoped Harper didn't think he'd lost his mind.

Knocking on her front door, he knew what he was about to do was madness. He rarely made impulsive decisions. His analytical brain wasn't wired that way. But the way he saw it, this wasn't so impulsive. He felt more for Harper in the short time he'd known her than any other woman. She made him laugh, she challenged him, and she made him feel at peace, something he could do with a lot more of.

Do you love her?

He'd pondered that at length last night too. A difficult question to answer for someone who'd never fallen in love. But if love made him do crazy things, like volunteer to be her foodie assistant, extend his leave to be with her, and almost ravish her in a public place beside a lake, yeah, he loved her.

Now he had to prove it.

She opened the door, smiling, and just like that he knew everything would be okay. "Hey, handsome."

"Hey yourself."

She stepped forward and into his arms, like it was the only place she wanted to be. Overcome with emotion, he crushed her to him, craving her warmth, wanting her with a ferocity that shook him to his core.

But this couldn't be about sex. Not now. Time enough to celebrate later.

When he released her, she stepped back and studied him, a tiny frown between her brows. "You okay?"

He had to be, otherwise she'd know there was something wrong, and he didn't want to tell her everything until he had her answer.

"Yeah, still tired from that massive shift yesterday."

"My man, the hero." She brushed her lips across his. "You do amazing work. It must be so satisfying."

"It has its moments."

He didn't want to stand around talking about his job. He wanted to ensure everything went smoothly tonight, starting now. "Ready to go?"

"Sure." She must've heard something in his tone because she continued to study his face as she closed the door. "I'm intrigued by this surprise you have planned."

"It's going to blow your mind."

He was still trying to get his head around it.

As he opened the passenger door and she slid inside, she glanced up at him. "There's something different about you today, and I can't put my finger on it."

"In a good way, I hope."

Her expression softened, and she got that look in her eyes, the one that made him feel like a superhero. "Everything about you is good."

"You'll give me a big head."

"Too late. I don't know how you fit through most doorways as it is."

He laughed and ducked down to kiss her before straightening, closing her door, and moving around to the driver's side. This is exactly what he needed, for her to make him laugh and take his mind off the momentous move he was about to make.

"Where are we going?"

"You'll see."

"I like this man of mystery thing you've got going on. It's very sexy."

"Speaking of sexy . . ."

Grateful they'd stopped at a traffic signal, he glanced across at her. "You look gorgeous and I'm sorry it took me this long to say it, but having you in my arms earlier made me lose my mind as usual."

"Thanks," she said, her gaze warm, her smile wide. "You say the nicest things."

"All true."

The lights changed and he refocused on the road, glad they didn't have to go far. Because with every passing second, he started to doubt his grand plan.

Was he seriously going to do this?

"Hey, I've got some good news," she said.

"Yeah?"

"My parents reunited."

"That's great. How long were they apart again?"

"Almost fifteen months."

"That's really good news. You must be thrilled."

"I am. It's restored my faith in love again. I always thought they were the perfect couple, and if they couldn't make it . . ." She trailed off, sounding pensive. "It shook me up when they separated, then Colin dumped me two months later, hence my man ban. I didn't want to believe in love anymore."

"And now?"

He held his breath, waiting for her answer, hoping it would be the right one.

"Now a fast-talking charmer who's easy on the eyes has swept me off my feet and I couldn't be happier."

"I like the sound of that."

"What about you?"

"You're about to discover exactly how you've captivated me."

"Tease," she said, resting her hand on his thigh, sending a surge about five inches higher. "You're definitely up to something. You've had this funny expression ever since you picked me up."

"From charming to looking funny. Nice."

She squeezed his thigh. "Are we there yet?"

He laughed, the first time he'd felt like it in the last forty-eight hours. Not every patient had survived that multicar pileup, and closely followed by Izzy's devastating news, he'd felt like crap since.

"We're about two minutes away."

It was the longest one hundred and twenty seconds of his life as her hand started to move along his thigh, lightly stroking, driving him wild.

When he finally pulled into the golf course, he wanted to drag her behind the nearest tree and bury himself inside her.

"We're playing night golf?"

He shook his head and killed the engine. "No. But one of my old patients owns this course, and there's something I want to show you down by the lake."

"Let me guess. It's balls."

He laughed again, reinforcing he was doing the right thing. If she could make him feel like this when sadness clouded him, she was definitely a keeper.

"You'll get to see mine, along with my number one driver, later if you're lucky."

She groaned and punched him in the arm. "Lame. Very, very lame."

"You're the one who mentioned balls."

"But you had to take it that one step further." Smiling, she shook her head. "Come on, let's see this surprise."

As they strolled toward the lake, hand in hand, Manny hoped Harper couldn't feel his palm slick with sweat. Nerves made his heart pound, and a strange buzzing filled his ears.

He was about to do this.

About to change his life in a way he'd never thought possible.

She caught sight of the table first. "Wow. Did you do that?"

"Yeah. Once the place closed for the day, I ducked down here. Turns out the guy who owns this place is a closet romantic, and he didn't mind me bringing you here for a surprise."

He'd ringed the long rectangular table in tea lights, the flames flickering gently in the barest of breezes. The surprise he'd arranged lay under white napkins, and as they neared the table, he almost balked.

This was crazy. The worst impulse he'd ever had, when he never had any usually.

But the image of Izzy's expression taut with worry flickered into his mind, and he knew he had to do this.

They stopped in front of the table and he clasped her hands, turning to face her.

"What I'm about to do may seem crazy, and in a way it is. But I'm a decisive man. I've made smart choices my entire life. And falling for you is definitely one of them."

Her eyes shone in the candlelight, and the corners of her mouth curved up. "Eloquent and gorgeous. No wonder I fell for you too."

"I want you to know I don't do this lightly either. It means something. It's scary but exciting, and I couldn't imagine changing my life this much with anyone but you."

Her eyes widened in surprise as he released her hands so he could remove the napkins.

"I'm hoping you'll think this is romantic rather than corny."

He whipped off the napkins one by one, revealing one word at a time.

WILL. YOU. MARRY. ME?

Spelled out in slices of kiwi fruit.

Harper stared at the table in openmouthed shock, before looking back at him.

"I . . . what . . . wow."

He smiled and tipped up her chin. "I wanted to do a bit of food styling of my own. And of course I chose kiwi fruit to do it, considering we got together in New Zealand. So what do you think?"

She gave a little shake of her head as if coming out of a trance. "You're asking me to marry you?"

"Yeah. And I know it doesn't make any sense because we haven't known each other long and we've been dating for less, but I know this is right. In here." He thumped a fist to his heart. "If I don't know what I want by forty, I'll never know, so this is definitely right."

He clasped her face in his hands. "You're the one for me, Harper. What do you say?"

She kissed him in response, but she didn't speak, and considering the indecision in her eyes, he braced for an answer he wouldn't like.

51

THOSE FOUR WORDS kept shimmering before Harper's eyes.

Will you marry me?

She'd alternated between shock and elation when she'd first read them, soon followed by *Are you freaking serious?*

In what crazy world would she accept a proposal from a guy she barely knew? A guy she'd fallen for way too quickly, but . . . marriage?

Ironic, she'd always craved the fairy tale—wedding, kids, the works—but with someone she'd known for more than five seconds. Though that was harsh. She may not have known Manny for long in terms of months, but in her heart she knew him better than Colin, and she'd been with him for over a year.

"It's the kiwi fruit, isn't it? Too much?"

She laughed, something she'd been doing a lot of since this wonderful man had swept her off her feet. Even now, when he must be feeling gauche and uncomfortable because of her prolonged hesitation, he was trying to make this easier on her.

"The kiwi fruit is a cute touch. I'm more shocked by the proposal."

"It's crazy and spontaneous and out of the blue and too soon, but I had to ask."

"Why?"

"Because I've fallen for you." His beautiful gray gaze bored into her, making her a believer. "It defies logic, I know, and I'm all about logic. Facts based in science are what I believe. My whole life revolves around it. But you and me?"

He released her hands to run his up and down her bare arms, pebbling her skin. "We're not logical or well-thought-out or planned. This is you and me. We're whipped cream and banter and fun."

His caresses slowed, almost hypnotic. "But we're also tenderness and strength and serenity. We fit, and it's easy and comfortable, with a constant undercurrent that blows my mind."

Manny's honesty broke her.

He spoke from the heart, stripping back her defenses, laying her bare.

His declaration wasn't eloquent, but it was real, and that's what she'd always wanted. A real relationship, stability, for the long haul. And here was this incredible guy offering it to her.

What was she waiting for?

"Yes," she murmured, waiting for the dread and regret and worry to fill her, to make her second-guess her decision, to reinforce she'd lost her mind.

But it didn't come. Instead, as he let out a jubilant yell, picked her up, and spun her around, all she felt was joyous elation.

"Hey, I'm dizzy," she said, slapping his shoulders. "Put me down."

"Anything you say, fiancée."

He lowered her gently, slowly, their bodies in full frontal contact, inch by delicious inch. "Damn, I like the sound of that."

"Me too," she said. "Even though I still think we're both officially nuts. I mean, I haven't met your gran yet, and you haven't met my parents. What are they going to think?"

An odd expression flickered over his face. "Gran will be ecstatic, and I'll do my best to win over your folks."

Harper wasn't worried about her parents. Lydia and Alec would be too wrapped up in themselves to be concerned about her impulsive decision. They wanted her to be happy, and Manny made a hell of an impression on anyone.

A small part of her wondered if agreeing to his proposal stemmed from her happiness for them. Was she so swept up in the romance of her parents reuniting that she wanted the fairy tale for herself?

She knew when the euphoria of Manny's shock proposal died down she'd start second-guessing the wisdom of marrying a man she hadn't known long.

But he was right about one thing. Logic didn't come into it, not when she could hardly believe this was happening and she wanted to celebrate.

"What are you thinking?" His strong hands framed her face as he peered at her as if trying to read her mind.

"That we're nuts, but I'm happy."

"Me too."

His hot, openmouthed, toe-curling kiss sealed it.

52

IN TRUE IZZY fashion, she refused to have her heart valve surgery at Manny's hospital. He tried to convince her, using persuasive arguments from "I can visit you more often" to "I can get all the inside info on your condition." Apparently, the latter was exactly why she didn't want to be anywhere near his hospital.

He understood. He was overprotective when it came to his grandmother at the best of times, and now his concern had shot into the stratosphere. Not that he was showing her. He thought he'd masked it well, but she'd been reading him since he was a little kid, and he couldn't get much past her.

At least he had some good news to tell her now, ensuring she'd fight like the devil to come through this surgery.

No way would Izzy not have a say in his wedding.

Manny entered her room, and in the second or two before she recognized him, he glimpsed exactly how terrified she was. Worry pinched her mouth, accentuating the fine lines fanning out from the corners, and she looked sad, like she expected the worst. All that changed when she saw him, and she visibly brightened, but her eyes didn't lie. She was just as petrified as he was.

"You don't need to be here while they take me in." She waved him away. "The anesthetist will be here any minute to prep me."

"That's exactly why I'm here, to give the guy the third degree and make sure he hasn't been drinking all night."

She made a *pfft* scoffing sound, but he saw the slight upturning of her mouth. He knew what he had to say next would definitely make her smile.

"I'm also here to tell you some news."

Her eyes narrowed as her eagle-eyed gaze swept over his face. "You look smug. What have you done? A crash course in cardiac surgery so you can replace my valves yourself?"

He grinned at her sarcasm.

"Better than that. What's the one thing you want?"

"To not see a bright white light in the distance over the next few hours."

He laughed. No surprises for guessing where he got his dry sense of humor.

"I'm engaged."

Confusion creased her brow. "To do what?"

Maybe the nurses had given her a little pre-sedative, because it took another second or two for his words to sink in.

"To get married?" Her eyebrows rose so high the wrinkles of her forehead reached her hairline.

"Yeah, big news, huh?"

"Huh," she said, staring at him like he'd lost his mind. "To that Harper woman, I presume?"

He nodded, unable to keep the goofy grin off his face. Even now, twelve hours since she'd said yes and they'd headed back to her place for the kind of celebration that invigorated in the best possible way, he could hardly believe it.

She'd understandably had reservations, and he shared them all, but as he watched Izzy process his news—the forehead wrinkles cleared, her eyes brightened, and she actually smiled—he knew without a doubt he'd done the right thing.

"You're getting married," she said, sounding wondrous and shocked and thrilled at the same time. "About time."

"If that's your way of saying congratulations, I'll take it."

"Come here." She beckoned him over, and when he stood next to her bed she reached for his hand. "You know I only want what's best for you, Manish, and if this Harper makes you happy, then I'm happy."

"Thanks, Iz." He leaned down to kiss her forehead, and she hugged him close for a moment before releasing him.

"Now I definitely have to turn away from any white lights so I can meet this fiancée of yours and make sure she's good enough for my grandson."

"I'm counting on it." He winked, thrilled his news had perked her up. "Now that I've given you an injection of endorphins, any questions about the surgery I can answer?"

"My cardiologist has done all that. Tell me more about your wedding plans."

Thankfully, the anesthetist entered the room at that moment, saving Manny from having to explain he hadn't got that far. Getting Harper to agree to his outlandish proposal had been his focus, and now that he was engaged he'd get to the rest; when his gran recovered from this potentially fatal disease.

"George, this is my grandson, Manish," Izzy said. "He's head of ER at another hospital, and he was just leaving."

George grinned and shot him a sympathetic look. "She's not so keen on having you advise on this procedure."

"You got that right."

Izzy waved him away. "I'll see you after the operation, Man-ish. Go. Be with your fiancée."

Manny wasn't going anywhere until his grandmother was safely wheeled out of the OR and into recovery, but he didn't want to rile her.

"Love you, Iz. See you when you're done."

"Not done, *done*, I hope," she said, making George and Manny chuckle.

Manny blew her a kiss, nodded at George, and left the room. He'd wait in his car. He didn't fancy a long stint in the cafeteria, surrounded by equally worried people trying to pass time by consuming brightly colored Jell-O or sloppy meat loaf.

And in the car he'd have privacy to call Harper.

If anyone could calm his nerves now, she could.

53

"YOU'RE *WHAT?*"

Lydia stared at Harper like she'd lost her mind. "How can you be engaged?"

"Quite easily, Mom. Manny asked; I said yes."

"This is insanity," Lydia muttered, shaking her head while Alec stepped forward to offer Harper a hug.

"Congrats, darling. If this is what you want, we'll support you. Won't we, Lyds?"

Lydia snorted, but her disapproving expression softened. "We haven't even met this man. How do we know if he's good enough for you?"

"Mom, I'm thirty. Don't you think I'm old enough to make my own decisions?"

"Well, yes, but . . . we don't know him; it's not right," Lydia blustered, her frown deepening. "And what kind of man doesn't ask your father for your hand in marriage?"

"A man who's forty, is worldly, and doesn't live in the dark ages." Harper rolled her eyes. "This is what I want. I hope you'll support me." She paused for emphasis, her gaze swinging between them. "Like I supported both of you through your separation."

"Touché," Lydia muttered, while Alec nodded.

"We've got your back, kid, one hundred percent," Alec said. "So when do we get to meet this fiancé of yours?"

"He should be here any second," she said, glancing at her watch. "He's coming straight from the hospital."

"He's a doctor?" Her dad looked suitably impressed, her mom mollified with the reminder.

"Yeah, but he wasn't working this morning. His grandmother had heart surgery, so he's been with her."

"Is she okay?"

"Yeah, she's in recovery and doing well."

Though Harper left out the details of how she'd spent an hour on the phone with Manny, trying to talk him down. He'd been wired with worry, and it broke her heart she couldn't do more. If she had any doubts about her feelings, offering him whatever comfort she could, wishing she could be there for him, reinforced that what she felt was real.

She'd fallen in love.

"But just so you know, he's popping in for a quick intro and then we're heading back to the hospital together."

"That's okay, we can celebrate later," Alec said, at the same time Lydia said, "So we won't even have time for a celebratory toast?"

"Mom—"

"Lyds—"

"Fine." Lydia threw her hands up in the air. "We'll wait for a more appropriate time to celebrate."

The doorbell rang at that moment, and Harper said, "I'll get it."

She'd tried to talk Manny out of doing this today, when she knew he'd rather be by his gran's side. But he'd insisted, and she admired his principles.

She opened the door, and her chest tightened with emotion. When he'd left her house in the wee small hours that morning, he'd looked happy and relaxed. Now fatigue ringed his eyes and worry furrowed his brow.

"You okay?" She stepped forward and wrapped her arms around him, tightening her hold when she heard his deep, long sigh.

"Yeah, I'm fine."

"And your gran?"

"Doing as well as can be expected."

That didn't sound as positive as when he'd rung her an hour ago when his gran had reached recovery and he'd seen her.

Releasing him, Harper studied his face. "This endocarditis you mentioned. It's more serious than simply having the heart valves replaced, isn't it?"

"Yeah." He swiped a hand over his face. It did little to eradicate the tension. "But Izzy's always been stubborn, and now that she knows she has a wedding to look forward to, she'll fight to get better."

Harper smiled and grazed his cheek with her knuckle. "Do you think she'll like me?"

"How can she not?" His eyes darkened to pewter, his adoration sending a shot of warmth through her. "I fell for you quickly, and Gran will too."

"Speaking of relatives approving . . ." She jerked a thumb over her shoulder. "I've told them I'm doing a quick intro and then we're out of here because we have to head back to the hospital."

His eyebrows rose. "It's okay if we stay awhile."

"You're sweet, but you should be with your gran now, not sitting through an interrogation of monstrous proportions from my mom."

"What about your dad? How did he take the news?"

"Dad's cool. He's a good buffer."

"And we need a buffer because . . . ?"

"You'll understand once you meet Mom."

He smiled. "On that note, are you going to let me in?"

Slipping her hand in Manny's, she led him into the lounge room, where her parents were standing on either side of the coffee table like sentinels.

"Manny, this is my dad, Alec, and my mom, Lydia."

She liked that he didn't release her hand as he shook theirs. "Pleased to meet you both."

"Likewise, son," Alec said, and Lydia shot him a death glare that had Harper stifling a giggle.

"You proposed awfully quickly, Manny." Lydia gestured at the couch, and Harper wanted to laugh again as they all sat simultaneously. "Are you usually so impulsive?"

"Mom." Harper shot Lydia a warning look that, predictably, her mom ignored.

"It's not like Harper to make such rash decisions either, so we want to make sure you've both thought this through."

Harper knew her parents loved her, but she wasn't some naive teen sitting here with her first boyfriend being grilled. But before she could speak, Manny squeezed her hand and glanced at her, his smile calming her.

"I understand your reservations, Lydia. I truly do. As I've explained to Harper, I'm not one for making impulsive decisions.

I base my decisions on facts, science; it's who I am. But some things defy logic, and how I feel about your daughter is one of them."

Harper melted, and she was pretty sure her mom's sigh echoed hers, while her dad beamed.

"Impressive speech, young man." Alec's gaze dipped to where Manny clasped her hand, before eyeballing him. "All we've ever wanted is for our little Harp to be happy, and we respect her decision. But if you hurt her, I'll have to kill you."

"Dad!"

Harper groaned but Manny laughed.

"I'll take good care of her, promise."

While Lydia's expression had softened somewhat, her gaze remained shrewd. "You don't have a ring yet?"

"I want Harper to have a say in what she wants."

Manny leaned over on the pretext of kissing her, and whispered in her ear, "My little Harp."

She elbowed him away, and they laughed together. Her dad had called her that when she'd been little, ever since she'd demanded a toy harp for Christmas one year. Now she knew Manny would never let her live it down.

When Harper glanced back at her parents, they wore matching expressions of surprise.

"You both look so happy," Lydia murmured, her eyes misting.

"That's because we are, Mom."

Harper stood, and Manny rose alongside her. "We really have to go, but we'll have that celebratory toast soon."

"Okay." Lydia nodded. "Please give your grandmother our best, Manny. Harper told us she's recovering from heart surgery."

"Thanks, I will."

This time when Manny extended his hand to Harper's dad, Alec pumped it enthusiastically, and when he did the same to Lydia, her mom swatted it away and embraced him in a quick hug. Harper didn't know who looked more surprised, Manny or her dad, who knew Lydia took a while to warm up to new people.

After Harper bid farewell to her folks, she followed Manny out to his car, waiting until the front door closed before collapsing against his chest.

"I'm so glad that's over."

"Your parents are fine, they love you, you're lucky to have them." He placed a finger under her chin and tipped it up. "But I have to admit, I almost lost it when your dad called you his little harp."

"Please don't ever refer to that again." She grimaced, not surprised to see a cheeky glint in his eyes.

"Why? I don't mind a little harp, as long as I get to pluck it all night."

A bubble of laughter escaped her. "You are so lame."

"Only because you love my bad puns."

"And the rest," she murmured, unable to believe she could be this happy, this quickly. She wanted to say *I love you*, but it didn't seem the right time while they were trading banter as usual and with her parents probably spying on them through the front window.

From his proposal last night to now, Harper had been floating, caught up in the fairy tale she'd always dreamed about. Gaining her parents' approval had made it all the more real. She knew they had a lot to learn about each other, and they didn't have to rush into a wedding anytime soon.

Because she still hadn't revealed her secret to Manny, and she couldn't get past the bone-deep fear that the last time she'd done it, the man she thought had adored her walked away.

Colin was nothing like Manny. They were worlds apart. But until she told Manny the truth, she couldn't fully embrace the excitement of being engaged.

Now wasn't the time, with his grandmother just out of surgery, but over the next few days she'd take the final step in trusting this amazing man with her heart.

54

IT HAD BEEN a long ten days.

Taking time off for that medical conference in Auckland, then tacking on extra vacation days, meant Manny was still struggling to get on top of his workload now.

It didn't help that he spent his limited downtime at the hospital with Izzy. Not that he begrudged the time by her bedside—she was the only family he had—but it meant he was more sleep-deprived than during his stint as a resident many years ago.

And it left him with no time for Harper.

She'd been incredibly understanding, but he still felt guilty they hadn't been ring shopping. Nor had she met Izzy, but that was more his doing.

His grandmother wasn't recovering well.

Physically, her cardiologist and registrar were pleased with her healing. After a few days in rehab, they would discharge her. But mentally, it was like Izzy had checked out. She didn't smile at his jokes. She feigned interest in the soap operas she was usually glued to. She hardly touched her food, even when he brought in a tiffin carrier of *dahl* and rice he'd made especially.

The only time she showed any sign of life was when she grilled him about his engagement. How had he proposed, where, when, what had Harper said, when was the wedding, blah, blah, blah, on and on it went, and he was tired of ad-libbing.

Interestingly, in all her focus on his nuptials, she hadn't asked to meet Harper beyond the first day, when he'd fobbed her off with a *She wants to come but doctor's orders say you can only see family.*

He'd half hoped Izzy would refute his claim with *Harper is going to be my family too, I want to meet her,* but with his grandmother in this strange mood he'd rather wait to foist her onto his fiancée.

His fiancée.

Even though they'd barely seen each other lately, the thought of being engaged to Harper brought him a comfort he'd never experienced before. She grounded him. Not that he'd ever been particularly jittery, but she brought calmness to his life that he loved.

Izzy managed a half-hearted wave as he entered her room, and he knew she wouldn't like what he had to say.

"Hey, Gran. A few more days in rehab and then you'll be home."

She mustered a weak frown. "Good. But I don't need any of that home nursing rubbish. I'm perfectly capable of taking care of myself."

He'd expected this battle and had an argument prepared. "I know you are, but I was thinking of throwing a small engagement party at your place, just family and close friends, and I can't expect you to do all the preparation, not when you're still recovering."

At last, some of her old fire sparked in her eyes. "An engagement party?"

"Yes, if you're okay with us having it at your place?"

She sat up straighter. "Of course. There'll be lots to plan—"

"Leave it all to me. You focus on getting better, and that means having a home nurse to help speed up your recovery."

If she guessed his underhanded blackmail, she didn't call him out on it. "I suppose you're right. I do want to be able to enjoy my only grandson's engagement, especially if it's at my house."

"Good, that's settled."

"Manish?"

"Yes?"

"I'm . . . not feeling myself."

Her admission out of the blue shocked him, but he was pleased she'd finally chosen to confide in him. "What do you mean?"

Her lips twitched, like she was trying to form the words but wasn't sure how. "I'm scared of dying."

His heart fractured, a tiny piece splintering off. He'd never seen Izzy so vulnerable, but facing up to her mortality and the prospect that the endocarditis could be life ending was a common response to serious illness.

"I'm angry and frustrated at lying here feeling so damn helpless, and I'm worrying about how I'll cope if my health deteriorates . . ." She shook her head, her mouth pursed with regret. "And I feel guilty. Have I done something to contribute to this? Should I not have eaten all those *gulab jamuns* when the doctor warned me sugar isn't good for my health? Or cooked with ghee that made my cholesterol shoot through the roof?"

She pressed a hand over her heart. "And the craziest of them all, I don't feel like me anymore. I feel like I'm defined by this stupid heart condition, and I want my old life back."

"I'm sorry you feel that way, but everything you've said is a common emotional response to dealing with a serious illness."

She waved him away. "You've got your doctor voice on. Please don't patronize me."

"I'm not." He scooted his chair closer to the bed and grasped her hand. "Everything you've described is perfectly normal." He lowered his voice. "Trust me, I'm a doctor."

Amusement flickered in her eyes. "Will I ever snap out of this?"

"Of course, but it may take time." He squeezed her hand. "But I won't lie to you. You may always feel resentful, a bit of 'why me?' On the upside, you'll have me to snap you out of any funk."

"And don't forget I have a wedding to look forward to."

The old Izzy was back, focused on one thing and one thing only: seeing him married.

"Exactly," he said, not having the heart to tell her they hadn't even discussed a date.

Proposing to Harper had been impulsive, but it had been the right thing to do. It gave Izzy a reason to fight, a reason to live.

Plenty of time to get the rest planned.

55

HARPER ARRIVED ON Manny's doorstep with groceries in one hand and an overnight bag in the other.

This was it.

The first time she'd stay over at his place.

The first time she'd reveal her vitiligo to him.

The last time she'd have to hide her true self.

She'd been a jittery mess all day, swerving between wanting to cook him a three-course meal and lead into her revelation, or jumping him as soon as he opened the door and doing it with the lights on.

She'd finally settled on whipping up homemade pizzas with store-bought dough, sauce, roasted vegetables, and pesto, with extravagant macadamia and honey nougat ice cream for dessert. Less time in the kitchen, more time feasting on each other.

Another thing she'd dithered on all day: her choice of outfit. The patches on her body had diminished considerably in size since she'd started UV treatment, but the ones around her eyes were still stark, considering she'd had a one in a billion reaction to the tacrolimus ointment and her white patches had turned dark brown.

She resembled a panda without concealer and foundation,

and the thought of Manny seeing the real her set an aviary of butterflies loose in her stomach.

But she had to do this. They'd been engaged for two weeks, fourteen long days in which she'd barely seen him. But his gran was home now, and they were throwing a small party tomorrow to celebrate, and she wanted there to be no secrets between them before that.

With her hands full she kicked the door twice, her nerves solidifying into a hard ball in her gut when he opened it and she felt the full impact of that spectacular gray gaze.

"You come bearing gifts," he said, reaching out to take the grocery bag from her and placing it on the floor before leaning in for a lingering kiss that made her weak-kneed. "What's in the other bag?"

"My stuff for the party tomorrow."

Smart guy, he understood the implication straightaway by the slightest widening of his eyes. "You're staying over?"

"If that's okay with my fiancé?"

"More than okay."

As she stepped over the threshold and dumped her bag inside the door, his arm snuck around her waist and he hauled her against him.

"I've missed you," he murmured, nuzzling her neck, setting her nerve endings alight. "You smell good."

"Missed you too," she said, burying her nose in his hair, loving the faintest hint of sandalwood in his shampoo. "How hungry are you?"

"Starving." He lifted his head, his greedy gaze focusing on her lips. "But whatever you have in that grocery bag can wait."

"I like the way you think, but there's ice cream to pop in the freezer and cheese for the fridge."

His hands drifted from her waist to her hips, caressing the curves before landing on her butt, pulling her flush against him. "But that means taking my hands off you."

"Only for a few seconds," she said, gasping as he ground against her. "Then I'm all yours."

"Ten seconds and counting," he said, releasing her to grab the grocery bag and dash to the kitchen.

She laughed, picking up her overnight bag and heading for the bedroom, unable to release all her insecurities at once. There was a vast difference between showing him her body in the harsh light of his living room and the muted lights of a bedroom.

"There, made it back in nine seconds," he said, sliding his arms around her waist from behind, his hard-on pressing against her ass, leaving her under no illusions how much he'd missed her. "Now, are you ready to satisfy my hunger?"

"I could ask you the same thing."

She turned in the circle of his arms, and this time, she grabbed his ass and writhed her pelvis against him. "Just for the record? I want everything you dish up and more. I'm greedy that way."

He growled and hoisted her over his shoulder, leaving her upside down and pummeling at his impressive ass with her fists. "Put me down, you crazy man."

"Crazy for you," he said, lowering her gently when they reached the bed. "And I'm about to show you exactly how much."

· · ·

WITH HER BODY languid from her third orgasm in two hours, Harper stretched, savoring the pull of muscles that had been given a thorough workout.

Sex with Manny was better than any gym.

He snuffled next to her, a cute little snore that made her want to hug him tight. Instead, she watched him sleep, feeling like a creeper but unable to stop.

This gorgeous, intelligent, sensitive man was hers.

They were engaged.

And she'd get to wake up next to him for countless days to come.

How had she got so lucky?

It felt like she'd stepped on a carousel since Nishi's wedding and had been moving at a whirlwind pace ever since. Heck, her best friend didn't even know yet, because Harper hadn't wanted to bother her on her honeymoon.

Nishi would be happy for her, but her friend wouldn't understand the impulsivity. Nishi had dated Arun for five years before they'd got engaged, and every aspect of their massive wedding had been coordinated down to the last *bhindi*. Harper didn't care if she got married at the registry office, as long as Manny was by her side.

Who knew, maybe she'd had to undergo a man ban to find the real deal?

Manny stirred, blowing out a puff of air from pursed lips, and she stiffened. This would be the time when she'd carefully slip from the bed, grab her handbag, and make a dash for the bathroom to check her makeup remained intact. She invested in the most expensive sweat-proof, budge-proof, water-resistant foundation on the planet, and so far it had done its job.

But tonight was different.

She wanted to take her makeup off.

With her heart racing, she lowered the top sheet and glanced down at her torso. At the large white patch extending from under her right breast to her tenth rib—she'd counted; at the patch shaped like Australia on her left hip bone; at the circular patch high on her right thigh, in the skinfold. There were several more on the back of her thighs too, and her ass, along with the ones circling her eyes and mouth and along her chin.

A regular patchwork.

That Manny would soon see.

Her pulse pounded and her palms grew slick as she picked up her overnight bag beside the bedroom door and headed for the bathroom. She didn't care about being particularly quiet, but Manny never stirred. He'd been staying at his grandmother's the last few days since she'd got home from rehab, and while nothing could diminish his outrageous good looks, he looked more exhausted than she'd ever seen him.

They may not have spent much time together since they got engaged, but it hadn't mattered. They'd spoken every day, and it was so effortless it felt like she'd known him forever. Theirs was the kind of relationship she'd always wanted; no muss, no fuss. Not that she was naive enough to think they'd never disagree or argue or have conflicting opinions. But she knew as long as they could communicate freely, they could sort out their differences.

Manny shifted, his head thrashing side to side before he settled into a fetal shape, and her heart almost exploded with tenderness. But she couldn't stand here and watch him sleep. She had important things to do, like strip away her mask and let him see the real her.

She'd never been inside his bathroom and couldn't resist peeking in his cabinet. Nothing terribly exciting; men's toiletries, a shaving kit, spare tubes of toothpaste, and aftershave in a funky spiral bottle. She uncapped it and inhaled, the smell making her receptors zing in memory of following this very scent trail all over his body . . .

Giving her head a shake, she recapped it and closed the cabinet. Not surprising, her hand shook as she removed her makeup with cleansing wipes she'd brought with her, revealing the patches that had defined her for over a year.

She stuck her tongue out at her reflection before getting in the shower and turning the jets to hot. As the water sluiced over her, she wished it could wash away her nerves as easily as the suds. Manny deserved to know everything about her, but the thought of walking into his bedroom, totally stripped of her usual armor, made her legs wobble.

After the longest shower in history, she toweled off and slipped into a robe. She'd brought her favorite one, a soft cotton with tiny poppies scattered all over it, that reached the floor. How many nights had she spent in this robe, curled up on the couch, alone and pretending to be content? Too many, and now she had a lifetime of having Manny by her side. And maybe others . . . they hadn't had the kids conversation yet; the proposal had come out of the blue, then his gran had been in the hospital, and the kids chat needed to happen face-to-face. Not that she was worried. It would happen.

Shaking out her arms like a prizefighter about to enter the ring, Harper dragged in a few deep breaths, blew them out, then opened the bathroom door.

This was it.

Showtime.

Literally.

She would show Manny her biggest physical flaw.

And pray he was the man she thought he was and wouldn't run.

He must've heard the bathroom door open, because his eyes opened. He knuckled them, blinked before focusing on her, and his slow, easy smile went some way to soothing her rampaging nerves.

"Hey, beautiful." He pushed up into a half-sitting position. "I like your robe."

"Thanks."

"But I prefer what's under it." He crooked his finger. "Come here."

"I hope you still feel that way in a minute."

With the room in darkness and her body silhouetted by the bathroom light at her back, he couldn't see her face yet. But as his eyes adjusted and she moved to stand beside him, he'd see everything.

"I love your body," he said. "I love everything about you."

Her heart pounded so loudly the sound filled her ears as she moved toward his side of the bed, forcing her feet to move forward when all she wanted to do was run out of the room.

When she reached the bed, she turned toward him so the light would show him the truth all over her face.

She watched him carefully for the slightest sign of revulsion. But other than the barest widening of his eyes, he showing nothing but curiosity.

"You have vitiligo?"

Biting down on her lip, she nodded. "For about a year. I hate the patches, which is why I hide them all the time." Her breath hitched as she murmured, "I feel ugly."

"Fuck," he muttered, all but leaping from the bed to reach for her. "Those patches don't define you. You're still you, and you're beautiful to me."

Tears stung her eyes as he plucked at the sash holding her robe, untied it, and pushed the robe off her shoulders. It slithered to the floor and pooled at her feet, leaving her exposed and trembling and wishing she could dive beneath the covers.

"Truly beautiful."

His fingertips skated over her skin, caressing, stroking, tracing every patch. He followed with his mouth, tiny kisses that made her shiver with want, his tongue outlining each patch like he wanted to commit them to memory.

Tears trickled down her cheeks as he worshipped her with everything he had.

As he made her feel beautiful.

She'd never loved him more than at that moment.

56

"I like having you here," Manny said, topping up Harper's coffee cup. "You should stay over more often. Like forever."

"I've been here since last night and all day, so it's nice to know I haven't worn out my welcome." She smiled, and his heart did that weird flip thing it had been doing ever since they'd met. "I guess that's another thing we need to discuss: where we're going to live."

"Plenty of time to figure out logistics."

One step at a time. Proposing had been the right thing to do, but planning an actual wedding made him want to get a script filled for hives. He hated fuss of any kind, and he hoped that wouldn't clash with Harper's ideas. Most women he knew wanted the big, fancy wedding, and their partners went along for the ride. Harper didn't seem the flamboyant type, and he hoped she'd appreciate low-key.

"Speaking of logistics, we haven't discussed kids."

He choked on his coffee and coughed, several times, while Harper grinned at him.

"Don't worry, handsome. Considering we haven't set a wedding date, I'm not planning on procreating within the next week or so."

"Phew." He made an exaggerated swipe at his forehead. If

setting an actual date made him break out in hives, the thought of being a father gave him a bad case of poison ivy.

"But you want them, right?"

Kids would depend on him to keep them safe and healthy. He would love them unconditionally. And they would leave, just like his mom had left him unexpectedly.

Eschewing relationships all this time had ensured he'd kept his heart intact. Letting Harper in was a big step for him. But kids took love into a whole new stratosphere, one where he wanted to run and hide.

When a tiny frown creased her brow, he knew he had to say something, other than *This is all happening too fast.*

"I do, but I'd want us to spend some time together as a couple first."

"Agreed. Makes sense, as we hardly know each other but you proposed regardless."

He smiled at her dry response. "What can I say? When I know what I want, I do whatever it takes."

"It's still crazy though."

"I know."

They sipped their coffees in silence, lost in thought. She hadn't applied her makeup yet, and he loved that she felt comfortable enough to do that now. Revealing her vitiligo explained so much: why she'd freaked out in New Zealand, why she always insisted he stay over at her place, why she always had an immaculately made-up face.

The thing was, when he looked at her, he didn't see the patches. He saw the woman he'd fallen for. And if she had any idea how much of a big deal that was for him, opening his heart to her, she'd know she could've trusted him much earlier.

"Are you sick of the treatment for the vitiligo?"

Her eyebrow arched. "That came from left field."

"I know it can be repetitive."

The adoration in her gaze made him feel ten feet tall. "I guess it's handy having a doc for a fiancé after all."

"I'm here for all your needs." He lowered his voice. "Medical or otherwise."

She laughed. "You have no idea what it means to me to be able to discuss this openly with you."

"Your parents must be supportive?"

Her expression blanked as she stared into her coffee cup. "I haven't told them."

"What?"

From his first meeting with them, he could tell they adored Harper. Her dad looked at her like she hung the moon and stars, and her mom was a tigress who'd fight to protect her daughter. Why wouldn't she tell them something that had obviously affected her so deeply?

"My diagnosis was at a stressful time for them. They hadn't been separated long, and I didn't want to add to their burden of dealing with all that."

"That makes you an incredibly caring daughter, but you must've been reeling from the diagnosis. Who helped you through it?"

"Nobody." Pain glinted in her eyes before she blinked, eradicating it. "I'm one tough chick, in case you haven't figured that out yet."

"You're amazing." He placed his cup on the island bench and moved around it to take her into his arms. "But it's okay for tough chicks to depend on fiancés. That's one of the unspoken rules of matrimony."

She laughed against his chest. "You're making that up."

"Maybe, but it should be written in stone."

He loved the peace that enveloped him when he held her like this, like all was right with the world.

But they had a party to get to.

"We need to leave in about half an hour," he said, reluctantly releasing her. "Though I still think you should've let me take you ring shopping before the engagement party."

"It's our closest friends, my folks, and your gran. Nobody to impress; we can be ourselves." She touched his cheek. "Besides, there's plenty of time to get a ring. I'd rather spend time with you than flash around a five-carat rock on my finger."

"Five carats?" He clutched at his chest. "I work in the ER; I'm not a brain surgeon."

"Well then, maybe you should introduce me to some of your colleagues—"

She squealed as he made a lunge for her, allowing him to catch her far too easily.

"You have a smart mouth, Ms. Ryland."

"Haven't you heard? Smart mouths make for the best kisses," she said, a moment before proving exactly that.

57

No AMOUNT OF makeup or hairstyling or wearing a killer new dress could've prepared Harper for walking into Manny's grandmother's house and meeting his beloved Izzy.

"Isadora Gomes, my dear." The sprightly old lady with tight gray curls and beady brown eyes held out her hand as if she expected to be greeted like the queen. "Pleased to meet you."

"Likewise," Harper said, shaking her hand, unsure whether to kiss her cheek or give her a hug too. Unfortunately, she ended up doing a weird one arm pat on the back that earned a raised eyebrow from Izzy.

"You can call me Isadora."

Harper didn't want to disagree and appear rude, but calling Manny's grandmother by her first name felt wrong, so she managed an awkward smile she hoped didn't look like a grimace.

"You're very pretty." Isadora tilted her head, studying her with an intensity that left Harper squirming. "I can see what my grandson sees in you."

"Thank you," Harper said, hating their stilted, almost clichéd conversation, wishing Manny would stop fussing with the caterers and get in here. "How are you feeling?"

"Like death warmed up. But don't tell Manish. He fusses terribly."

"It's sweet that he cares about you so much."

"Yes, I am lucky." Isadora eyed her speculatively. "So, what's this I hear about you styling food?"

At last, a subject they may have something in common about. Manny had told her Izzy was a great cook and he'd learned a lot from her.

"Food is my passion," Harper said. "When I was young I'd sit with my mom and we'd look at cookbooks together and I loved the pretty pictures. I did okay at school but knew I wanted to do something in hospitality when I finished, so I ended up working with various catering companies while trying to hone my hand at styling."

Her enthusiasm caused her to babble, and by Izzy's beady stare, she had no idea if she'd impressed her or confirmed a less favorable opinion.

"So you intend on making a career out of this food styling?"

Izzy made it sound like Harper wanted to dance naked in Federation Square in the heart of Melbourne for a living.

"I do. When it's your passion it doesn't feel like work, and I've just done a big job in New Zealand for the magazines to be placed throughout Storr Hotels, so I should get plenty of referrals out of that. And my hours can be flexible, which should fit in well with Manny's."

"Indeed."

Uh-oh. Manny may have implied his grandmother was a sweetheart, but Harper found her slightly terrifying.

Thankfully, Manny reentered the lounge room at that moment, preventing what felt like an incoming interrogation of monstrous proportions.

"How are my two favorite girls in the world getting along?"

"Famously," Isadora said, reaching across to pat Harper's hand, as she tried not to flinch at the iciness of the older woman's palm. "Don't you worry, Manish. We may not have time to talk now, but I intend to grill Harper after the party."

Great, something to look forward to. Harper settled for saying, "I'll be prepared," and smiling, as Manny looked on fondly.

She liked that he doted on his grandmother and placed value in family loyalty, but Harper had a feeling Isadora had meant it when she said she was in for a grilling.

Manny had kept the guest list small—Samira and Rory, Pia and Dev, Nishi and Arun, and her folks—and they all arrived within minutes of one another. Once everyone had drinks in their hands, the catering staff set the food out and left, leaving everyone to help themselves. Casual, just the way she liked it, and she tried her utmost not to criticize the canapé presentation.

Harper's head spun as she clung to Manny's hand, laughing as he regaled everyone about details of his proposal, adding the odd snarky comment of her own, while their friends and family hung on their every word.

This whole party had a surreal quality, like she was an actress playing a part, the happy woman swept off her feet by the dashing doctor, into a happily-ever-after scenario she'd only ever dreamed about.

But all through the party Harper felt Isadora's shrewd gaze on her, assessing and judging. Hopefully not finding her lacking. It took the gloss off what would've been a joyous affair otherwise.

"Girlfriend, I need to steal you for a moment." Nishi grabbed her arm and tugged. "I go on my honeymoon and come back to this? I need details."

Harper smiled. "Let's duck out to the backyard."

She caught Manny's eye as Nishi dragged her toward the kitchen, and he nodded in understanding, mimicking a chatterbox with his hand. She grinned, loving how in sync they were, even across a crowded room.

When they slipped out the back door and into the yard, Nishi spun on her. "You and Manny are engaged? I can't believe it. Tell me everything."

"It's all happened pretty fast."

"Fast? Girl, you've given me whiplash. Is it true things started up between you two at my wedding?"

"Sort of."

Harper didn't want to go into details of how she'd paid Manny back for his insulting her food, so she settled for an abbreviated version.

"We kissed, and I guess it spiraled from there."

Nishi snickered and poked her arm. "You're not telling me everything."

She should've known Samira or Pia had blabbed.

"Come on, Harper, this is me. The girl who shared your crush on Gregory Green in year seven, who lied to her mom so we could go to the Royal Melbourne Show together in year nine, who drank way too many margaritas with you when you broke up with that dweeb Colin."

"Okay, okay, you're my best friend, and I'm guessing you already know about the whipped cream incident and you're sending me on a guilt trip for not telling you myself."

Nishi giggled and held up her hand. "Guilty as charged. Sam told me. It's hilarious. Imagine you two going through something like that and ending up engaged. How cool is that?"

"Cool or madness," Harper said dryly, but unable to keep the grin off her face. "And I am mad. Totally crazy about him."

"He's a good guy," Nishi said, but Harper heard a hint of something in her tone.

"But?"

Nishi shook her head. "Nothing."

"Hey, you just gave me a lecture about besties sharing everything. What aren't you telling me?"

Nishi huffed out a breath. "Look, this means nothing, because we all have pasts, right? And Arun says Manny is one of the good guys. But he's also got a reputation . . ."

Considering Manny had been up-front with her about never having been in a serious relationship, Harper had a fair idea what her friend was about to say.

"A reputation?"

"As a ladies' man. He's dated every nurse, physical therapist, and doctor in the hospital, and never calls them back after one date." Nishi wrinkled her nose. "I know things are totally different with you, because he's actually popped the question so he must be absolutely smitten, but Arun was genuinely shocked when he heard the news because he thought Manish would never get married and he's heard him say it."

"People change," she said, hating the sliver of doubt undermining her joy.

Harper had finally come to terms with the speed of their engagement, and Manny's acceptance of her vitiligo last night had solidified what she'd already known in her gut.

He was the one.

So why was she letting Nishi rattle her?

"You're right: people can change," Nishi said, with an emphatic nod. "But I just wanted to let you know, because I'd be a shitty friend if I'd heard that and didn't tell you."

"I appreciate your honesty," Harper said, in sudden need of a reassuring hug from her fiancé. "Shall we head back inside? I think Manny wants to make a speech and wrap things up soon because his gran tires easily."

"She seems like a bit of a tyrant," Nishi said, glancing over her shoulder at the back door as if she expected Isadora to bear down on them at any moment. "I don't know her well, but my mom knows of her through the community, and while she's always pushing Manish to get married she's very picky with his prospective brides." Nishi laughed. "Maybe that's why he's never had more than one date with a girl? And if that's the case, what's your magical power?"

Harper faked a laugh as another shard of foreboding lodged in her doubts. "No magic. I'm irresistible."

"I've always known that," Nishi said, slinging an arm across her shoulders. "I'm rapt some smart guy has finally figured it out too."

"Thanks, Nish, I'm happy."

And she was.

So why was she allowing her simmering doubts to ruin it?

Definitely time to find her fiancé. With Manny by her side, she could do anything. Him and her. The dream team. Her motto, she was sticking to it.

58

MANNY HAD KEPT a close eye on Izzy for the last hour, looking for any signs of fatigue. But Izzy seemed to be in her element, perched on her favorite armchair, presiding over his friends and Harper's parents. Everyone seemed to be having a good time, but he couldn't shake the feeling he was trying too hard.

Not in his relationship with Harper; it was a given how he felt about her. But accepting congratulations, getting to know Lydia and Alec better, playing the jovial host felt like a role he'd slipped into, that of a happy groom-to-be. It was the weirdest feeling, like everyone was revolving around him but he wasn't actually part of the festivities.

Probably a result of exhaustion, juggling shifts, staying with Izzy, and the long drives between her place and the hospital. But whatever the reason, he didn't like it.

"You're looking a little shell-shocked, my friend." Arun slapped him on the back. "Don't worry, happens to the best of us." His friend's doting stare landed on Nishi. "When we find the one, we're powerless to stop the juggernaut."

"How did you do that?"

"Do what?"

"Figure out exactly what I was feeling."

Arun guffawed. "It's your expression, man. It's priceless, and one I've seen many times, each morning I looked in the mirror ever since I popped the question."

"Why do we do it?"

"For love of a good woman."

Nishi glanced up at that moment, and her expression softened when she saw Arun staring at her across the room. She blew him a kiss, and Manny tried not to gag as one of the most well-respected doctors he knew caught the imaginary kiss in his hand and pressed it to his cheek in a parody of a scene straight out of a rom-com.

"Man, that is so corny."

"Honeymoon period," Arun said, as if that explained his goofy behavior. "You'll see."

Manny guessed he would, but right now he couldn't see past today. Heck, he couldn't even envisage standing at the end of an aisle waiting for Harper, let alone beyond that.

"Harper's lovely," Arun said, "but I've got to ask. What made the eternal bachelor boy change his tune?"

"Everyone changes over time."

But not him. He'd stuck to his no-relationship rule for fifteen years now, ever since he'd finished med school, his mom had died, and he'd discovered it was easier to play hard to get than be tied down to one woman.

So why was he really doing this?

"I guess you have changed, because the number of times I've heard you say you'd never get married over the years is well into the thousands."

"I liked to date. Nothing wrong with that."

"Until you find the one."

Manny struggled not to grimace. Again with "the one" talk.

His friend had really turned into a lovestruck schmuck the moment Nishi had slid that gold band on his ring finger.

But with Arun studying him through narrowed eyes, he had to give his friend something, so he nodded. "Yeah. And for me, that's Harper."

"Well, all I can say is about bloody time." Arun raised his whiskey glass. "To us and how the mighty have fallen."

"To us," Manny echoed, clinking his glass against Arun's, grateful when his friend wandered back toward his bride.

Arun's congratulations hadn't settled his funk. If anything, Manny felt more uncertain than ever.

He'd fallen for Harper.

He wanted her in his life.

So why did the thought of being married make him want to loosen his tie, run a finger between his collar and neck, and drag in great lungfuls of air?

59

HARPER'S PARENTS WERE the last to leave, and she walked them out to their car. She'd been ecstatic to see their hands glued to each other's throughout the party, and they'd been absorbed in deep conversation in the few times they weren't mingling with the other guests. It gladdened her heart and added to the all-round surrealism of the day.

"We already thanked Manny, but please thank him again for us," Alec said, slipping an arm around her waist. "You've got a good one there, sweetheart."

"Yeah, I know."

Harper was pretty sure she stood taller when next to Manny because he made her feel so good. Even when they weren't working the room, chatting with their friends, she could feel that all-encompassing gray gaze on her, drawing her to him like a magnet.

But he'd been edgy today. She'd seen him hovering near his grandmother several times and put it down to worry. And he'd virtually set the whole party up himself, refusing her offer to assist with the food at least, so tiredness had to have something to do with it.

She refused to believe it was anything more. He'd been fine this morning at his place, his usual playful self, and she didn't want her well-buried doubts surfacing when she'd done a good job of submerging them today.

"You're radiant," Lydia said, bracketing her from the other side, so Harper stood between her parents in a comforting embrace. "Being engaged suits you."

"I'm happy."

Harper meant it. So why couldn't she shake the niggle that something was going on with Manny?

The old, paranoid her might blame it on her revelation last night. He'd taken one look at the real her and wanted to bolt. But Manny wasn't Colin, and he'd done everything in his power to reassure her how attractive he found her. The way he'd kissed all her patches, the way he'd made love to her afterward . . . he couldn't fake that depth of feeling, and having his acceptance had solidified what she already knew.

She loved him.

Wholeheartedly. Unreservedly.

"I can say this now, but I've been worried about you," Lydia said, as her parents released her. "You pretend to be okay, but I can see something's worrying you. I put it down to your father and me separating, then your breakup two months later, but whatever it was, I'm glad to see you so happy."

Some of that happiness fizzled. Her mom had given her the perfect opening to tell them about her diagnosis. Yet she knew discussing it on a day like today would take some of the gloss off. They'd want to know why she hadn't told them, what was the treatment, was there a cure . . .

But she owed them the truth. It didn't seem right Manny knew and her parents didn't.

"I'll be honest and say you two separating really shook me up, but there was something else I was dealing with in those months after."

"What?" her parents asked in unison, then laughed.

"A few weeks after you guys split, I noticed these weird white patches around my eyes. I didn't think much of it because I'd developed a bit of a rash after using a new serum a few months earlier and thought it was a result of that. Then I noticed the patches on my body." She gestured at her torso. "In skinfolds around here. And some on my back, so I went to the doctor."

Her dad paled. "Are you okay?"

"Yeah, but it turns out I have vitiligo. It's an autoimmune disease."

"Oh no." Lydia swayed like she was about to faint, and Alec reached out instantly, steadying her.

"It's not as serious as it sounds. Basically, the cells that produce melanin are destroyed, hence the loss of pigment. I've been having phototherapy, which is UV treatment to re-pigment my skin, and using an ointment. I've had blood tests to check for other autoimmune conditions it can trigger, but I'm okay, which is good news."

Her dad's expression remained terrified while her mom fixed her with a pitying stare. "Why didn't you tell me? Us? We're your parents; we need to know things like this so we can help you."

Feeling suitably chastised, like the time she'd ridden to Nishi's house to show off her new bike without telling her folks where she was going, she nodded. "I should've told you, but you both had enough to handle, and there wasn't anything you could do, really. I just had to get on with it and do the treatment."

Lydia tut-tutted. "You still should have told us."

"Yes, you should've," Alec reinforced, slipping his arm around her waist again. "You're our girl, and we love you. We're always here for you, whatever is going on in our self-absorbed lives, okay?"

"I know," Harper said, relieved she'd finally told her folks—though not the part where stress could trigger it—and happy to be part of another group hug.

When they disengaged, she said, "I should head back in. I think Manny's gran wants to interrogate me."

Her mom hesitated, before saying, "She seems like a lovely woman, but I get the feeling she's very protective of Manny."

"Why, did she say something?"

"Not really, just a general feeling," Lydia said. "But you've got nothing to worry about. You're amazing, and she'll love you."

If only Harper had her mom's confidence.

60

HARPER SHOULD'VE BEEN floating.

She'd just celebrated her engagement to a lovely guy with her folks and closest friends, and had revealed the truth about her vitiligo to her parents. While she did feel lighter about the latter, the moment she spied Isadora sitting on the sofa, patting the empty space next to her, that familiar feeling of doubt was back.

Manny's grandmother didn't like her.

She usually had an inkling for these things and tended to overcompensate by trying to make the other person like her. It always ended badly. At thirty, she was too old to pretend to be someone she wasn't, and if a person didn't like her, they could go screw themselves.

She couldn't take that attitude in this instance.

"Manish had to take a call from one of the residents at the hospital," Izzy said, beckoning her over. "He's taking it in his old bedroom for privacy."

"Okay. I better start cleaning up—"

"Leave it. Sit. Let's talk."

Great, so much for escaping. Harper had no desire to wash platters and glasses, but anything to dodge the incoming inquisition. She'd seen Izzy talking to Lydia and Alec earlier, and by the intent expressions on her parents' faces, Izzy had been grilling them too. And for her mom to mention a feeling about Izzy's overprotectiveness . . . Harper braced for an interrogation.

"Is there anything I can get you? A cup of tea?"

"Can you make masala chai?"

Her first test, and by the glint in Izzy's eyes, she'd asked her deliberately, knowing she'd fail.

"No, but I'm happy to take instruction. I'm a fast learner."

Izzy shook her head. "Never mind. I'll make it later. Let's talk, just the two of us, while Manish is busy."

Unable to come up with any other reasons to avoid this, Harper reluctantly sat next to Izzy.

"Did you enjoy the party?"

Izzy's eyes narrowed and fixed on her with unerring precision. "More to the point, did you?"

Feeling like the older woman was setting a trap again, Harper nodded. "It was a lovely celebration."

"If you can call it that."

Izzy made a dismissive sound that had Harper on edge in an instant.

"What would you call it?"

"A farce." Izzy eyeballed her, daring her to disagree, as Harper tried to mask her shock.

There was a huge difference between Izzy not liking her and being so blatantly rude.

"Why do you say that?"

"Because this engagement can't be real. My grandson has eschewed many choices of a more suitable bride, then he meets you and asks you to marry him in a rush?"

Izzy pointedly glared at Harper's belly. "Either you're pregnant and he's living up to his rescue complex, or he's doing this for me."

"I'm not pregnant," Harper said, keeping a tentative hold on her temper. This woman meant everything to Manny, and she'd never get in the way of their relationship. But Harper expected civility, not these blunt proclamations like the older woman knew more than she did.

"Then my first supposition is right." Izzy had the audacity to lay a comforting hand over hers. "I hate to tell you, my dear, but my grandson is only doing this because I'm seriously ill and he knows my dying wish is to see him married."

"You're wrong," Harper blurted, snatching her hand out from under Izzy's, appalled by the older woman's rudeness.

Izzy arched an eyebrow. "Am I?"

Harper studied Izzy, looking for some sign of hatred, of intense dislike, for her to say something so outrageous. But all she saw was sadness mingling with resignation, as if Izzy didn't want it to be this way.

"I have nothing against you personally. You and your family seem like lovely people, but you're not suited to my grandson, and I don't want him entering into marriage for the wrong reasons."

Only doing this . . . dying wish . . . not suited . . . wrong reasons . . .

If Harper had any doubts before, Izzy had just played into each and every one of them.

Hell, Harper had had similar doubts herself. She had little in common with Manny. Would he tire of their differences? Why propose so quickly? Why marry when they could date first?

Hearing Izzy echo her doubts and articulate them so clearly made her want to cover her ears and yell *la-la-la*.

Izzy took her ongoing silence as permission to continue. "My grandson thinks he's progressive and modern, but deep down he's a traditionalist. He respects me and my wishes, and wants to give me what he thinks I want. But I don't want him marrying you out of obligation. It isn't right."

What wasn't right was Harper sitting here, helpless and frustrated and taking whatever this woman dished out. There was a fine line between respect and cowering, and she'd remained silent for too long.

"We both know Manny adores you, but it's a shame you feel compelled to belittle what we share." Harper stood, aiming for graceful, not surprised when her legs trembled. She really wanted to get the hell out of here. "Neither of us is obligated. We love each other—"

"Has he actually said those words to you?" Izzy interjected rudely. "Has he said 'I love you'?"

"Of course."

Harper's rebuttal came quickly, a natural reaction to prove this woman wrong at any cost in the spur of the moment. But she wracked her memory, trying to remember if he'd actually said those three all-important words, and came up blank.

He'd said he'd fallen for her. He'd said he loved her body. He'd said he loved everything about her. Declarations she'd lapped up but mistakenly translated into *I love you*.

"You are lying to yourself." Izzy gave a dismissive wave. "I'm counting on you to do the right thing and break this off, because Manish certainly won't. He thinks I want to see him married so badly he'll do it with whoever happens to be handy." Izzy jabbed a finger at her. "And right now, that's you."

Speechless, Harper gaped at the woman she'd hoped to win over. She understood older people lost their inhibitions sometimes and felt compelled to say whatever popped into their heads, but it sounded like Izzy actually believed the drivel she was spouting.

"Our relationship isn't like musical chairs—"

"I need to rest," Izzy said. "We'll speak no more of this now, but you need to do what's right."

Right now, that meant Harper had to leave the room before she said something she'd regret.

61

HARPER NODDED OFF on the drive back to Manny's place, and he let her sleep. It had been a big day, starting with her vitiligo revelation in the early hours of the morning, the party, tidying up, and now heading back to his place. At least, that's what he hoped caused her tiredness.

Something hadn't been right when he'd come back into the lounge room after taking that call from the hospital. Harper had been huddled in on herself like a wounded deer, and Izzy had been stiff and unyielding, refusing his offer of help to clear away. It was almost like she wanted to get rid of them, and he'd ignored her wishes, enlisting Harper's help and ensuring the place was spotless and his grandmother ensconced in bed with a cup of masala chai before they left.

He hadn't minded staying over and caring for her the last week, but it was nice to head back to his place with his fiancée, knowing he could chill.

When he pulled up out the front of his place, Harper instantly opened her eyes, and in that moment, he knew she'd been pretending. She hadn't been sleeping; she'd been avoiding talking to him.

"What's going on?"

He expected her to laugh off his concern, to fob him off, so when she snapped, "You tell me," he reared back.

"Tell you what?"

"Apparently, your grandmother thinks you're settling with me. That you had no intention of getting married, something Nishi and Arun concur with, by the way. That because it's her dying wish to see you married and because she's so ill that's the only reason you asked me . . ."

She trailed off, horror widening her eyes. "Oh my god, that's why you asked me before she went in for her surgery, isn't it? You wanted to give her hope, something to focus on, to get her through it."

She slapped her forehead. "I'm such an idiot," she said, glaring at him like he was the last man on earth she wanted to be near let alone marry, and he sat there like a dummy, letting her vent, hating how she was partially right.

"She actually said I was a convenience, I just happened to be the one you were dating at the time and that's why you asked. That we weren't suited . . ." She trailed off, and he hated the sheen of tears in her eyes.

Numb, he let her rant, each word ramming home what a prick he was. He wanted to say all of it was a lie. That he never wanted to hurt her. That he cared for her deeply, more than he'd cared for any woman before.

He'd been committed to making this work. Harper had become a part of his world so quickly he couldn't imagine her not in it.

But if Izzy knew the truth, did he have to go through with this?

The very fact his first instinct was to renege gave him his answer.

In that instant he knew he'd have to break Harper's heart.

"Do you know you've never said you love me?" Harper pressed a hand to her chest, her devastated expression making him feel like the biggest bastard in the world. "And I'm so stupid I believed every slick word you said about falling for me. How could I have been so dumb?"

"You're not stupid, you're wonderful—"

"Shut the fuck up!"

He jumped at her sudden vehemence.

"Do you hear yourself? With everything I've just said, not once have you refuted it or tried to convince me I'm crazy or that you do, in fact, love me." She shook her head. "The first words you say are I'm *wonderful*? Well, if I'm so freaking wonderful, why do you want to walk away from me?"

She'd given him a chance. A chance to say something to save their relationship. A chance he didn't deserve.

"I don't want to walk away from you." He reached for her, and she shrank away until her back hit the passenger door. "You're the best thing to ever happen to me."

"But was your grandmother right? About why you asked me to marry you?"

Manny hated men who lied. He'd been privy to secrets at the hospital, wealthy consultants and specialists who earned seven figures a year and split their money between their real families and their mistresses. Those men thought nothing of lying. It soon became second nature, but he never understood their compulsion.

He loathed deceit, but in that moment, with Harper staring at him with a spark of hope, he wished he could lie.

"Yes," he eventually said, hating how she crumpled, hugging

her arms around her middle. "I'd already fallen for you and the timing seemed right and—"

"Don't." She held up her hand. "There's no way you can justify what you did."

"I know it seems harsh, but we're so good together, and if we'd had a chance to date for longer I would've probably proposed—"

"Bullshit. You would've sabotaged us because . . ." She trailed off, her expression morphing from fury to devastation, her eyes filled with pain and disappointment—in him.

"Because why?"

"We're done," she said, fumbling for the handle to open the door. "You can courier my overnight bag over."

He had to stop her.

He had to beg and plead and do whatever it took to save this.

But he was floundering, out of control, as helpless as he was when he lost the last woman he loved.

So he sat there like a jackass, flinching when she slammed the car door shut on him and their fleeting relationship.

62

HARPER DROVE HOME in a daze.

What the hell had just happened?

One minute she was celebrating her engagement to a guy she loved, the next they'd broken up.

She didn't blame his grandmother. Izzy had been right. She'd only been telling the truth, a truth Harper had probably recognized deep in her gut, in that place where instinct ruled, an instinct that should never be overridden by stupid pheromones.

She'd known this had happened too quickly, that it was too good to be true. But she'd gone along with it anyway, all in the name of *love*.

What a crock.

The unfortunate thing was, once she started to analyze this ridiculous relationship, she'd come to an even more sickening revelation.

Was Manny exactly like Colin?

She'd revealed herself to Manny, and the next day, he dumped her. Worse, he'd fooled her into believing it hadn't mattered to him, that he adored her regardless.

At least that asshole Colin had the decency to not touch her once she showed him and had withdrawn before breaking up with her.

But Manny's acceptance of the real her had made her fall in love with him even more, if that were possible, and that made him a hundred times worse bastard than Colin.

The rational side of her didn't want to believe this was the case. Manny wasn't that good of an actor. Then again, he'd conned her into getting engaged for the wrong reasons, so maybe he was?

Muttering a string of unladylike curses under her breath, she stomped inside and turned up the heat. Like that would do anything to ease the chill invading her body. Her cell rang as she tore open a fresh pack of Tim Tams, intent on demolishing all eleven of those little slices of chocolate heaven.

It better not be Manny. Then again, her cell had remained silent on the thirty-minute drive home, when a guy who wanted to win her back would've called or texted nonstop.

His silence spoke volumes.

Resisting the urge to fling her cell across the kitchen, she glanced at the screen.

Mom.

Harper wanted to let the call go through to voice mail. She wasn't in a fit state to talk to her mother. But if she didn't answer, Lydia would think something was wrong; her mom had good instincts like that.

Like how Lydia had known something was wrong with Izzy and had warned Harper about it before she'd left the party.

She'd have to break the news to her parents sometime, and putting it off wouldn't make the task any easier.

With a sigh, she picked up the phone and hit the "answer" button.

"Hey, Mom."

Harper tried to inject as much fake enthusiasm into her voice, but predictably, Lydia wasn't buying it.

"What's wrong?"

"Nothing . . ." The lie ended on a sob, and the sorrow Harper had been holding in finally burst in a torrent of tears.

"Are you home? I'm coming right over," Lydia said, all brusque efficiency.

"I'm home," Harper managed, with a hiccup. She'd planned on having a pity party for one, but her mom, along with Nishi, had been her best friend growing up, and it might help to have her around.

"That woman said something to upset you, didn't she?" Lydia asked, tut-tutting. "But why isn't Manny with you? Did he stay with her?"

"Mom, come over. I'll explain everything then."

Harper hung up before she blurted the whole sorry tale over the phone. What she had to say had to be said face-to-face.

With gin.

And Tim Tams.

Two packs' worth.

63

AFTER HARPER DROVE away, Manny trudged inside, and the first thing he saw was her makeup bag on his dining table, her robe draped across a chair and her overnight bag underneath. He'd teased her about making herself at home and she'd come back with "You better get used to it."

Not anymore.

The pressure in his chest expanded, compressing every organ until he could hardly breathe. Had he been naive in not thinking it would come to this? That his astute grandmother wouldn't see through him, like she had his entire life? That she wouldn't call him out on it?

But that's the thing; Izzy should've confronted him, not Harper. He loved his grandmother more than life itself, but what she'd done was unforgivable. Harper didn't deserve to bear the brunt of Izzy's blunt home truths; his fiancée didn't deserve to be treated that way.

Ex-fiancée.

"Fuck," he muttered, striding toward the table where he shoved her makeup and robe into her bag and zipped it up, trying not to remember sliding the robe off her, the silkiness of her skin beneath it, burying himself in her . . .

He couldn't have this reminder of her in his place, taunting him, a testament to what a prick he'd been. It wasn't like he'd get any sleep tonight anyway. So he grabbed the bag and headed back out, knowing when he got to Harper's house he couldn't go in like he yearned to do and try to convince her he'd never meant to hurt her, that he did care for her, that it was worth risking a second chance.

He wouldn't do that to her. Couldn't give her false hope, because one thing she'd said had struck home.

Do you know you've never said you love me?

He thought he'd made his feelings clear. He thought she understood he'd never opened up to another woman.

But he knew he'd been lying to himself, the part of him hell-bent on self-preservation avoiding making the ultimate declaration of commitment.

He'd never said those words to his mom before she died, and that's a tragedy he had to live with every fucking day.

Maybe he was incapable of verbalizing his love? Because he did love. He'd loved his mom, he just hadn't said it in so many words, and then she'd died in his arms and he still hadn't said it. He loved Izzy, but he rarely spelled it out.

And he loved Harper.

The realization slammed into him and he pulled over fast, earning a honk from the driver behind him.

The engagement party had freaked him out, then Harper had come at him with those accusations and . . . he'd done nothing. He'd sat in this very seat like a dummy, making her think she'd never been anything more than an adjunct to making his grandmother happy.

He should've fought harder.

He should've tried to convince her he could love, that he did love her.

Instead, he'd talked himself out of it, convinced himself he only *cared* about her, that it was better this way because he'd never wanted to get married in the first place.

And he'd lost her.

Harper wouldn't want to see him now, of that he was certain. So he'd drop off her bag, give her some time, and head to the one place that would ground him.

With a frustrated thump on the steering wheel, he pulled back onto the road and drove the remaining twenty minutes to Ashwood. He saw her car in the drive when he parked outside her house, but the front rooms were dark. Had she gone to bed? Was she taking a bath to wash away all traces of him? Did she expect him to come after her and wanted to show she wouldn't answer the door?

It didn't matter; he wouldn't be bothering her regardless. She deserved better than some jerk who didn't have a fucking clue what he really wanted trying to convince her she'd made a mistake and they should give their relationship another go.

He snatched her bag from the seat and stomped to her front door, where he dumped it. He'd text her after he left so they wouldn't have a chance of running into each other. He'd made it halfway down the drive when a car swerved into it, almost running him down. It screeched to a stop and the engine had barely shut off before the door flew open and Harper's mom got out, glaring at him like she wished she'd flattened him.

"What's happened? Why aren't you with Harper? She needs you right now. She sounded distraught . . ." Lydia trailed off, and he saw the exact moment concern morphed into anger in her eyes.

"You're the reason she's upset."

A statement, not a question, and he gave the slightest of nods.

"What. Did. You. Do?"

Lydia slammed the car door and advanced toward him, her arms rigid by her sides, her hands clenched into fists like she wanted to slug him. "I thought your grandmother must've upset her, but you wouldn't be out here unless you've done something to upset my daughter too."

Manny didn't want to have this conversation, but if it made it easier on Harper he'd take the heat off her, because he knew once Lydia made it inside she'd start interrogating, and that's the last thing Harper needed.

"We broke up," he said, hating how each word drove a stake through his heart.

Lydia gasped, shock making her stagger a step back. "What? I thought you might've had an argument . . ."

"No, it's more than that. Harper chose to end our engagement, and I respect her decision."

He refrained from saying, *You should too*, because it wasn't his place. He had no say in Harper's family, not anymore, and they'd hate him as much as she did when they discovered the truth shortly.

Lydia shook her head, as if trying to clear it. "I'll repeat my earlier question. What did you do?"

More a case of what he didn't do—convince Harper what they had was the real deal despite the brevity of their relationship, show her how much she meant to him, tell her he loved her—but it was too late for any of that.

"I think this is a discussion you need to have with Harper."

"I will, but I want to hear it from you first." Lydia jabbed a finger in his direction. "I had my doubts about you from the start, Mr. Too Good To Be True, but I quashed them because I've never seen Harper so happy. I wanted to believe in the fairy tale because she did. And I respected her decision because you seemed like a stand-up guy." She jabbed her finger again, her eyes glowing with resentment. "But you're nothing but a liar, because you conned my daughter into falling for you. I have no idea why you proposed so quickly. Maybe this is what you do, your MO, using women for goodness knows what reason."

Lydia sucked in a breath and drew herself up, formidable in her fury. "But I'm here to tell you Harper isn't like other women. She's special and far too good for the likes of you. So get the hell away from my daughter."

Manny wanted to make a stand. To convince Lydia he wasn't the bastard she thought he was. But he had no right to try and convince her of that, when he agreed with her opinion.

"I'm sorry," he said, the only thing he could say as he walked away, her glare boring into his back until he got in his car and waited for her to reverse out of the drive so he could escape.

64

HARPER HEARD HER mother's tires squeal in her driveway. Considering her dad often teased Lydia about driving like a ninety-year-old, her mom must really be concerned about her, so she peeked out the blinds in the lounge room.

To see her mom in a standoff with Manny.

Harper shrunk back from the blinds instantly; stupid, considering Manny was facing her mom and couldn't see her. She hated that her first reaction was to recoil from him, and the tears she'd shed during and after her mom's call prickled her eyes again.

She didn't want to shy away from Manny.

She wanted to run to him and bury herself in his arms and forget everything.

Opening the door quietly, the first thing she saw was her overnight bag on the mat; the second, Lydia stabbing her finger at Manny. Harper couldn't hear what they were saying, though it looked like her mom was doing all the talking. When Manny walked back to his car her mom watched him, then got back in hers and reversed so he could leave, before pulling back into the drive, parking, and heading for the house.

Lydia didn't know the half of it, and Harper doubted Manny

would've told her, but by the looks of it, her mom had given him an earful anyway.

Harper opened the door wider, picked up her bag, and waited for her mom, who took one look at her and flew across the few remaining feet separating them.

"Darling, I'm so sorry." Lydia enveloped her in a hug, and for the second time in an hour Harper burst into tears. "It's okay, sweetheart, cry it out, then forget that bastard."

Lydia never swore, so her mom must know they'd broken up. Harper should've known Manny would own up to it. He was that kind of guy.

What kind of guy is that? her conscience screamed. *The kind of guy to dupe you into believing a vacation fling meant more? The kind of guy to ingratiate his way into your life, meet your parents, hang out with your friends, when his proposal was nothing but a sham? The kind of guy who thought marriage was some warped way to gain kudos with his grandmother?*

Maybe her mom coming over now wasn't the best thing. Rehashing what had happened would only exacerbate her pain, and she wanted to forget, not relive, the nightmare of this evening.

But Lydia wouldn't leave without discovering exactly what had happened and voicing her strong opinion, so Harper wriggled out of her embrace. "I've got gin and Tim Tams."

"Make it tea. I have to drive home, unless you want me to stay?"

The last thing Harper wanted was her mom hovering over her all night and then facing her pity in the morning, so she said, "Thanks, Mom, but I'll be fine."

"You didn't sound it on the phone, and you don't look it."

Harper flinched. After her crying jag, she'd gone to the bath-room to wash her face, seen what a mess she looked with streaked mascara, and removed her makeup, so this was the first time Lydia had seen her vitiligo patches.

Realizing her faux pas, Lydia touched Harper's cheek. "I didn't mean it like that. I meant you've been crying." Her mom's thumb brushed the outer corner of a patch high on her cheekbone. "I wish you'd told me about what you've been going through."

"I'm dealing with it, Mom," Harper said, sidestepping so her mom's hand fell, not in the mood for recriminations over some-thing she couldn't change. "Now let's go have that tea."

Lydia followed her into the kitchen and gently pushed her into a seat at the table, before picking up the gin bottle next to the half-demolished first packet of Tim Tams. "Maybe a small G&T wouldn't hurt?"

Harper nodded and reached for another chocolate rectangu-lar slice of comfort. "I saw you ran into Manny."

"I should've run him over," Lydia muttered, dumping ice cubes into two glasses before sloshing gin over them and adding tonic. "He said you'd broken up. That you ended the engage-ment."

"Yeah, it was the only option."

"Why?"

"Because he only proposed to make his grandmother happy."

Harper took the glass her mother held out and sipped the gin, before taking three big slurps. G&Ts didn't exactly compliment chocolate, but she'd take all the comfort she could get right now.

"I'm confused," Lydia said, sitting and placing her glass on the table, before reaching for a Tim Tam. Her mom had her priorities right. Chocolate before alcohol. "I got the impression the old lady didn't like you, so why would Manny marrying you make her happy?"

"Because it's her dying wish or some such crap and he thought popping the question before she went in for her surgery might make her fight harder."

Lydia's mouth dropped open. "You can't be serious."

"Pathetic, huh?"

Lydia chomped down on the Tim Tam, demolishing half in one bite.

"His grandmother told me all about it after everyone left. How unsuited we are, how he only proposed because he thought that's what she wanted, how I needed to do the right thing and end it."

Harper took another slug of gin to ease the tightening of her throat from articulating exactly how little she meant to Manny. "So I confronted him, asked him if it was true, and he confirmed it."

Lydia laid the other half of the Tim Tam down, her eyes filled with sorrow. "I had my doubts about the speed of your engagement, but he seemed like a decent guy, a man worthy of you."

"Turns out he's a jerk. Who knew?"

Harper's forced laugh sounded hollow and way too sad, and Lydia dragged her chair around the table so they were almost knee to knee. "I'm just as angry at him as you are, sweetie, but I'm going to play devil's advocate for a minute. I saw the way Manny looked at you, and it's pretty hard to fake that depth of caring." Lydia hesitated, took a sip of her drink, before continuing. "Colin never looked at you like that, and I never saw you glow around him the way you did with Manny. So although his grandmother is an interfering cow, are you sure there's not more to this?"

Harper hated the flare of hope her mom's words elicited. "What more can there be? If he loved me, he would've fought for me. He would've tried to convince me I meant more to him than some weird pawn in his dumbass game to impress his gran."

He would've said he loved me, she thought, but Harper didn't want to tell her mother every single detail of her heartbreak.

"I don't want to make this harder for you, but the man I confronted in your yard looked shattered. And he wouldn't look like that if you'd been nothing more than some ploy to help that dragon recover."

"Whose side are you on?" Harper shoved the Tim Tam packet toward her mother. "Here. Have a few more of these. The chocolate will make you see sense."

"Have the five you've eaten helped you see sense?"

Harper tipped the rest of her drink down her throat. "From where I'm sitting, things are looking pretty damn clear, Mom. I fell for a charmer who proposed for all the wrong reasons. I made the mistake of loving him, and I'll have to deal with that the best I can . . ."

"Oh, sweetie." Lydia reached out to hug her again, but Harper was done with the tears and she held her off.

"I really appreciate you coming over, Mom, but I think I need to be alone to wallow for a while, you know?"

"I do know, considering I wallowed way too much after I kicked your father out of the house. But the thing about wallowing is, you eventually have to face up to facts, and I don't want you making the same mistake I did."

"What mistake?"

"I took too long to come to my senses, but it was different for me because I was married to your father and he never let me forget that. But in your case, if you let Manny go too easily, I'm afraid he'll move on and you'll lose him forever."

Harper shook her head, unsure if it was the gin or the sugar overload clogging her brain. "But don't you hate him? Isn't that what you want?"

"What I want is for you to be happy, and I know you can't see a way out of this right now, but as your mother I owe it to you to try and think logically, not emotionally."

Harper needed another G&T, but she slumped in her chair, exhausted to her bones. The faster her mom got whatever she had to say off her chest, the faster she'd leave.

"If Manny would go to such lengths out of worry for his grandmother, he must love her a lot."

"Not helping, Mom," Harper muttered, folding her arms.

"From what you said, his father died young, his mom died fifteen years ago, and his gran is the only family he has. So in a way it's admirable he'd go so far for her. It also means he's had no male influence in his life, he's surrounded by loss in his job every single day, and perhaps he felt helpless when faced with losing Isadora too?"

Lydia shook her head. "Proposing may not have been the smartest thing he did, but it came from a good place, love and loyalty to the only woman in his life until now." She touched Harper's arm. "Because I think he loves you too, sweetie, and he has a hard time expressing real emotion. He got everything jumbled up, wanting to prove his love for his grandmother, but sacrificing his love for you in the process by not telling you the truth."

"Mom, you've been watching too much *Dr. Phil*."

Hearing her mother spouting a bunch of psychobabble made Harper's head hurt. Or that could be the gin on a stomach devoid of anything but chocolate.

"The other thing is, I think you'll kick yourself later once you realize you let an old woman dictate what you should do." Lydia drew her shoulders back. "I raised a strong woman, and my daughter wouldn't let anyone tell her what she should do. She'd believe in herself and fight for what she wanted rather than throw in the towel."

Harper loved her mom's passionate support, but what would be the point of fighting for a man who didn't want her enough?

"I really thought you'd be on my side."

"Honey, your father and I are always on your side. And the sensible thing to do would be for me to lecture you against Manny, to call him every unsavory name rattling around my head, and to whisk you away for a weeklong spa retreat to help you get over him." Lydia pressed a hand to her chest. "But the heart knows what the heart knows. And I think deep in your heart, you love Manny, and all I want is for you to be happy."

Hating that her mother was right, Harper huffed. "Don't you want to castrate him just a little?"

"He only needs a little castration? In that case, honey, forget everything I said and find yourself a man to satisfy you."

"Mom!"

Lydia laughed, a blush staining her cheeks. "Hey, at least I made you smile."

"So that's what that weird upward thing my lips are doing is."

Lydia cupped her cheek. "I love you, your father and I both do. So maybe sleep on it tonight, and I promise you'll have a clearer head in the morning."

Not if her date with the gin bottle had anything to do with it, but her mom was right. Things always seemed better in the morning.

Besides, let Manny stew over what a dufus he'd been, preferably all sleepless night.

65

MANNY DIDN'T SLEEP a wink all night.

He hadn't expected to, which is why he'd gone to the hospital straight from Harper's last night. The loathing in her mother's eyes . . . he should be dead from that killer glare. The kicker was, he'd deserved it too.

He'd come to the hospital because he didn't want to be alone at home, mulling over his monumental screwup. Most people hated their workplace and saw it as a jail, time served to be endured in the name of a paycheck. But not him. Walking through the sliding glass doors, breathing in the pungent fumes of ammonia-based cleaning products, listening to the constant buzz of conversation, never failed to calm him.

Not that he'd be dumb enough to go near patients in his condition, but hiding in his office had sufficed. He always had a stack of paperwork waiting for him, so he'd stared at the computer screen for hours, reading through reports and journals until his eyes blurred from the blue light. He hadn't absorbed a lot of it, but by the time dawn broke he'd made it through the night without picking up the phone or hightailing it back to Harper's like he wanted to.

He had to get past this. Move on. He'd hurt her badly, and he had to live with that. Whatever that entailed: feeling like crap, constantly clamping down on great memories, taking extra shifts, submerging himself in work.

But first, he had to see Izzy.

However, as he cracked open his door just after seven, Arun stood on the other side, his fist raised to knock.

"First day back on the job, boss, so I'm checking in."

"You know what to do, Arun. You don't need to see me."

His retort came out harsher than intended, and his friend reared back, hands raised.

"Hey, what's biting your ass? Thought I'd pop in and see if you wanted to grab a coffee."

"Sorry, haven't slept."

Manny swiped a hand over his face; like that would erase his fatigue.

"Were you called in for an emergency last night? Because you weren't rostered on, and no man should have to deal with gore the night of his engagement party."

Manny's declaration to Harper about how much he hated lying rang in his ears but he had to do it, because no way in hell did he want to stand here and discuss his broken engagement with Arun before he'd had a chance to talk with Izzy.

"No emergency, but I'm sick of being swamped up to here." He made a chopping motion at his neck. "Harper and I were both exhausted after the party, but I need to get ahead on my workload so I dropped her home and came here."

Arun stared at him like he'd lost his mind. "Let me get this straight. You've finally taken your head out of your ass and fallen in love with a spectacular woman, you celebrate your uncharacteristic proposal to her, you're tired, yet you choose to abandon her in favor of *work*?" Arun shook his head. "Man, you are such a dumbass."

"Fuck off, Arun."

Once again, harsher than intended, but he didn't need one of his few friends reiterating how much of a dumbass he actually was.

"Man, you are shitty when you're tired." Arun backed away with exaggerated steps. "I'm off to start my shift now. You really need to get some sleep before Harper dumps your sorry ass."

Too late for that, Manny thought, as he waited for Arun to traverse the long corridor in the direction of the ER before slipping out the side door for a confrontation with his grandmother.

66

OF ALL DAYS Harper had to front up to a job and look professional, today wasn't it. After her mom left last night, she'd taken a long, hot shower, had another two G&Ts, finished the rest of the Tim Tams, and fallen into bed without brushing her teeth. She'd slept fitfully, dozing and tossing, until her alarm went off at seven thirty.

Driving to an inner-city hospital in peak-hour traffic wasn't fun either, but without the influx of referrals she'd expected from Nishi's wedding and the Storr job, she needed to grab every scrap of work.

In all the excitement of the engagement, she'd forgotten to ask Manny if he'd had anything to do with her landing this job. What a joke. She'd initially been annoyed, wanting to stand on her own. She'd got her wish and then some.

At least the parking gods were on her side because she found a rare spot, fed the meter coins, grabbed her portfolio, and headed for the hospital, her steps faltering the closer the got. Crazy, because Manny didn't work here and there was zero chance of running into him, but the sight of two guys in white coats holding takeout coffee cups and striding toward the same door she was made her heart palpitate.

She'd never seen Manny in a white coat, so her visceral reaction didn't make any sense. And she sure as hell hoped she wouldn't feel the same when she watched her favorite hospital dramas on TV. She may have ditched her doc, but she had no intention of breaking up with her dashing docs on-screen.

Giving herself a mental slap upside the head, she entered the hospital and approached the front desk. Elaine Legham, her contact person, was at the desk and after introductions Elaine whisked her to the function rooms buried in the admin section of the hospital, down several confusing corridors.

"I'm so glad you could do this job for us," Elaine said, as they entered a conference room dominated by a monstrous mahogany table. "I'm one of the senior psychologists here, and I'd usually leave this to our functions coordinator, but this event is too important." She lowered her voice. "It's a send-off for our head of department, and I'm gunning for his job."

"I'll do my best."

Elaine smiled. "Good. You come highly recommended."

Damn Manny for his interference. The polite thing to do would be to thank him, but she wasn't feeling so polite.

"What did Manish say?"

"Manish?" Elaine blinked, confusion clouding her eyes. "Manish Gomes?"

"Yes, my fiancé." Damn, slip of the tongue, but Harper had no intention of correcting it and inviting a host of unwelcome questions and explanations. "I take it he referred me?"

"No," Elaine said, staring at her with open speculation. "One of the junior psychologists on my team attended an Indian wedding recently and said the food looked amazing and took one of your cards."

Elaine gestured to a seat. "Let's sit and you can tell me how on earth you managed to snare the elusive Manish."

So this woman knew Manish? Not unreasonable considering the hospital fraternity in Melbourne couldn't be huge, but damn, now Harper would have to tell her the truth. "Well, Manny and I—"

"Excuse me for interrupting, but I have to say I'm stunned. I mean, you're gorgeous, but Manny getting married? It's like discovering I can get a direct line to Freud to consult with him anytime I want." Elaine shook her head, admiration in her eyes. "He once told me I was his longest girlfriend, and I lasted a week. So what's your secret?"

Manny had *dated* this glamorous woman? Elaine topped her by four inches, had expressive brown eyes, perfect features, glossy russet hair to her waist pulled back in a ponytail, and managed to make a rather staid uniform of navy shirt and skirt look elegant. Throw in her psychology degree and perfect poise, and it made a small part of Harper feel better that she'd made the cut when this woman hadn't.

A ridiculous thought when all she'd succeeded in doing was being duped by Manny for longer. "We actually broke up last night."

"I'm sorry." Elaine's hand flew to her mouth. "Let me guess, he hit the scary two-week mark with you and decided to end it."

Harper barked out a laugh at Elaine's droll response. "It's actually been a bit longer than that, but I ended it."

Elaine did a dramatic double take worthy of an actress. "You dumped him? I think the world just tilted."

Harper really didn't want to discuss her private life with a potential client, but before she could steer the conversation onto work, Elaine said, "I've spent twenty years working as a psychologist, so you'd think I'd be able to figure out Manny, but he's an enigma. He swans through life like it's one big party outside of work, but he's hurting inside."

Against her better judgment, Harper asked, "Why?"

"I got him drunk on our second date, and he muttered something about losing everyone he loves eventually. That's when he said I should be happy I'd made it to a second date because he usually stops at one. He also warned me I probably wouldn't make it past the end of the week, and he was right."

Elaine shrugged. "Don't get me wrong, I'm not pining for Manny if that's what you're thinking. I'm a few years older than him and happily married to my job. I made a choice long ago to not have a long-term partner or kids, which is why I thought Manny and I would be suited. But I think for all his bachelor bluster, he craves a connection, and if he proposed to you, he found it."

Harper wanted to dismiss Elaine's babble as that of an ex surprised to be jilted in favor of someone like her. But Elaine didn't sound jealous, merely curious, and she was a psychologist, meaning she knew what she was talking about.

"At his age, Manny wouldn't have proposed to you for any reason other than love. And it must've blindsided him so hard he proposed to keep you close, then when he had you he must've totally freaked out because he thinks he'll eventually lose you too." Elaine eyed her with respect. "I don't know you, so whatever reason you dumped him for, I'm assuming it's legit, because you've played into his greatest fear."

Harper was done. She didn't need this woman undermining her decision to end things with Manny. She'd done it out of self-preservation. As for all that crap about Manny loving her enough to propose, Harper wanted to yell, *With all due respect you're talking out your ass, psych degree or not.*

Instead, she mustered a smile, slipping into her professional persona so she could ignore the doubts whirling through her head.

"Thanks for your insights, but we really need to get on with planning this menu."

Elaine winced. "Sorry, I got a bit carried away there. Sometimes it's hard to shelve the psychology degree, especially when I'm at work. Now, where should we start?"

Harper tried to focus as she presented Elaine with pictorial proof of what she could do for the hospital fundraiser. But in the back of her mind, she couldn't dismiss what the other woman had said.

Harper believed Manny's proposal had been driven by devotion to his grandmother, but what if there was more to it?

If someone like him couldn't date any woman beyond a week, did they have something special and she'd dismissed it because of her own rampant insecurities?

The vitiligo and resultant dumping from Colin had seriously messed with her confidence. But now it seemed trite to label Manny as shallow and pushing her away for the same reason. He was a better man than that. He was her man. At least, he had been.

The burning question was, did she want him to be her man again?

67

THE LOCAL COMMUNITY nurse had just finished Izzy's morning checkup when Manny arrived. After a brief chat where the nurse reiterated Izzy was doing surprisingly well for her age and surgery, he waved the nurse off and braced for a confrontation he hoped wouldn't affect his gran's health.

Over the years, he'd laughed off her interference in his life, particularly his love life. They rarely argued, and when he'd lived with her she'd been surprisingly liberal in her views on his dating life. It had only been the last five years or so, as he hit his mid-thirties and showed no signs of slowing down, that she'd become less than subtle in her prods to get him married.

Both Izzy and Samira's mom, Kushi, had been instrumental in pushing the two of them together, and when that hadn't worked he knew Izzy had been scouring her friendship group for appropriate granddaughters to match him with. He knew she wanted to see him settled, so what had brought on her blunt discussion with Harper after the party?

It irked that Izzy had guessed his motivation behind popping the question, but his feelings for Harper ran deeper than she thought, and Izzy had no right to interfere.

Something he intended on making perfectly clear.

And then what?

Telling Izzy to butt the hell out wouldn't change a thing. He'd still screwed up. He'd still lost Harper. He'd still end up wondering if he should've done things differently.

The front door swung open, and Izzy stared at him with raised eyebrows. "Are you going to come in or are you planning on standing out there all day thinking up ways to tell me off?"

"Why did you do it, Iz?" He dropped the obligatory peck on her cheek as he entered, waiting until she closed the door before offering his arm for her to lean on.

She waved him away and tottered into the lounge room.

"Still refusing to use the walker, I see."

"You see correctly. I'm old, not immobile."

"You're recovering from major surgery, and the last thing you need is to have a fall and end up with a broken hip."

"Thanks for that positive prediction." She sighed and lowered herself into her armchair gingerly, wincing. "Now, have at it. I know why you're here. Harper tattled."

"What did you expect, for her not to tell me?" He paced a few steps, struggling to get his temper under control. "She confronted me, then she dumped me."

Izzy's eyes widened in shock. "She broke off the engagement?"

"She broke everything." *Including my heart*, he wanted to say but didn't. "That's what happens when you tell her the only reason I proposed is because it's your dying wish and I thought you needed the extra motivation to recover."

Izzy shrugged, infuriatingly calm. "Well, isn't that why you did it? The timing was very suspicious, just before my surgery, so I put two and two together."

"It was part of it," he admitted, dragging a hand through his hair. "But you don't know everything."

"Then tell me." She pointed to a chair opposite. "And for goodness' sake, stop that infernal pacing."

He sank into the chair, bracing his elbows on his knees. "I proposed because we get on well together, I love spending time with her, she makes me happy and gives me a sense of peace I haven't felt since . . ."

"Since?"

"Mom died. Losing her gutted me, and I've shut off from everyone but you."

"You don't think I know that, Manish?"

He glanced up to see anguish contort her face.

"I've left you alone for many years. You needed to find your own path, to make your own decisions. I always hoped you'd find the right woman, and despite my many suggestions, it never happened. Then I saw the way you looked at Harper at Arun's wedding, and I knew this woman could be different."

"Then why did you disparage her?"

She screwed up her nose. "Because I'm getting senile in my old age and I wanted to test you."

"Test me?"

"That's what last night was about. Anybody can see you two are head over heels for each other. It's so obvious, like two magnets drawn to each other and unable to pull away. I already suspected your motivation for asking her to marry you, so I wanted to test you, to make sure you really loved her. And the fact you let her break up with you means you failed."

She tut-tutted and shook her head. "You may have asked her

to marry you for all the wrong reasons, but if you've fallen in love for the first time in your life, don't you think she's worth fighting for?"

"I don't believe this," he muttered, dropping his head into his hands.

His grandmother had done all this out of some warped plan to test his true intentions? He'd always been lousy at love; the last thing he needed was an exam he'd be destined to fail.

And he'd failed spectacularly.

Harper despised him, and he didn't blame her. He'd treated her badly when he should've treated the woman he loved like a princess.

He did love her.

It had taken a mighty big wake-up call for him to see that.

"What are you going to do, Manish?"

He raised his head. "I don't know."

"You're a smart man. You've got a medical degree to prove it. Surely you can come up with something?"

"The thing is, I don't think groveling is going to do much. I let her down, badly. She was herself with me, she revealed so much of herself, and I still held her at arm's length. How can I make her trust me again?"

"By doing what she did for you." Izzy pressed a hand to her heart that had him surging to his feet. "No, no, sit, there's nothing wrong. What I meant was, if she opened her heart to you, you owe her the same courtesy."

Open his heart.

Why did something so simple entail a world of complicated possibilities?

68

ONCE MANNY MADE his mind up, he could be an unstoppable force. Take his proposal to Harper, for example. He'd arranged it on short notice and made it happen. So after his pep talk with Izzy, he wanted to do the same. Make a grand gesture. Something Harper couldn't shy away from. Something to show her how much she meant to him. Make it unforgettable so hopefully, if she needed time to think, she wouldn't forget him.

But the more he thought about it, the more he realized expressing his love shouldn't be about pomp and show. Harper had never been impressed by his job or his apartment. The best times they'd spent together had been curled up next to each other, chatting, laughing. Shared intimacy. It had been everything to him.

This time, he had to keep it real.

Standing on her doorstep, wearing his oldest faded jeans and a T-shirt, clutching a bunch of flowers, was low-key. He'd thought the flowers could be trite until he remembered her expressing her love for them in New Zealand. Besides, it wouldn't matter what he presented her with; it was his words that counted.

He just hoped she'd hear him out.

Sweat pooled in his armpits and he flapped his arms, trying to cool down. He hadn't been this nervous since his final year exams at med school, and even then, he'd known deep down he had it covered.

This time, he had no such confidence.

After rolling his neck side to side to loosen the kinks, he took a deep breath, blew it out, and raised his hand to knock. Before he could, the door swung open. Revealing a disheveled, tired Harper with fire in her eyes. She wore black yoga pants and a hoodie, her hair snagged in a low ponytail and no makeup, fatigue accentuating the patches under her eyes. He hated that he'd caused her angst. He loved that she hadn't slammed the door in his face.

"I'm not sure why you're here, but doing bird impersonations on my porch is a surefire way to get the neighbors calling the cops."

Great, she'd witnessed his nerves. Then again, why did he care? He was ready to prostrate himself in front of her if she'd give him a second chance.

"You saw that?"

"Yeah. Hopefully if you flap hard enough you'll fly away and leave me the hell alone."

Nothing about this situation was remotely funny, but to hear her signature sass . . . he wanted to fling the flowers aside and bundle her into his arms.

"I'm nervous. Can't you give a guy a break?"

"When it's you, no."

He hadn't expected this to be easy. Hell, he'd fully intended on groveling for as long as it took. But he wished he'd glimpse something other than anger in her eyes.

"These are for you."

He held out the flowers, exhaling a little sigh of relief when she took them.

"How did you know orange gerberas are my favorite?"

"I heard you telling that assistant chef when we were working that job in Auckland."

Her right eyebrow arched. "You remembered something like that?"

"I remember everything about you," he said, clearing his throat when an unexpected wave of regret washed over him. "Can I come in so we can talk?"

"The flowers won't soften me up, if that's what you're thinking," she muttered, but at least she opened the door wider so he could step inside. "We can talk in the kitchen."

"Thanks." He followed her, trying his best not to stare at her ass and failing, remembering the feel of it in his hands, the sounds she made when he hoisted her up against the wall . . .

She spun around, and he didn't drag his gaze away quick enough, earning a scowl.

"If you expect me to apologize for appreciating you, I won't."

"I gave up expecting anything from you around the time I discovered I was merely an adjunct in your warped plan to impress your grandmother." She snapped her fingers. "Maybe you could call me Harpercillin? An effective medication in the prevention of post-op complications—"

"I didn't come here to argue."

He had to interject before he laughed. Her snark got to him every time, and he wouldn't be doing himself any favors if he actually laughed when this was serious business.

"Then what did you come here for?"

She propped against the sink, her hands behind her, which only served to thrust her breasts forward, and he struggled to keep his gaze fixed on her face. Was she deliberately taunting him with what he was missing out on? If so, she wasn't playing fair. But her gaze was guileless.

"I came here to apologize."

"So you're sorry? Big deal." She shrugged. "It doesn't change anything. You still ran when you saw this."

She pointed at the patches on her chin, around her eyes. "These repulsed you, but you just hid it better than Colin."

"What the fuck . . ." He took a step toward her but stopped, knowing touching her at this point wouldn't be conducive to talking. He'd either earn a slap for his troubles when he had no right to lay a finger on her anymore, or she'd lose her mind like he currently was and they'd end up having makeup sex without making up first.

"You think I'm like that shallow son of a bitch?"

It burned that she thought so little of him, but maybe she was hurting as much as he was and had tried to deflect.

"Let's see. Are you shallow?" She tapped her lip, pretending to think. "You've dated half the female population in Melbourne, not more than once. You dress like a male model most of the time. You manscape. And according to your longest-running girlfriend before me, you never get attached to anyone." She snapped her fingers. "So yeah, shallow."

"When did you meet Elaine?"

"For a job, but that's irrelevant. I showed you the real me; the next day we're over."

"But you broke it off."

"Because you couldn't refute why you proposed, and you certainly couldn't say you loved me . . . and maybe I don't believe you dumped me for the vitiligo and that's just my own insecurities at play, but . . ." She glanced away, biting down on her bottom lip, and he saw the moment her bravery gave way to hurt. "You used me."

This was it. Manny had to lay it all on the line.

"I did."

She hadn't expected him to admit it, because her gaze flew back to his, accusatory and resentful.

"Deep down I knew what I was doing, but I was so shit-scared of losing Izzy I jumped before contemplating what it would do to you, to us, if you found out. I should've trusted you. Maybe if I'd explained the situation, you might've gone along with a fake engagement to fool Izzy into fighting to recover. Instead, I hurt you in the worst possible way . . ."

He shook his head; it did little to clear it. "My grandmother is sorry, by the way, and she wants to apologize to you personally, but all that stuff she said to you yesterday? She wanted to test me."

"Test you?"

"Apparently, she knew I was smitten when she saw me looking at you at Nishi and Arun's wedding. Then I kept mentioning you, and we were together in New Zealand, and after we came home I had this look . . . she knew you were the one I'd set my heart on, but she wanted to see if I truly loved you."

"You and your gran are nuts." She made circles at her temple. "Off the charts, cray-cray nutjobs."

This time he couldn't stop a chuckle escaping. "You're probably right, but she meant well. It's just been the two of us for the last fifteen years, and she's overprotective."

Harper merely rolled her eyes.

"She was right about one thing though. You gave me your heart, and I didn't do you the same courtesy. I knew I loved you, but I couldn't admit it, particularly to myself, because I'm so caught up in self-preservation . . ."

He'd never told anyone the rest, but he had to flay himself open or risk losing her forever.

"My mom died because of me. I was a cocky med student, newly graduated, who thought I knew everything. I insisted she start exercising; she did and ended up having a heart attack right in front of me. I froze initially, and by the time I got my shit together and started CPR, it was too late. She died in my arms . . . from then on I've shut myself off from people. You're right. I have superficial relationships and never get attached to any of my dates because with commitment comes the risk of loss, and I wasn't prepared to take that chance."

His voice had turned croaky with emotion, and he swallowed, twice, before continuing. "Until you. I can't explain it, because it's not logical, but you swept into my life, brandishing that damn whipped cream, and I haven't been the same since."

Tears filled her eyes, and he didn't know whether to be wary or relieved, but he took another chance and crossed the kitchen to stand in front of her.

"I love you, Harper. I may not have said it before, but if you'll give us another chance I'll make sure I say it every single day. And we don't have to be engaged. We can date for however long it takes until I can convince you I'm not some emotionally stunted idiot and I am good husband material."

"How many times a day will you say it?" she deadpanned, but the glint of cheek in her tear-filled gaze told him he'd done it.

She believed him, believed in him, but he needed to hear her say it before he could fully celebrate.

"I love you. There, I've said it twice in under thirty seconds, and if we multiply that by the hours in a day, I can easily manage five thousand seven hundred and sixty 'I love you's' in twenty-four hours."

"Stop being such a show-off, smart-ass," she said, the corners of her mouth curling into a smile.

"I assume your insults mean you love me back?"

"Idiot," she muttered, before flinging herself at him, burying her face in his chest, and sniffling loudly.

Manny grinned like the idiot he was and held her tight, that familiar sense of peace, of rightness, washing over him. This was fate, destiny, or whatever other crap Izzy's horoscope predicted for him on a daily basis.

"And for the record, I love you too, but you already knew that," she said, lifting her head to eyeball him. "I love you, you big, infuriating, gorgeous man. So multiply that."

"I will, after you prove how much you love me."

Her eyes widened in faux innocence. "Any ideas how I can do that?"

"I'll show you," he said, a second before he kissed her.

EPILOGUE

"It seems rather fitting that our last date mirrors our first," Manny said, sliding his arms around Harper from behind. "Have you ever seen such chaos?"

Harper leaned back against her fiancé and surveyed the dance floor at the Springvale Town Hall, where roughly four hundred people wearing colorful saris and kurtas were currently engaged in some kind of flash mob, Bollywood-style.

"This is the sixth Indian dance I've been to in the last six months, so I'm used to the festivities by now."

"Yeah, but this is the first one you haven't been working." He snuggled her, something she'd never get tired of. "Who knew you'd become the queen of styling Indian food?"

"It was inevitable, because I like eating it so much."

"We are talking about Indian *food*, right?" he murmured in her ear, and she elbowed him, earning a loud *oomph*.

"Stop being so naughty in public." She spun in the circle of his arms. "Besides, you're Anglo-Indian, so does that mean I only get to eat half of you?"

"Now who's being naughty?"

They laughed, something they'd been doing a lot of since they'd got back together seven months ago, and engaged a month later. Turns out, when it's right, you don't wait.

"Uh-oh, my grandmother is beckoning us over."

"Is it too late to hide?"

"You're the one who insists we eat with her twice a week, so don't blame me if you're her new favorite person."

"We've got a lot in common," she said, brushing a kiss across his lips. "We both love you."

"Women with exquisite taste." He snagged her hand. "Come on, let's go see Izzy."

Harper knew how much it meant to Manny to have his grandmother here tonight. It was the first function of this size she'd felt well enough to attend. While her heart valves were now functioning, she hadn't fully recovered from the surgery, and her frailty terrified Manny.

He'd confided so much to Harper since they'd reunited, and it had been a no-brainer when he'd proposed again, while the two of them were snuggled on the sofa at her place, drinking masala chai. There hadn't been a kiwi fruit in sight, and she'd been glad. She didn't need grand gestures. She just needed him.

Izzy beamed as they joined her and patted a vacant seat either side of her. "Sit, you two, quickly. I see three of the aunties eyeing me off, and I don't need another person to ask me how I am or can they drop off a pot of chicken curry."

"Everyone cares about you, Izzy." Manny pressed a kiss to her cheek. "It's nice."

"There's nothing nice about those aunties." Izzy shuddered. "I have nightmares about them smothering me with their saris or force-feeding me their ghee-laden *laddoos*."

"Good to see you sticking to the dietician's meal plans," Manny said, with a wink over Izzy's head that had Harper stifling a laugh.

The dietician had nothing do with Izzy's new strict eating routine and everything to do with Harper revealing they wanted to start having kids sooner rather than later. Turns out the prospect of being a great-grandmother was a more powerful motivator than seeing Manny married or any empty threats from a dragon dietician.

"And how's my favorite granddaughter-to-be?" Izzy clasped Harper's hand between hers, a gesture she'd done many times over the months since she'd apologized for her behavior the night of the first engagement party.

Harper had never been excessively touchy-feely, but Izzy had welcomed her into her heart—the least she could do was hold her hand every now and then.

"I'm fine, though please tell your grandson I prefer *aloo chops* as one of the mains at our wedding rather than roast beef."

If it was Harper's choice, she'd have the Anglo-Indian patties—spicy beef mince wrapped in mashed potato then fried—for breakfast, lunch, and dinner. She'd grown addicted to them and had learned the authentic way to make them from Izzy.

"You don't play fair," Manny grumbled. "Enlisting the help of Izzy so you two can gang up on me."

"Get used to it, buddy," Harper said, smiling when Izzy leaned into her in a show of solidarity. "Sisters before misters."

Izzy bumped her. "I heard that on one of the soap operas I watch. Are you hooked on them too?"

Harper didn't have the heart to tell Izzy she'd rather clean her bath than watch the soapies Izzy was glued to all day, so she settled for a smile.

Thankfully, she saw Samira and Pia waving her over, facilitating a graceful escape. "I'll be back soon. Just popping over to say hello to the girls."

"Kushi tells me those two are trouble," Izzy said, but her fond smile belied her words. "If they've taken you under their wings, watch out."

"If anyone's a bad influence around here it's your grandson," Harper said, laughing at Manny's outrage. "And on that note, I'll let him defend himself."

Harper hitched up her sari and strode toward Samira and Pia. They'd all agreed to wear saris once she'd told them attending this function was like a commemoration for her and Manny, a coming-full-circle kind of thing.

Amazing, that her sari slipping had been the catalyst for their tumultuous relationship, which thankfully had developed into one of bliss now.

She neared the women, both wearing matching smug smiles as they waved her over.

"What's going on with you two?"

"We've got news," Samira said, grabbing her arm and tugging her close. Pia poked her, and Samira amended, "Okay, Pia has some news."

"What is it?"

Pia's smile could've lit up the hall better than the disco ball spinning in the center high above the dancers. "Dev and I have taken a big step and put our names down for several adoption agencies in India."

"That's wonderful. I'm so happy for you." Harper flung her arms around Pia and hugged her tight, knowing how much this meant to her.

Once Pia and Dev had reconciled, it had taken them a while to get to this point, and she couldn't be happier.

"So have you and Manny set a date yet?"

"Not yet, but we will, soon."

A little white lie because the two of them had already decided to elope, with her folks and Izzy as their witnesses. Harper may have once had the idealistic dream of the big white dress and two-hundred-strong reception, but she'd changed. All she needed was Manny and her family. The rest didn't matter. They'd throw a party for their friends when it was done, a low-key celebration with a much happier ending than the last party they hosted seven months ago.

"Don't look now, but the doctor is in the house and he's headed this way." Samira smirked and nudged Harper. "He's such a goof-off."

"Yeah, but he's my goof-off." Harper raised her hand. "Later, girls. I have a date with one hot doc."

"Yuck," Pia and Samira said in unison, before high-fiving and laughing so loudly Manny shook his head.

"Are you two celebrating the fact Harper has landed such an amazing guy?"

"I think it went more along the lines of you're a goof-off, but whatever floats your boat," Samira said, with a grin.

"Ladies, ladies, please. We all know you're jealous." He gestured at himself. "Harper has this and you don't. Deal with it."

"Still the same Manny," Samira said, rolling her eyes. "Thinks he's gorgeous when in reality he's a—"

"On that note, I'm taking my man away before you can insult him further." Harper slid her hand into his. "See you later, girls."

Samira and Pia waved as Manny whispered in her ear, "I have a surprise for you."

"If it's the same surprise I saw twice before we left home, can it wait till later?"

He chuckled and swooped in for a kiss. "Did you know I find your sass as attractive as the rest of you?"

"Good, because I plan on putting you in your place for a long time to come."

"On that note, come check out the surprise."

He led her to the side door leading to the back car park, the same door she'd led him to at Nishi's wedding when she'd planned her stealth attack.

She paused when he opened the door. "You're not going to spray me with whipped cream, are you?"

"Would I do something like that?" He feigned innocence, adding, "I'm not you."

She smiled and allowed him to lead her outside, the silence welcome when the door closed on the boisterous Bollywood festivities inside.

"It's around the corner."

They passed the band's van and a few cars belonging to the service staff, before she spied her car.

With a giant I HEART U on her back window, in whipped cream.

He'd actually drawn a heart, though it was wonky and tilted to the right. She liked it even more that way, signifying there was no such thing as perfect, and she was just fine with their version of an imperfect love.

"You are such a romantic," she said, leaning her head on his shoulder when they came to a stop in front of it.

"I've toned down the grand gestures since the kiwi fruit, in case you haven't noticed."

"I have, and I much prefer understated." She reached out, snagged a dollop of cream on the tip of her finger, and plopped it on his nose. "There. It's only fair I re-create some of that night we first met when you've done all this."

He smiled, and her heart somersaulted the way it had been doing ever since he'd first looked at her.

"Just so you know, I plan on re-creating that evening later at home. Covering your naked body head to toe in whipped cream. Before I lick it off."

"Now that sounds like a plan I can get on board with, and a much better use of cream than plastering it all over your handsome face."

"I thought so."

He jerked his head at the car. "We could always get in a little practice in the back seat?"

"You think we need practice?"

"Hell no, but any excuse to get my hands on you."

To demonstrate, he rested his hands on her waist and slid them slowly upward, until he hit the bare skin beneath her choli. She inhaled sharply when his thumbs caressed her, teasing her, a promise of what was to come.

"I love you," he murmured. "With or without whipped cream."

"I love you too," she said, plastering herself against him so hard his back hit her car's window and she heard the squelch of whipped cream.

Neither of them cared as they re-created their first memorable kiss—just as sexy, just as scintillating, but this time was better.

Because this time they knew it was forever.

Author's Note

As an author, each story I create has a little piece of me in it, whether it be a phrase or a hobby or a quirk. Something uniquely me that only I recognize.

In *The Boy Toy*, I particularly identified with Rory because he had a stutter, like me, and in this follow-up novel *The Man Ban*, it's Harper I'm drawn to.

Like Harper, I have vitiligo.

I was diagnosed with the autoimmune disease a few years ago and have undergone the same treatment she does. The white patches haven't vanished, and I don't wear makeup all the time to hide them, but they're a part of me now and I accept that.

It's so satisfying to be able to invest more into a character through personal experience, and I hope you enjoy reading the journey of my characters as much as I love creating them.

Nicola x

Acknowledgments

When I first wrote *The Boy Toy*, one character demanded attention more than others.

Manny.

Dr. Manish Gomes strutted out of my imagination and onto the pages of *The Boy Toy* and he almost stole the show, to the extent I had to tone him down during the editing process. He's utterly charming, and I had an absolute ball telling his story in *The Man Ban*. Many readers asked if he'd be getting his own tale and I'm so glad he has.

Thanks to the following people for helping me bring Manny's story alive:

My fabulous editor, Cindy Hwang, who shared in my vision for Manny and let me run with it. I love working with you.

My agent, Kim Lionetti, who's always in my corner.

My marketing team at Berkley: Jessica Brock, my publicist; and Jessica Plummer, my marketer; thanks so much for getting my books into readers' hands. You do a fab job, and I'm eternally grateful.

Vi-An Nguyen, for the gorgeous cover illustration, and Katy Riegel, for the lovely page design. It absolutely pops and I love it!

Angela Kim, for always being available to answer questions and sort stuff out, thank you.

And to the team at Jove, Berkley, and Penguin Random House for bringing my books to life. Being published with you is a great experience.

Jamie Humby, a food stylist and chef in Melbourne who I reached out to for research assistance. Your answers to my questions really helped develop the food styling angle of Harper's career and brought it alive for me, so thank you.

My parents, Olly and Marina, for immersing me in Anglo-Indian culture growing up. I'll never forget those dances at the Springvale Town Hall (or the food!), even if I never got to meet a real-life Manny.

My hubby, who thinks a boy toy (him) is better than a Manny.

My gorgeous boys, you make me want to be the best I can be. Love you always.

Photo by Jemm Photography

USA Today bestselling and multi-award-winning author **Nicola Marsh** loves all things romance. With seventy novels to her name, she still pinches herself that she gets to write for a living in her dream job. A physiotherapist for thirteen years, she now adores writing full time, raising her two dashing young heroes, sharing fine food with family and friends, cheering her beloved Kangaroos footy team, and curling up on the couch to read a great book. She lives in cosmopolitan Melbourne, Australia.

Ready to find
your next great read?

Let us help.

Visit prh.com/nextread

Penguin
Random
House